W9-BRQ-681

MURDER, SHE WROTE: KILLER IN THE KITCHEN

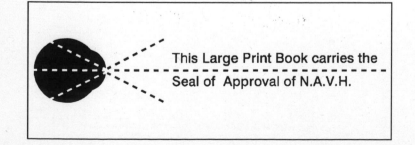

This Large Print Book carries the
Seal of Approval of N.A.V.H.

MURDER, SHE WROTE: KILLER IN THE KITCHEN

JESSICA FLETCHER & DONALD BAIN

Based on the Universal Television series created by Peter S. Fischer, Richard Levinson & William Link

THORNDIKE PRESS

A part of Gale, Cengage Learning

GALE
CENGAGE Learning·

Farmington Hills, Mich • San Francisco • New York • Waterville, Maine
Meriden, Conn • Mason, Ohio • Chicago

Copyright © 2015 *Murder, She Wrote* © Universal Network Television LLC. Licensed by Universal Studios Licensing LLC 2015. *Murder, She Wrote* is a trademark and copyright of Universal Studios.
Thorndike Press, a part of Gale, Cengage Learning.

LIBRARY OF CONGRESS CATALOGING-IN-PUBLICATION DATA

Fletcher, Jessica.
  Murder, She Wrote: Killer in the kitchen : a Murder, she wrote mystery / by Jessica Fletcher & Donald Bain. — Large print edition.
    pages cm. — (Thorndike Press large print mystery)
  "Based on the Universal Television series created by Peter S. Fischer, Richard Levinson, & William Link."
    ISBN 978-1-4104-7711-8 (hardcover) — ISBN 1-4104-7711-8 (hardcover)
  1. Fletcher, Jessica—Fiction. 2. Women novelists—Fiction. 3. Restaurateurs—Fiction. 4. Murder—Investigation—Fiction. 5. Large type books. I. Bain, Donald, 1935– II. Murder, she wrote (Television program) III. Title.
  PS3552.A376K55 2015b
  813'.54—dc23   2015012495

Published in 2015 by arrangement with New American Library, an imprint of Penguin Publishing Group, a division of Penguin Random House LLC

Printed in Mexico
1 2 3 4 5 6 7 19 18 17 16 15

For Johnny Mercini and his wonderful Della Francesca restaurant in Danbury, Connecticut, our go-to place when we have something to celebrate

PART ONE

CABOT COVE INCIDENT REPORT
CABOT COVE SHERIFF'S OFFICE
TOWN OF CABOT COVE,
STATE OF MAINE

On April 18 an officer from the Cabot Cove Sheriff's Office was dispatched to the area of the new waterfront restaurant at 23 Old Wharf Road on a 911 assault complaint. Responding officer found a white male lying faceup, apparently dead of wounds from a kitchen knife protruding from his torso. A pool of blood was under the body's left side. The victim was identified as the restaurant's chef and owner. Officer notified Sheriff Metzger, who arrived on the scene at 3:24 a.m.

The medical examiner pronounced the death at 3:43 a.m. The knife was turned over to the state regional crime laboratory and a receipt taken for same. Crime-scene technicians observed a half-empty wine bottle on the counter and two glasses, one with red-colored residue. Four cigarette butts were collected from outside the rear entrance to the kitchen.

A statement was taken from the man who found the body and put in the call. Witness had been taking inventory in the basement after the staff had been dismissed for the night. He said he was not aware of any visitors at that late hour, did not hear any arguments. When he returned upstairs, he found the chef as described. He said the back door was propped open, but no one else was in the kitchen. He admitted that it was not unusual for the back door to the kitchen to be left open to facilitate airing out cooking smells. He said he did not know if the victim had been drinking prior to the incident. He said the victim was not a smoker. He said he could not recall any altercations that might have led to the incident. He provided a list (attached) of kitchen and waitstaff who had been dismissed earlier in the evening.

Deputies were dispatched to notify next of kin.

Sheriff Metzger interviewed the witness who made the 911 call, and released him.

State investigators have been assigned to offer mutual aid.

CHAPTER ONE

Maureen Metzger, the wife of our sheriff, Mort Metzger, had hosted Thanksgiving dinner and invited a dozen people, including Isabel Fowler. Isabel was a widow who lived alone on the eastern fringe of Cabot Cove. I'd met her when she worked as a dispatcher in the sheriff's office, and we became fast friends. A lifetime Cabot Cove resident, Isabel was a delightful person to be around, always with something good to say about others. She was a volunteer for numerous town charities, some of which I worked for as well, and had a reputation as a superb cook. Every potluck fund-raiser, every holiday celebration at the senior center, every pancake breakfast at the fire station, every annual PTA kickoff dinner, featured dishes provided by Isabel Fowler. And there wasn't a hostess in town who hadn't implored her to share a favorite recipe, requests to which she always complied.

"I was hoping to see Brad and Marcie here today," I said as Isabel and I sat in a corner of the Metzger home, sipping coffee and wondering how many pounds we'd put on at Maureen's dinner table.

Isabel's only child, Bradley, was a handsome thirty-year-old fellow who had spent most of his post–high school years working on the many lobster boats that call the Cabot Cove port home. Lobstering is hard work, and only the hardy manage to make a go of it. I knew that Brad had taken a year off from working the boats to attend a community college with a curriculum designed to prepare students for jobs in the restaurant business, but he had gone back to hauling lobster traps from the deep after earning his certificate. His wife, Marcie, worked as a secretary in the Cabot Cove school superintendent's office and also as a part-time waitress after school.

"They went off to spend the long weekend in Portland with their young friends," Isabel said. "I was invited but didn't want to be the only person at dinner on the wrong side of fifty. When Maureen called, I decided to enjoy this Thanksgiving right here in Cabot Cove with old friends — well, maybe not 'old,' but friends my age."

"I'm delighted that you decided to stay, Isabel," I said. "We haven't had a chance to catch up since last summer's Lobsterfest, when Brad supervised the Down East shore-dinner lobster bake. You know, I always wondered why he never did anything more with the culinary classes he took in college. He's a very good cook. Of course, he had an excellent teacher at home."

A sly smile crossed Isabel's lips. "Promise to keep a secret?" she asked in almost a whisper.

"I'll do my best," I said, "but I promise nothing."

She held her index finger and thumb an inch from each other and continued to speak in the same conspiratorial tone. "Brad and Marcie are this close to getting the funding to open their own restaurant."

"That is exciting news," I said. "I didn't know they had those plans."

"It's always been Brad's dream, but it seemed beyond their ability to come up with enough money to turn it into reality. They're such hard workers and live frugally, saving every penny they can. Marcie has always worked a second job, and Brad is constantly taking on extra shifts with the lobster boats. Still, what they managed to put away wasn't enough to open a place, so I decided to

15

help. I've refinanced my house, and Steven Wagner at the Savings-and-Loan has granted them a sizable loan. They now have enough to go forward."

"That's wonderful," I said, keeping another thought unsaid. It was admirable that Isabel would risk her home — the mortgage for which, I was certain, must have been paid off years ago — to help her son and daughter-in-law. I wasn't sure it was the most prudent of decisions. I knew from my previous research that owning and operating a restaurant was not only an all-consuming, challenging job, but the failure rate was high.

I had to assume they knew the risks. Certainly, it wasn't my place to throw a wet towel on the idea. Isabel glowed with pride at what Brad was about to undertake. Her being able to help him and his wife go forward with their plan was obviously satisfying to her. I was happy for her.

"Have they decided where their restaurant will be located?" I asked.

"The old Wharf Seafood Shop, on the dock," Isabel replied. "It's an ideal location, with all the summer tourists we attract. Of course, it will take a lot of construction to turn it into the sort of fine-dining spot Brad and Marcie envision, but a lot of restaurant

16

equipment, like ranges and refrigerators, tables and chairs, even napkins and silverware, can be gotten on credit from suppliers."

"That should be helpful," I said.

"Brad is going to feature some of my favorite recipes," Isabel said proudly, "and name them after me on the menu."

Her pleasure was palpable and contagious, and I squeezed her hand and laughed along with her. "I can't wait to be one of their first customers," I said.

We were joined by Seth Hazlitt, the town's beloved physician and my treasured friend.

"Hope I'm not interrupting something important," he said as he lowered himself into a chair next to Isabel. "Has she been filling your ears about the restaurant her son and daughter-in-law are about to open?"

So much for keeping a secret. I looked at Isabel in surprise.

"I guess I have told a few people," she said sheepishly.

"Because you're proud," I said.

"As well you should be," Seth said, "although they're facin' themselves a daunting challenge."

Isabel's face turned serious.

Seth raised a finger to forestall her

response. "Don't get me wrong. I love a good restaurant. But with this bein' a seasonal town and all, they'll have to come up with ways to keep the locals comin' when there's six feet of snow. Not an easy task."

"Now, Seth, let's keep a positive outlook. We have other restaurants in town that manage to survive the winter."

"That's all right, Jessica. The kids have been talking about that very thing," Isabel said. "Brad has a lot of good ideas, and Marcie has a wonderful sense of advertising and promotion."

"Then I imagine they'll do just fine." Seth craned his neck to steal a look into the kitchen. "I wonder if Maureen has any more of that pecan pie left. It's one of her better creations."

"Let's go find out," I said. "Would you like a piece, too?" I asked Isabel.

She waved a hand. "I actually have a pecan pie in my refrigerator at home that I made for the kids for when they get back. You two go on. I'm going to talk with Mary-Jane Koser. Her husband, Richard, promised to take photos of the restaurant for our website."

I accompanied Seth to the kitchen, where Maureen and Mort were cleaning up.

"Did I see right that there was a little slice

of that pecan pie left?" Seth asked.

"Help yourself, Doc," Mort said, handing him the fork he'd just finished drying. "Save me those extra calories. Maureen really hit a home run with that one, didn't she?"

"Ayuh, it's very good," Seth said as he sat at a small table in a corner of the kitchen and dug into his second dessert.

"I can't take all the credit," Maureen said. "It's Isabel's recipe, practically foolproof. I didn't change a thing. Don't tell her, but I have a few ideas to tweak it a bit the next time I make it."

Maureen had put together an excellent Thanksgiving dinner, including pecan, apple, and cherry pies. She'd stuck to the basics, which wasn't always the case. Her gastronomic creations, especially those that involved "tweaking," too often left something to be desired — I won't use the harsh language that has occasionally spilled from the mouths of Seth and others when evaluating her dishes. Maureen is a dear person and I would never insult her efforts, but considering what a major meal such as Thanksgiving entails, it was nice to see that she'd kept it plain and simple.

"It's exciting about Brad and Marcie Fowler, isn't it?" Maureen said from where she scrubbed a pan.

19

"Opening a restaurant?" Seth said between mouthfuls.

"Yes. Isabel told me all about it," Maureen said over her shoulder. "Oops! I wasn't supposed to say anything, was I? Don't let on I told you. It's supposed to be a secret."

Seth and I looked at each other and smiled.

"Wonderful pie," Seth said, patting his mouth with a napkin. "Maybe Brad and Marcie Fowler will buy pies from you and sell them at their restaurant."

"Ooh, I like that idea," Maureen said. "There can be a separate page in the menu for 'Pies by Maureen.' What do you think, hon?" She looked at her husband, who'd substituted an apron for his usual sheriff's uniform.

"If you're a big hit, I can retire early," he said.

She playfully slapped him with a dish towel.

"Thanks for a great dinner," Seth said, bringing his plate to the sink. "I've got to get up early tomorrow, so Mrs. Fletcher and I will be toddling along if she still wants to hitch a ride from me."

He drove me home but declined my offer of a nightcap. "Got a full slate of patients tomorrow, including Isabel Fowler," he said.

"Anything serious?" I asked.

"No. Just getting older. I hope her son and his wife know what they're doing. Restaurants are a tough business."

"They'll find out soon enough," I said.

"I suppose they'll name the place 'Brad and Marcie's,' " he said. "People like to see their own names on the sign out front."

"Maybe they will," I said, "but I'm sure they have a long list of other names in mind. The way news travels in Cabot Cove, everyone will be talking about it tomorrow — and throwing out their own suggestions. There's something wonderful about young people chasing a dream, no matter what the risks. I hope they make a success of it."

At home I made myself a cup of tea and sat at my desk. It had been a lovely Thanksgiving, full of good food and good conversation with dear friends. What could be better? I thought of the restaurant that Brad and Marcie Fowler would be opening, smiled, and said aloud, "Go for it!"

To want something badly and never take the chance to make it a reality can eat away at people for the rest of their lives. A friend of mine, a psychiatrist, preaches "Any action is better than no action." They were young and could bounce back should their dream not succeed. I thought of myself and

21

my decision to write my first murder mystery. It was something I'd aspired to for a very long time and finally had decided that if I didn't try, I'd regret it to my dying day. Fortunately, it had worked out for me, but if it hadn't, I could have taken comfort in having given it my best effort.

A new restaurant opening, I thought. Cabot Cove was certainly expanding, and I was pleased to see its growth. What *would* Brad and Marcie call their restaurant? The minute they decided, it would be the topic of conversation all over town. Keeping a secret in Cabot Cove was like trying to slam a revolving door.

CHAPTER TWO

I slept later than usual the morning following Thanksgiving dinner at the Metzgers — they say that turkey can have that effect on you — and took my time getting ready for the day. Since I planned to spend the afternoon doing some final editing on the mystery I'd recently completed, I decided to treat myself to a leisurely start to the day, including breakfast at Mara's Luncheonette on the town dock. A big dinner always seems to make me especially hungry the next morning, and a short stack of Mara's signature blueberry pancakes was appealing.

A November chill had settled in, which made me debate riding my bicycle into town. Then, too, this was the day after Thanksgiving, when all the shops launch their holiday sales. Traffic would be especially heavy, and I didn't fancy competing with four wheels while I was on only two. I called the local taxi service, where I had a charge account.

"It's Black Friday, Mrs. Fletcher. Big shopping day. All our cars are out," the dispatcher told me.

"Well, do the best you can," I replied, trying to ignore the rumbling in my stomach.

An hour later, I walked into Mara's, where an assortment of familiar faces greeted me, including Mayor Jim Shevlin, who was having an early lunch with an aide. He motioned for me to join them, which I happily did.

"Good Thanksgiving, Jessica?" the mayor asked.

"Yes. You?"

"Couldn't have been better, although I wish this infernal cold snap would end. I could do without an early winter."

"Issue a decree banning it," I said playfully. "After all, you *are* the mayor."

"I just may do that," he said through a laugh. "By the way, have you heard the news?"

"That you've banned an early winter?"

"That we're about to have a new restaurant in town."

"You mean Brad and Marcie Fowlers'. Yes. It was a topic of conversation at the Metzgers' house last night. Brad's mother was at dinner with us. She told me about the restaurant and swore me to secrecy, but it seemed that everyone there had also been sworn to keep that same secret."

"Boy, I'd love to bottle Cabot Cove's rumor mill," Jim's aide said. "Make a fortune."

"It is active," Jim agreed. "As I understand it, the Fowlers are taking over the old Wharf Seafood Shop. It'll be nice to see it spruced up and open again. It's been an eyesore since Ginger and her husband closed down more than a year ago."

Mara, who'd come to the table to pour coffee refills, overheard the conversation and said, "We don't need another restaurant in town. Just means more competition for me."

"No, it doesn't," Jim said. "They'll be opening a real restaurant and —"

"What do you call *this* place, Mr. Mayor?" Mara said, not attempting to keep the pique from her voice. "A fast-food joint?"

"What I mean is —"

"You and the Fowlers will be running two distinctly different types of establishments," I quickly interjected.

"I hear they're going to feature a bunch of different lobster dishes," Mara said, "recipes that Brad's mother came up with."

"Isabel is an excellent cook," Jim Shevlin offered.

"So am I," Mara said. "I've got lobster rolls on the menu and my aunt's recipe for lobster bisque."

"And they're always excellent," I said, hoping to defuse what was becoming a contentious conversation. "But there's something you serve that the Fowlers will never be able to duplicate."

"What's that?" Mara and Jim asked at the same time.

"No one will ever make better blueberry pancakes than you." I indicated my now empty plate. "As usual, they were sublime."

My words seemed to appease her, at least for the moment. As Mara walked away, Shevlin rolled his eyes and smiled. "I hope the Fowlers' new place doesn't pit one restaurant owner against another," he said. "That would be a shame."

"I don't think it will come to that," I said.

"Brad Fowler's got a reputation as a hothead," Jim's aide said.

"Yeah, but he's more bark than bite," Shevlin said.

I appreciated Jim defending Brad, but I didn't know if that was true. There had been stories about fights Brad had gotten into with fellow lobstermen, and I knew from

Mort Metzger that he'd once been locked up overnight after starting a brawl in a local bar. Brad had always been a perfect gentleman around me, but I'd sensed a tautness and tension that hovered not far beneath the surface. Hopefully, his alleged short fuse wouldn't be on display when the restaurant was open and he had to deal with demanding — and not always polite — customers.

I was about to ask Mara for my check and head home when the subject of our conversation, Brad Fowler, entered. He looked around the luncheonette, spotted me, and headed our way.

"Speak of the devil," Jim Shevlin said. "Not that we were calling you a devil, but — just a phrase. Sit down and we'll toast your new restaurant." Jim held up his coffee cup.

Brad grinned and took the remaining seat. "That's okay, Mr. Mayor. Seems like everybody in town is talking about me — and Marcie."

"And where is your lovely wife?" I asked.

"Taking a well-deserved rest. Marcie and I got back late last night. No, make that early this morning. We had Thanksgiving dinner with friends in Portland. We had to get back because we had an appointment at the bank. I've never signed so many papers

27

in my life. Mr. Wagner has been great, led us by the hand through the whole loan process."

"Then it's settled," Shevlin said. "You have the loan and are going forward with the restaurant."

"Looks like it," Brad said, beaming. I noticed that he'd swapped his usual work clothes for a suit and tie, which testified to his growing maturity.

"My mom says she was with you last night at Thanksgiving dinner," Brad said to me.

"Yes. That's how I learned about your plans."

"We wanted to keep it a secret until the final papers were signed, but Mom is too excited to keep anything under wraps. But yeah, the deal is done."

"Congratulations to all of you," I said.

"Marcie says she's finally going to get to use the lessons she learned at the Culinary Institute."

"I didn't know your wife attended the Culinary Institute," Shevlin said. "I thought you and your mother were the cooks in the family."

Brad's face reddened. "She didn't attend, exactly. It was just a summer course she took between high school and junior college." He shrugged. "She wanted to stay on,

28

but couldn't afford it. Those schools cost a fortune."

"But between the two of you, you're starting out with a good foundation," I said.

Brad shot me a grateful look. "Yeah. I think so, too."

Mara came to the table and asked whether Brad wanted breakfast.

"Thanks, but I don't have time. Just a fast cup of coffee. I have to pick up my mom at Doc Hazlitt's office."

"How is your mother?" Shevlin asked.

"She hasn't been feeling well, only you'd never know it by talking to her. Ask her how she is and she always says 'great.' I finally got her to admit that she's been feeling lousy and make the appointment with Doc Hazlitt."

"She certainly was in good spirits last night at dinner," I said. "She's so proud of you and Marcie."

"We couldn't have done it without her," Brad said as Mara brought him his coffee. "It's a shame my dad isn't around to see it happen."

"I'm sure he'll get the word from somebody up there," the mayor said.

"That's good to hear," said Brad, raising his eyes to the ceiling.

"When will you start renovations?" I asked.

"Marcie and I have already met with the architect who's drawing up the plans, and Billy Tehar will be doing the construction."

"Looks like you and Marcie have a busy couple of months ahead of you," I said. "Do you have a date yet for when you'll be opening?"

"As close to spring as possible," he replied. "Tourists start showing up earlier every year, it seems." He gulped down what was left of his coffee. "Got to run." He fished for change in his pocket.

"My treat," I said.

"Okay, so long as you agree that your first cup of coffee in our new place is on me."

"It's a deal."

As Brad started to walk away from the table, Shevlin called after him, "Have you got a name yet?"

Brad turned and nodded. "We're thinking, maybe, the Fin and Claw," he said. "Marcie came up with it. Pretty sharp, my wife, isn't she? See ya."

"The Fin and Claw," Shevlin repeated. "Good name. Has a nice ring to it."

"The Fin and Claw?" Mara said as she came to collect our money. "That's what they're calling it? Sounds pretty fancy for

Cabot Cove."

"Cabot Cove is getting fancier all the time," our mayor said. "A sign of progress."

Shevlin, his aide, and I exited Mara's into a stiff, frigid breeze off the water.

"Can we give you a lift somewhere?" Jim's aide asked.

"Thank you, no. I'm going to see if I can take advantage of some of these sales before I head back home. Good seeing you both."

They walked toward City Hall, and I headed for Charles Department Store.

The Fin & Claw, I thought as I hunched forward to brace myself against the wind. It did have a nice ring to it.

CHAPTER THREE

The next few weeks flew by.

Christmas decorations were up in all the stores, and a crew had strung tiny colored lights from telephone pole to telephone pole downtown, giving Cabot Cove a festive air despite the overcast sky.

The premature chill of Thanksgiving had given way to a brief thaw, surprisingly mild weather for Maine in December, which lured shoppers out of their homes and gave a boost to the town's retail economy. I'd finished my final edits on my latest novel and proudly sent it off to my publisher, Vaughan Buckley, in New York. Of course my excitement — and relief — at having finished and submitted another novel was tempered with concerns. Would Vaughan and his editors like it? You'd think after all these years I'd have more confidence as a writer. But I'd learned from interacting with other authors that my paranoia was not at all unusual. We all want to be appreciated and dread having our work rejected.

Construction started on the Fin & Claw before Christmas, and the site became a frequent stop for people curious about its progress. The architect's plans called for a complete gutting of the interior, which meant that big trucks dominated the street in front of the pier as workmen hauled out and loaded the rubble onto the truck beds, to be carted away.

I had an appointment one day with Seth Hazlitt — a burn on my hand from being careless in the kitchen — and after he tended to my wound, we strolled downtown to see how things were moving forward. A temporary wall of plywood had been erected to keep people out and the dust in, but Seth spotted Billy Tehar, whose construction company was working the job. "Can we take a look?" Seth called.

Tehar waved us inside. "If you don't mind getting dusty, I'll show you around." He handed us two plastic hard hats. "Just in case."

"Starting from scratch, I see," Seth commented.

"It's the only way to go," Billy said. "Better to clean it out and begin with a clean slate than try to work around existing

33

things. More economical in the end."

"Starting a project like this must be daunting," I commented as Tehar led us around a pile of debris to the back of the space.

"Not a problem if you know what you're doing, Mrs. Fletcher. I have a good crew. They've been with me for a long time."

"Nothing like experience," Seth said.

"You should know," Tehar said, laughing. "How many years have you been practicing medicine here in Cabot Cove?"

"Too many to count," Seth replied.

"Is this where the kitchen will be?" I asked, indicating the rear portion of the rapidly emptying room.

"That's what the drawings call for," Tehar said, "only —"

"Only what?" Seth said.

"Well, the plans keep changing." He didn't sound happy.

"The architect keeps changing them?" I asked.

"No. His original chart for the space is terrific. He's designed restaurants before, in Bangor and Portland, and he did one in Montreal last year. He knows what he's doing."

"Then — ?"

Tehar shook his head. "It's Brad Fowler,

34

but don't tell him I said that."

"What's *his* problem?" Seth asked, raising his voice to be heard over the sound of hammers and saws and workmen tearing down walls.

"Oh, I shouldn't be too hard on him," Tehar said. "This is his first experience with opening a restaurant, and I suppose he's eager to see it just the way he wants it. But every time he gets a new idea, the cost goes up and the time it takes to get it done gets longer. Nothing is ever simple; when you change one piece, all the other pieces are affected. It's like tipping over the first domino. I've tried to point that out to him, but he's — well, he tends to be bullheaded about how he sees the picture in his mind."

We stepped out of the way as two men pushed a cart overflowing with trash toward the front.

"Looks like the young Mr. Fowler could use some good advice about listening to people who know more than he does," Seth said.

Tehar laughed. "Care to volunteer to pass that message along to him, Doc?"

"Not my concern," Seth said. "I run into it enough with young physicians who think because they got their MD license they know everything there is to know about medicine. When you've been practicing as long as I have and see all the progress being made by research, you learn that not only don't you know everything, but you know less and less every year."

"I've been treated by one or two of those know-it-alls over the years," Tehar said. "Luckily, I'm still here." He helped us navigate the demolition as we returned to the pier.

Seth and I handed him back the hard hats, and I fluffed my hair with my fingers. "Nice to breathe fresh air," I said.

"A construction site is always dusty," Tehar said, "but demoing is the worst part."

"Does Brad often stop in to check on progress?" I asked.

"*Too* often," Tehar said. "He's out lobstering today. Better he stays out on the water and leaves the construction to me."

"What about his wife?" I asked. "Has she been playing an active role in the planning?"

"Marcie? She's a sweetheart," Tehar said. "Dealing with her is a pleasure. Brad? Well, like I said, please don't repeat what I've told you."

The temperature had dropped while we were inside the construction zone, and I pulled my coat collar tighter around my neck.

"I have to get back to the office," Seth said.

"Don't let me keep you," I said.

"Follow my instructions about that burn," he said, nodding toward my injury. "Try to keep your hand out of water. Get a pair of rubber gloves."

I'd forgotten about the burn, which Seth had bandaged with gauze. "Yes, sir!" I said. "You go on. I think I'll stop into Cabot Cove Books and see if they'd like me to sign copies of my last mystery."

It was midday, and I was pleased to see the bookstore full of holiday shoppers. I spotted Mayor Shevlin and our sheriff poring over a display of new cookbooks and went to say hello.

"We have to stop meeting like this," said the mayor with a chuckle.

"People will think I'm lobbying you for something," I said.

"Are you, Jessica?"

"Not today. How are you, Mort?"

"Just fine, Mrs. F. Been out and about?"

I told them about having visited the construction site of Brad and Marcie Fowler's restaurant with Seth.

"Some folks are complaining about the noise," Mort commented.

"It is noisy," I agreed, "but the demolition

phase will soon be over."

"Only to start up again," the mayor said.

I looked quizzically at him.

"Seems like Cabot Cove is on its way to becoming the Down East restaurant capital," he said.

"What are you talking about, Jim?"

"Mrs. F. hasn't heard the news," Mort said, paging through a tome with the celebrity chef Gérard Leboeuf's face on the cover. "You think Maureen would like this one?"

I read over his shoulder. "The recipes look pretty complicated," I said. "What haven't I heard?"

Shevlin laughed. "Hard to believe that the news hasn't reached you."

Mort picked up another cookbook. "What about this one?"

"She'll like that one better. *What* news?"

"Your old pal is about to open a new restaurant."

"What old pal?"

"Gérard Leboeuf."

"Where?"

"Here."

"Leboeuf is opening a restaurant *here*?"

"Yes, *here.*"

"Do I hear an echo?" Mort asked, looking around.

"I don't know that I'd characterize him as 'my old pal,' " I said.

"Looks like it'll go through," Shevlin said. "I spent a good part of this morning in a meeting with the zoning board. Leboeuf sent two of his attorneys from New York to submit the plans. It's a pretty ambitious undertaking."

I had met Gérard Leboeuf years earlier, when I was in New York researching a novel I'd titled *Murder Flambéed,* which I later put aside. The plot just wasn't gelling. I had been hoping that meeting a famous chef would help me work out the kinks in my story. Our mutual agent, Matt Miller, had introduced us and, after a bit of arm-twisting on Matt's part, the chef had grudgingly allowed me to peek behind the scenes at one of his restaurants.

"He intends to take over that abandoned warehouse down by the lobster pound and open a French bistro," Jim continued.

"Wait! That's right across from where the Fowlers are opening their place," I said.

"One thing's for sure," Mort said, tucking a copy of *Mike Isabella's Crazy Good Italian* under his arm. "Maureen and I won't have to go far for a good dinner out."

My mind was racing, and what I was thinking had nothing to do with how far I would have to go for a meal. I wondered whether Brad and Marcie Fowler knew about Leboeuf's plans and what it would mean to the success of their own place.

"Anything wrong, Jessica?" Shevlin asked. "You look lost in thought."

"Wrong? No. I'm just afraid that Mr. Leboeuf's restaurant will make things difficult for Brad and Marcie Fowler. They don't have the experience he does, much less the financial backing."

"That's free enterprise at work, Mrs. F.," Mort said.

He was right, of course. Competition could be healthy, prompting competitors to put their best feet forward, which benefits consumers. But Leboeuf was a wealthy and powerful restaurateur, with a string of successful establishments in New York, Las Vegas, Chicago, and other big cities. He had a lot of money behind him and could bide his time until a new restaurant took hold. Stories abounded of his having forced smaller places to close simply by staying open even though his new enterprise lost money. What would he do to the Fowlers' Fin & Claw? Would it even be possible for them to compete? Would his presence doom their dream?

"Does he ever stay at the palace he built

north of town?" the mayor asked, putting down the cookbook he'd been perusing.

"You mean his summer place?" Mort said. "We keep an eye on it, but as far as I know, Mr. Leboeuf and his family hardly ever spend time there. You probably know more than I do, Mrs. F. You're friends with him."

"I wouldn't call it being friends," I said. "Mr. Leboeuf was good enough to grant me an interview in New York, but we've rarely touched base in Cabot Cove. I haven't seen him since I attended a large cocktail party he held for his business associates last year. If he doesn't spend much time at his summer home, I suppose it's because he's simply too busy running his restaurant empire."

"His plans for the restaurant didn't go over too well with the Zoning Commission," Shevlin said. "His lawyers are asking for a series of variances to the zoning code to allow Leboeuf to put his architect's plans into action. He wants the kitchen to be large enough to accommodate television cameras and sound equipment."

"Does the commission really think Cabot Cove can support a new place, along with the Fowlers'?" Mort asked.

Shevlin shrugged. "That remains to be seen. I understand Leboeuf decided to open

41

a place in town because recent legislation that came out of Augusta gives tax breaks to out-of-state companies that bring business to Maine. He's got himself a sweet deal."

"Will the Fowlers get a similar 'sweet deal,' Jim?" I asked.

"I think it only applies to businesses that come here from another state, Jessica."

"That hardly seems fair," I said. "Why shouldn't local citizens like the Fowlers also benefit from a tax break? Besides, Leboeuf has a home here in Cabot Cove. Why is he considered to be from out of state?"

Shevlin chuckled. "Go ask the legislators up in the state capital. I've never been able to figure out half the decisions they come to in Augusta." Shevlin picked up another book and riffled the pages. "You think Susan would be offended if I bought her a cookbook? I don't want my wife to think I'm hinting at something."

"She might prefer a mystery," Mort said, cocking his head toward me.

"Good idea, Sheriff! Where are your books, Jessica?"

"There's a pile on the front table," I said.

"Thanks," Shevlin said, putting down the cookbook. "Should be interesting to see what develops. At the very least, looks like we'll all be well fed this summer." He shook Mort's hand and gave me a peck on the cheek. "If I don't meet up with you again, have a good holiday."

We wished him the same.

The store manager was delighted to have me sign my latest novel. She set me up at a counter with a pile of books and a roll of SIGNED BY AUTHOR stickers, and I went to work. Mort paid for Maureen's gift and offered to drive me home, but I declined. When I finished writing my name a dozen times, I took a walk around town, trying to clear my thinking about what I'd learned. Although Mort had been right — competition is usually healthy — I couldn't shake the feeling that two new restaurants were more than our town could support. Someone was going to be very disappointed, and I had a premonition that something unpleasant was in the wind for Cabot Cove.

CHAPTER FOUR

A lot had happened in the years since I'd interviewed Gérard Leboeuf in New York. He and his much younger wife, Eva, a successful model and creator of a popular line of cosmetics, went through with their plan to buy waterfront property in Cabot Cove, on which they'd built a stunning summer house for their family, which also included their by-now twenty-year-old son, Wylie. What Leboeuf termed a "country cottage" was framed in redwood and featured huge, soaring windows that gave them a 360-degree view of their surroundings, particularly the water. A few neighbors had complained to the Zoning Commission that the home partially blocked their own views of the sea, but Leboeuf's attorneys successfully challenged or settled these complaints, in one case by buying off the neighbor. While the house was a permanent fixture in town, its occupants weren't.

Gérard Leboeuf and his wife were seldom seen . . . until he arrived one day to hold a press conference to announce his plans to open a new restaurant. The press event, which I'd been invited to attend, was held at a lovely small hotel called the Blueberry Hill Inn that was owned by friends of mine and that sat on a grassy knoll overlooking the water. With Leboeuf were two of his lawyers, a New York PR woman whose agency handled the celebrity chef's publicity, a couple of young aides, a man who was introduced as the future general manager of the newest jewel in Leboeuf's culinary holdings, and the great man's dog, a German shepherd named Max. I knew that the editor of our local paper, Evelyn Phillips, would be there, but I wondered if the occasion would attract more than a smattering of people looking for something to do, or maybe a free buffet. When I walked in, I was surprised to see almost every chair in the room occupied.

Evelyn spotted me and came to my side. "Exciting, isn't it?"

"Any new business coming to Cabot Cove is exciting," I replied.

"I wasn't sure the Zoning Commission would let it go through, but they did," Evelyn countered. "This is really big-time.

Imagine, someone of Gérard Leboeuf's stature in the restaurant industry choosing to open a restaurant here. Next thing we'll have Bobby Flay, Paula Deen, maybe even Emeril Lagasse opening *their* restaurants in Cabot Cove. We might become the Las Vegas of the East Coast."

What a dreadful thought!

Evelyn returned to the chair she'd staked out directly in front of the speakers' table, and I found a vacant one next to Maureen Metzger on the opposite side of the room. I'd just taken my seat when Leboeuf's PR woman took the microphone and welcomed everyone.

"Gérard has been talking for years about opening one of his signature restaurants in this charming town," she said, "and once he decided to build his summer retreat here, there was no stopping him. Cabot Cove is about to get an authentic French bistro, the first of its kind in this part of Maine. As most of you know, the name Leboeuf is synonymous with fine dining. His standards are the highest in the industry, and he'll be bringing those values to Cabot Cove. I might also add that simply having Gérard's name attached to this new fine-dining establishment will encourage the tourist dollars to flow. Plus, your unemployment rate, no doubt, will go down."

"I didn't know our unemployment rate was high," I whispered to Maureen.

The PR woman introduced Leboeuf, who stood to the applause. He wore a double-breasted blue blazer, white shirt with vivid red and blue stripes, and a jaunty white yachtsman's cap, an obvious — and slightly silly — acknowledgment that Cabot Cove was a seafaring community. After the clapping had died down, he said, "I've opened many restaurants around this great country of ours, but none has excited our family as much as opening my bistro in Cabot Cove. We are thrilled to be so close to our lovely home here, especially my wife, Eva, who says it will be nice to have her husband around for a while."

"Which one is his wife?" Maureen whispered, turning her head to scan the women in the room.

"Alas, my sweet wife, Eva, sends you her regrets. She desperately wanted to be here today, but business has taken her out of the country. Even so, I know that, were she here, she'd join me in thanking you for welcoming us as you have as your new neighbors, and I promise that my new restaurant will make you as proud as I am."

47

"He's so handsome," Maureen said into my ear.

I ignored her comment as Leboeuf continued.

"It takes a lot to run a successful restaurant," he said, "not just a charming location, as you have here in Cabot Cove, but expertise in creating delicious food, pleasing not only people's palates, but their enjoyment of the entire dining experience. I've spent many years honing my craft, and I'll bring that unique knowledge and feel to Leboeuf's French Bistro. Now, I'd like to introduce you to Walter Chang, a graduate of Le Cordon Bleu in Paris, who'll be moving here shortly to manage the restaurant. And I might add that my furry friend, Max, agrees with everything I say." He waited until the laughter ebbed to add, "He'd better, or that's the end of his doggy bones."

Chang, a portly Asian gentleman wearing chef's whites, took the mike and waxed poetic about Leboeuf and his success as a world-famous chef and restaurateur. He spoke of what the restaurant would offer and pointed to a pile of menus at the end of the table. "Naturally, we'll adjust the daily fare based upon what fresh ingredients are available each season, but please feel free to take a menu from some of our other French brasseries. They'll give you a hint of what's to come."

Leboeuf replaced him at the dais and indicated a pile of books at the other end of the table. "Some of the cookbooks I've authored are for sale. I'll be happy to autograph them for you. And you'll also have an advance peek at what my new restaurant will look like. The famed designer Tony Chi and his people have come up with beautiful and innovative designs, and their renderings are available for you to peruse. And since we're talking about food, the good folks here at the Blueberry Hill Inn have provided a lovely assortment of pastries based on recipes from my latest cookbook. So you can sample the results before you buy the book. Thank you for coming."

"That's for me," Maureen said, pulling out her wallet. "His recipes are a bit tricky, but it'll be helpful to know what they're supposed to taste like. I can't wait to try them."

Leboeuf acknowledged the polite applause greeting his closing remarks but remained at the microphone. When the room quieted again, he said, "I see that Jessica Fletcher is with us this morning. I hope that she doesn't decide to set one of her bestselling murder mysteries in my restaurant."

The crowd joined in his laughter as he

pointed a finger of recognition at me, the way politicians do when acknowledging someone in the crowd. I waved in response, although I wished that he hadn't done it.

I mingled with others at the long table and eyed the drawings of what Leboeuf's new restaurant would look like. It was all very impressive, and there were a lot of oohs and aahs.

Maureen had cornered the manager, Walter Chang, and, from the snippets of conversation I overheard, was extolling the virtues of her latest favorite dish. Evelyn Phillips had managed to isolate Leboeuf for an interview, the young photographer on her staff snapping photos.

"What do you think?" Mayor Shevlin asked as we walked from the room. He'd grabbed a cherry pastry on the way out.

"They certainly are ambitious plans, according to the architect's and designer's drawings."

"Mr. Leboeuf is big-time, that's for sure. Will you honor his request not to set a murder in his place?"

"I promise nothing, Jim," I said, laughing.

He laughed, too. "You have the makings of a politician, Jessica."

Out in the parking lot I was surprised to see Marcie Fowler. Dressed in only a thin white silk blouse and green skirt, she leaned against her car, crying.

I hurried over. "Marcie! What's wrong?"

She shook her head and wrapped her arms about herself, trembling in the cold.

"Where's your coat?" I asked.

She wiped the tears from under her eyes and sniffled. "I forgot it. I just ran out and I left it inside."

"Then let's go back inside and retrieve it," I said.

She didn't move.

"Were you at Mr. Leboeuf's press conference?"

"Oh, Mrs. Fletcher. We're ruined." She started crying again.

"Come on," I said, tugging on her arm. "Let's get your coat. It's crazy to be out here without it in this weather. You'll catch pneumonia."

She managed to get herself under control. We reentered the inn and went to a coatrack in the lobby, where she retrieved her coat, draping it over her shoulders.

"Do you have time for a cup of coffee?" I asked.

I didn't think that she would agree, but she nodded. We helped ourselves to the coffee Leboeuf's entourage had provided for the press and took our cups into the inn's

51

cozy sitting room, taking matching wing chairs that flanked a window overlooking the cold gray ocean. The wind had churned the water into angry waves, accurately reflecting the roiling emotions of the young woman sitting across from me.

"I know it's not my business," I said to break the silence, "but you're obviously in distress. Would you like to talk about it with me?"

"Oh, Mrs. Fletcher, it's just that —" She dabbed at her eyes with a tissue. "Why does he have to open a restaurant *here*?"

"There are quite a few other restaurants in Cabot Cove. And there will be more in the future, I'm sure. Tell me, how are things coming along with the Fin and Claw? That's the name you've chosen — am I right?"

"The Fin and Claw is turning into a nightmare," she replied, the tears threatening again. "Why wasn't it enough for Gérard Leboeuf to come here and build his minimansion? Why does he have to open a restaurant just when Brad and I are opening ours?"

"It's bad timing, I admit," I said, "but it doesn't mean that your restaurant and Mr. Leboeuf's can't happily exist side by side."

"I wish you were right," she said, "but we're sure to suffer by comparison. Leboeuf is so powerful and has so much money to spend on promoting his place."

"Sometimes competition is good, Marcie," I said. "People who stop in at Leboeuf's will want to also try the Fin and Claw. I would assume that variety is appealing to restaurant patrons."

She ignored my attempt at viewing the glass as being half-full and said, "Brad and Billy Tehar had a terrible argument last night."

"I'm sorry to hear it."

"Brad wants to change things again. He got freaked out when he learned Leboeuf had bought the old lobster pound property. Billy keeps pointing out that every time Brad decides to change something in the construction, it costs more money."

"That's usually the case," I said. "Why does Brad want to change things at this late date? I understand that you're opening in a month."

"It'll make it more like two months now."

"Still in time for spring and the tourist season," I offered, again trying to put a positive spin on things. My words, meant to be encouraging, wafted into the air like a puff of smoke.

"Brad is being unreasonable about everything, Mrs. Fletcher. Even before this news, he did nothing but argue with the people supplying the fixtures and kitchen equipment, kept changing his mind. It's driving everybody crazy, including me. And it's eating up our budget. We had to ask his mother for more money. She took out a personal loan."

Isabel Fowler is getting in deeper and deeper financially, I thought, and hoped she knew what she was doing.

"And now Leboeuf!" Marcie said in what was almost a snarl, "strutting around in his captain's outfit and with that big dog at his side, like some third-world dictator."

I realized that there was nothing I could say that would lift Marcie out of her despair. Her coffee sat untouched, her eyes were red-rimmed, and she displayed her upset by the constant interlacing of her fingers on the tabletop. We sat in silence before I said, "I think what you're facing is what happens in business, Marcie. I can't comment on Brad's behavior, but the reality is that Gérard Leboeuf is opening a restaurant here in Cabot Cove, and that means that you'll be in competition with him and all the other restaurants in town. Your mother-in-law told me at Thanksgiving that you're very good at marketing and publicity. If I were you, I'd stress that you and Brad are native Cabot

Covers. You know how people are in this town. They take care of their own, support local businesses. While Gérard Leboeuf might have a big reputation and lots of money, don't sell yourself and Brad short. The town is flooded with visitors in the spring and summer, and you'll just have to take advantage of that and be prudent with money the rest of the year."

"I hate that man!" she said abruptly.

"I don't think you mean that," I said. "Leboeuf's plans may make things more complicated for you, but it seems to me that your focus has to be on reining in Brad where the construction is concerned. This is no time to be creating cost overruns."

She looked out the door where Leboeuf, with Max pulling on his leash, was leaving the inn with his entourage. I smiled at her. "Don't pay attention to Gérard Leboeuf," I said, placing my hand on hers. "Get your own wonderful restaurant open and make it the best Cabot Cove has ever seen. I'll be there on opening night, and so will half the town."

She simply nodded, stood, and said, "Thank you for listening, Mrs. Fletcher. I'd better be going."

"My pleasure. Don't forget your coat again," I said, pointing to where she'd

55

tossed it over the back of the chair.

It was her first smile since we'd met in the parking lot.

I watched her walk away and couldn't escape the feeling that while it was easy for me to offer platitudes and feel-good advice, this young couple was facing an uphill battle. All I could do was hope that the hill wasn't too steep and that they'd manage to climb it together.

CHAPTER FIVE

By the middle of March, the construction on Brad and Marcie's Fin & Claw restaurant was nearing completion. Marcie had evidently found a way to temper Brad's penchant for changing the plans because, according to Billy Tehar, Brad had backed off and stayed out of the contractor's way as the final finishes were installed.

Evelyn Phillips called me one morning and asked if I'd like to accompany her to see the progress that had been made on the restaurant, which she said was close to opening. "If I remember correctly, you were going to set one of your books in a restaurant. You'll probably notice things I won't. Are you game?"

I readily agreed. I'd felt housebound the past few weeks and was grateful for the chance to get some stimulation and fresh air. Evelyn and her photographer picked me up at ten, and we drove into town and parked in the recently paved lot that would serve the Fin & Claw's customers.

The temporary plywood wall was gone, but the windows facing the street were lined with brown paper to keep the curious from peeking inside.

"What an incredible difference from the last time I was here," I commented as we walked through a handsome mahogany door with colorful etched glass panes embedded in it. What had once been a scene of destruction had been transformed into a dazzling space, with a ceiling dotted with recessed lighting, wall sconces spaced close together, a mosaic tiled floor that looked as though it had come from the most expensive restaurants in Italy or France, spacious padded banquettes, and heavy tables surrounded by solid armchairs with upholstered leather seats.

"It's beautiful," Evelyn said. "Look over there." She pointed to a mural-size color photograph of Brad on a lobster boat, holding up two live lobsters, like an Olympic competitor raising his gold medals. He was dressed in a tuxedo. On the opposite wall, long picture windows looked out on the Cabot Cove harbor and were angled to capture at least part of an evening sunset.

I agreed with Evelyn — the Fin & Claw

would rival any upscale restaurant in appearance — but I silently questioned the choice of décor for a dockside eatery serving lobster and crabs. I suppose I had expected a less formal interior, more like other seafood restaurants I'd enjoyed, in which the tables were bleached wood and patrons could open crabs with a hammer on sheets of newspaper. The original plans that Billy Tehar had shown me appeared to call for that sort of interior. This certainly was a drastic departure from those early sketches. It all spoke to me of an expensive steakhouse — all dark wood and polished brass — undoubtedly reflecting the many times that Brad had changed his mind and raised not only the stakes but the budget.

While Evelyn's photographer snapped shots of various areas of the room, I drifted to an ornate dais located just inside the front door, where guests would be greeted. Across from it, on the other side of the entrance, was a small bar with four stools and a mirrored backbar. Next to it, stretching from floor to ceiling, was a copper wine rack designed to hold at least two hundred bottles.

As I admired the dais's burled wood and the gleaming brass rail that defined its surface, angry voices were heard from somewhere in the back, where the kitchen was located. Two men were arguing. As I tried to make out what they were saying, the kitchen door swung open and a tall, gaunt man stormed through, followed by Brad Fowler. Immediately behind him was Marcie. The tall man was obviously enraged. His face was red, and his lips were set in a combative slash. He was breathing hard.

"You'll do it my way," Brad shouted after him, "or you can find another job."

The man turned and said, "That's fine with me. You don't know squat about running a restaurant, but you're too dumb to know it. I can always work at Leboeuf's place."

"Brad, please," Marcie implored, "stop it. Jake was only suggesting a change in the way the workstations be set up. He's been in the restaurant business for a long time and —"

The three of them suddenly realized that we were there, and the heat of their quarrel abated.

"Mrs. Fletcher," Marcie said, smiling warmly and coming to greet me. She said to Evelyn, "My apologies, Mrs. Phillips. I forgot you were arriving this morning to do a story on how things are shaping up."

"Looks like you're almost ready to open,"

Evelyn said, groping in her shoulder bag for her pen and spiral notebook.

All eyes went to Jake, who stood by the dais. He was so angry that I wouldn't have been surprised to see steam coming out of his ears.

"We can work this out," Brad said, slapping him on the shoulder and forcing a smile.

"Just don't treat me like some damn amateur," Jake said before leaving through the front door.

"A little misunderstanding with my sous chef," Brad said. "So, what do you think?" He took in the restaurant's interior with a sweep of his hand.

"It's beautiful," Evelyn said. "Very elegant."

"Mrs. Fletcher?" he said. "Your take on what we've accomplished?"

"It's ah — yes, it is elegant. Very elegant."

Brad raised his hand. "That's just the start. Can you wait a minute? I want you to taste something." He hurried into the kitchen and returned a moment later with a saucepan and three spoons. "Please, try this." He dipped a spoon into the sauce and gave it to Evelyn, his eyes expectant.

Evelyn tucked her pen behind her ear, took the spoon, and sipped at the sauce.

"Oh, my, that's really delicious. What is it?"

"Mrs. Fletcher, would you like to try it?" He dipped another spoon into his pan and held it out for me. He did the same for his wife and gave her a big grin.

"Wonderful, Brad," I said. "Is this on the menu?"

"It will be. I'm working on perfecting it right now. It requires just the right balance of butter, lobster sauce, a special liqueur, and a pinch of saffron."

"Tastes pretty perfect to me," Evelyn said, handing Marcie her spoon and retrieving her pen from behind her ear.

"It's based on one of my mother's recipes, but I've added a few other elements."

Marcie rolled her eyes. "Easy on the saffron. I had a devil of a time finding a good supply."

"When's the official opening date?" Evelyn asked, her pen poised over her notepad.

"A week from today," Marcie replied. "I'm delivering a full-page ad to you this afternoon."

"That's great," said Evelyn. "Have you had many reservations yet?"

Brad and Marcie looked at each other.

"The ad will bring people in," Evelyn said.

"We have reservations." Brad's tone implied he wasn't pleased.

"Gérard Leboeuf is coming with a party of ten," Marcie explained.

"That's wonderful," I said.

Brad grimaced. "Call me suspicious — this is not for publication, Mrs. Phillips — but why does Leboeuf want to come here?"

"To see what his competition is offering," Evelyn provided. "You might want to consider doing the same."

"He's grandstanding," Brad said.

"But he'll be a paying customer," I said, giving Marcie my spoon. "I'm sure that he'll be very impressed with what you and Marcie have accomplished. Put me down for a table for two on opening night. I'll bring a guest."

"Who'll be your guest?" Evelyn asked.

"I'll see if Seth wants to join me," I replied. "He mentioned that he wanted to be here on opening night but has probably been too busy to make arrangements."

We turned as the door opened and Sheriff Mort Metzger came in.

"What brings you here, Mort?" I asked.

"Hello, Sheriff," Brad said. "I hope you're not here on official business. All our permits are up-to-date, and the city has given us the go-ahead."

"Just checking out how things are going," Mort said. "Looks like a pretty fancy place, Brad. Hope your *prices* aren't too fancy."

"We'll be in line with what other fine-dining establishments charge," was Brad's reply.

I silently hoped our young restaurateur hadn't exceeded his ego boundaries. The elaborate décor of the Fin & Claw and the expensive ingredients in this planned dish suggested that its menu would come with a big tab.

"You given any more thought about featuring Maureen's pies on the menu?"

"No, Sheriff. I've been so busy. . . ."

"I was going to call your wife this afternoon to discuss it," Marcie quickly added. "If we do the sort of business we hope to, it would mean your Maureen making a lot of pies."

"That's no problem," Mort said. "She can turn 'em out by the dozens."

"Then I'll be in touch."

"She'll appreciate that," Mort said, and left.

"Speaking of menus," I said, "have you come up with yours?"

Marcie went behind the dais, emerged holding a thick leather-bound book, and handed it to me.

"It is certainly impressive-looking," I said as I opened the binding and read. "Oh, look," I said, handing it to Evelyn. "Isabel

Fowler has a special page featuring her recipes."

"She must be thrilled," Evelyn said.

"Yeah, she likes it," said Brad, smiling genuinely for the first time.

"How is your mom?" I asked.

He rocked his head. "Okay some days, not so good others. Doc Hazlitt is taking good care of her."

The front door swung open behind us, and this time a half-dozen young people filed in. There were *ooh*s and *aah*s and whistles of appreciation.

"Please excuse us, ladies," Brad said to me and Evelyn. "We have our first staff training today."

Evelyn asked to take away the menu, to which Marcie readily agreed, and we said good-bye and exited to the pier.

"Must have cost them a pretty penny," Evelyn commented. "Did you notice the prices? I'll have to sell one of my cats to afford it."

"They are steep," I agreed.

"Anything strike you that I might not have picked up on?"

"I think it's nice that Gérard Leboeuf is bringing a party to the opening. Very courteous and not something you see all the time, I imagine. Have you heard when he'll be opening *his* new place?"

"He told me that he's a few weeks behind," Evelyn said, "something to do with a delay in original French art coming from Paris. I think they've scheduled the opening for three weeks from now."

"Lots of culinary excitement in town," I commented.

"That's what Cabot Cove needs, Jessica, some excitement. If they bring in more tourists, everyone in town will benefit. See you at the opening."

I called Seth Hazlitt when I returned home. He said that he would be delighted to share a table with me on opening night of the Fin & Claw. "How's the place looking?" he asked.

I told him of my reaction to the décor and mentioned the lofty prices on the menu.

"Sorry to hear that," he said. "Don't know if we have that many high rollers in Cabot Cove. Most folks around here don't like to pay a lot for a meal."

"They're young and in business for the first time. They'll have to make adjustments as they go along."

"Not our concern, of course, but I hope they can hang on long enough to learn the lesson. Thank you for making the reservation. I'm lookin' forward to it."

Seth was right, of course. How Brad and Marcie Fowler elected to price the dishes on their menu wasn't our concern, at least not in a literal sense. But I couldn't help wondering whether they were in over their heads. It's been my experience that people will pay for an expensive dinner to audition a new restaurant, but if it makes too much of an impact on their wallets, they won't return for another visit.

I thought about the contentious conversation between the sous chef and Brad that Evelyn and I had witnessed. Jake had accused Brad of not knowing anything about running a restaurant. Maybe he was right. Had Brad and Marcie consulted someone with expertise in restaurant management before forging ahead with the Fin & Claw? I didn't know.

When I'd interviewed Gérard Leboeuf years earlier for the novel I was writing, he'd commented, "The restaurant business is like being in show business, only it isn't. The problem is that too many people think it's a glamorous business. It's not. It's hard work, long hours, and tracking every penny. You'd better know what you're doing or you'll join all those people who've lost their life savings."

At the time I'd simply accepted what he

said and used that analysis of the business in the novel. But now it had taken on greater meaning for me. Isabel Fowler had remortgaged her home and had taken a personal loan from the bank to help her son and his wife fulfill a dream. Brad and Marcie had scrimped and saved every penny they could to make that dream a reality. They'd both taken some courses, I knew, but was that enough? Had they barged ahead without the benefit of the advice from someone who knew how the restaurant business worked? Had they neglected to do all the prep work to learn how a successful establishment needed to be operated? All signs seemed to point in that direction.

Of course, their problems were compounded by the unexpected arrival of Gérard Leboeuf and his grandiose plan to open a restaurant a stone's throw from the Fin & Claw. He was a seasoned pro with an impressive track record of opening and running multiple restaurants around the country, and had plenty of financing to carry him through until a new place began earning back its investment. As I was thinking about this, I wondered whether Leboeuf saw the Fin & Claw as a competitor, or if he considered it nothing more than an ill-fated, amateurish foray into his business, one that would fail as so many others had. If he viewed it as a legitimate competitor, would he pull out all the stops to destroy it? That was his reputation. Journalists had written of how he'd been known to crush rivals, regardless of the personal hurt it inflicted on those who'd lost a life's dream.

My negative reverie was interrupted by a phone call from the man in question.

"Jessica, it's Gérard Leboeuf."

"Oh, hello, Gérard. Your timing is impeccable. I was just thinking about you."

"Always pleased to capture a writer's imagination."

"I understand that you're getting close to opening your restaurant."

"Just a matter of weeks. I've commissioned original art from two French artists, but you know how artists are, fiercely independent and oblivious to the business end of things. I assume you are still turning out great mystery novels."

"I don't know about great, but yes, I am still writing."

"Hopefully your next victim won't be found in my restaurant."

"Never! I took your warning at the press conference seriously."

"I was joking, of course."

"As am I."

He hesitated a moment before forging ahead. "Splendid. I was wondering whether you would like to be my guest at the opening of our little competitor down the street, this Fin and Claw."

The way he put it rang to me of arrogance, a dismissal of Brad and Marcie and all they'd worked so hard to achieve, but I didn't comment.

"I appreciate the invitation, Gérard, but I've already made plans to go with a friend."

"Oh. My loss. I'm putting together a party and hoped to include you. Eva, my wife, and our son, Wylie, will be there, along with some of my business associates. Have you seen this new place yet?"

"As a matter of fact, I was there earlier today. It's very handsome."

"So I understand. I'm told that you're acquainted with the owners."

"Brad and Marcie Fowler. Yes, I know them. Brad's mother, Isabel, is a friend of mine."

"Oh, yes, the mother. I hear that she supplied some of the recipes. Isn't that sweet?"

I didn't reply and he hurried on. "Young people get seduced by all the TV shows about running a restaurant." He laughed. "Those of us in the industry know that's not even half of the story, but I suppose we should always help the little people, welcome them into the business." Another laugh. "Even mom-and-pop operations."

I ignored the snide comment and thanked him for calling, hoping to end the conversation.

"Before you go," he said, "I have a question."

"Which is?"

"Do you think this young couple, the Fowlers, might be interested in being bought out?"

I wasn't sure how to respond. Did his question indicate that *he* was concerned with the competition Brad and Marcie could give his restaurant? If so, that was a real surprise. After all, Gérard Leboeuf was a major force in the nation's restaurant business. Why would he be worried about Brad and Marcie's initial foray into it?

"I rather doubt it," I said. "Having the Fin and Claw represents a lifelong goal for Brad Fowler."

"Running a restaurant is a tough business, Jessica."

"I imagine they're aware of that," I said.

"I'd hate to see them strike out their first time at bat."

"That's very kind of you."

He chuckled. "I'm never kind."

71

I thanked him for calling, and for the invitation. "I'll see you at the Fowlers' opening night."

Hearing from him had come out of the blue, and I pondered what he really wanted to know while I got busy running a vacuum over my living and dining room carpets. I'd half completed the chore when the phone rang again. It was my agent, Matt Miller, calling from New York.

"Interrupting your creative endeavors, Jessica?"

"If you consider vacuuming a creative endeavor, yes."

"As they say, cleanliness is next to godliness."

"In that case I'm very saintly today. What prompts your call?"

"I wondered if you'd heard the latest rumor about Gérard Leboeuf."

"Funny you should ask," I said. "I just got off the phone with your culinary client."

"He didn't ask you to ghost one of his cookbooks, did he? They actually sell quite well."

"Not this time. Were you thinking I wanted to branch out?"

"Heaven forbid! I'm sure that my esteemed client didn't mention that he is having a little run-in with the authorities."

"Why? What has he done?"

"This is not for public consumption, at least not yet, Jessica, but there's a rumor around that Leboeuf is in the pocket of organized crime, that they finance his operations and use his restaurant empire to launder money."

"My goodness," I said. "Those are serious accusations."

"And totally unproven, I might add. Just thought you'd be interested in some gossip about your neighbor."

"Do you think there's any truth to those charges?" I asked.

"You know as much as I do. Of course, bad publicity can sell books as well as good publicity."

"Even cookbooks?"

"It's all name recognition, Jessica. People will remember the name but not always what they heard about it. Speaking of names, your publisher, Vaughan Buckley, ran some ideas by me, and I promised to fill you in."

After chatting about marketing plans for my latest novel — and not raising the subject of Gérard Leboeuf again — we ended the call. But although we ceased talking about him, the famous chef and restaurateur occupied my thinking for a

73

while. Could it be possible that Leboeuf was using his string of restaurants for illegal activities? That the authorities were investigating didn't mean that Leboeuf had done anything wrong. People are innocent until proved guilty, a tenet of our democracy that I've always embraced. Then, too, successful businesses often inspire jealousy and on occasion false accusations. Unfortunately, when people are accused of something that turns out to be unfounded, it's too late to take the charges back. The damage to their reputation has already been done. But I didn't ponder it. The whir of the vacuum not only removed dust from my carpets; it also vacuumed out my thoughts, at least for the moment.

CHAPTER SIX

The grand opening of the Fin & Claw took place on a windswept, chilly, rainy evening, as Mother Nature lent an untimely contribution to the festivities. Brad had hired two local teenagers to wield large green and white golf umbrellas with the restaurant's name emblazoned on them to escort patrons from the parking lot. Others had to park a distance away and held on to their umbrellas and hats as they made their way to the entrance. Gérard Leboeuf's empty parking lot had been roped off to prevent any Fin & Claw customers from using it, which disappointed me. It would have been a good time for Leboeuf to extend a hand of friendship, but maybe I was being too much of a Pollyanna. As he'd stressed to me during our recent phone call as well as during my interview with him years ago, the restaurant business was just that, *a business*. Still, allowing patrons to park in his close-by empty lot would have been a nice gesture.

Inside the Fin & Claw, there was an atmosphere of excitement. Marcie had arranged for giant spotlights to highlight their location, and even though they also illuminated the low-hanging clouds, they brought Hollywood-style attention to the opening, at the time a unique experience for Cabot Covers. I wondered had the weather cooperated whether a red carpet would have been laid down outside for customers to pose upon. Marcie looked absolutely lovely in a stunning teal sheath that she'd bought for the occasion. She stood at the dais, welcoming their guests for the evening, a dazzling smile on her pretty face. I'd heard from Loretta Spiegel at the beauty salon that Marcie had spent a considerable portion of the afternoon there for a hair and cosmetics makeover. Although she seemed very much on top of things, I sensed her nervousness as she checked off my reservation and led Seth and me to our table, from where we could take in the entire dining room. Almost every table was occupied. A large round one next to us with ten place settings was vacant. I assumed it was for Gérard Leboeuf and his party, and I hoped that he wouldn't commit the cardinal sin of not honoring his reservation.

Seth and I knew most of the other diners in the room. Mayor Jim Shevlin and his wife, Susan, the town's leading travel agent, were with another couple, Cabot Cove's unofficial historian, Tim Purdy, and his date for the evening. At the next table were Jack and Tobé Wilson, whose animal hospital had treated half the dogs, cats, and horses in town, and untold wild critters brought to them in need of medical assistance. Their dinner companions were Sheriff Metzger and his wife, Maureen.

Billy Tehar came in with his girlfriend and stopped near our table, turning in a slow circle to admire the room. He gave Seth and me a wink. "I have to say, for all the trouble he gave me building this place, the final result looks spectacular. Brad had a vision I wasn't seeing. Don't tell him I said so, but I guess he was right." He chuckled as he escorted his companion to the table where Marcie stood waiting for them.

I looked for Isabel Fowler but didn't see her right away. Surely she wouldn't miss this auspicious evening in her son and daughter-in-law's life. I was about to ask someone when she came through the kitchen door. Like Marcie, she'd dressed up for the occasion, and wore a broad smile to go with her red silk dress. I had the feeling that she wasn't accustomed to the high heels she wore, because she teetered a bit, but she managed to skirt tables, greeting guests before she arrived at ours.

"Jessica, Seth, how wonderful to see you."

"You look stunning, Isabel," I said.

"Had to look my best for the opening," she said, tilting her head to the side with a flirtatious grin.

"Feeling tip-top?" Seth asked.

"Yes, I —" Her face clouded over and she gripped the back of a chair, as though needing support. But her smile quickly returned and she straightened. "Feeling just fine, thanks to you, Dr. Hazlitt."

"That's what I like to hear," Seth said, "but don't overdo it."

"I'd better see if I can help my daughter-in-law," Isabel said. "Enjoy your evening."

We watched her take unsure steps in the direction of the dais where Marcie was welcoming customers. I glanced at Seth, whose expression could only be construed as concerned.

"Something wrong?" I asked.

"Nothin' I can talk about, but I am looking forward to a good dinner."

Our waiter was a familiar face — the son of a friend — who'd been waiting tables in another restaurant the last time I saw him. He took our drink order, white wine for me and a "perfect Manhattan" for Seth.

The waiter looked confused. "Perfect?"

"Ayuh," Seth said, "a touch of both sweet and dry vermouth. Tell the bartender to make it with rye, not bourbon, and not to forget the dash of bitters."

He dutifully noted Seth's details and walked away, a puzzled expression on his face.

"Seems to me a waiter should know what a perfect Manhattan is," Seth said, opening his napkin and laying it across his lap.

"He's young," I said. "He'll learn."

"I know that, but it's no excuse for Brad Fowler not to have trained him." He looked in the direction of the bar, where the bartender was busy mixing drinks and uncorking wine bottles. "That bartender looks young, too," Seth said. "Probably has to consult a book to see how a perfect Manhattan is made. But I'll bet he knows what Jell-O shots are."

"What are they?"

"Dreadful things young people make themselves sick on."

Once Seth fixates on something, he won't let go until another topic takes its place, so I was about to change the subject when

79

Gérard Leboeuf arrived with his entourage and was led to the large table next to ours. His wife, Eva, and their son, Wylie, were with him, along with the man who'd been introduced at the press conference as the manager of Leboeuf's new restaurants, Walter Chang, though he had substituted a suit and tie for his chef's whites. I also recognized two other young men who'd attended the press conference with Leboeuf. They were sullen, unsmiling fellows whose duties had not been explained.

Leboeuf stopped at our table to greet Seth and me, and Eva wiggled her fingers to acknowledge us.

"You look radiant this evening, Jessica," Leboeuf said, taking my hand after I introduced him to Seth.

"Thank you."

"And you, Doctor? I trust all is well in the world of medicine."

"Things are just fine, Mr. Leboeuf. I see you don't have your dog with you this evening. I've had several patients ask me if you had trouble with your eyesight."

Leboeuf laughed heartily. "My vision is perfect, Doctor. No, Max is home guarding the compound. He's the best alarm system there is, although I also have one of those electronic ones." He looked around the dining room, his smile morphing into a smirk. "Not bad for a novice decorator, but why they used that shade of blue on the walls is beyond me. Not good for the digestion, but of course they wouldn't know that, would they?"

I didn't challenge him. The pale blue color of the walls was pleasant, although I had to admit it didn't flatter Isabel's complexion. She was looking a bit wan as she orbited the room.

Leboeuf's party of six was not the ten the table had been set for, and I wondered if he'd bothered to update his reservation. After another minute of aimless chitchat, he joined his companions.

"Full of himself, isn't he?" Seth muttered in my ear.

When I didn't respond, Seth said, "Jessica?"

"Oh, I'm sorry, Seth. My attention was elsewhere. Excuse me. I just want to ask Marcie Fowler a question."

I went to the dais, where Marcie was greeting a couple who didn't have reservations. When she returned after finding them a small table next to the kitchen door, I asked, "Is Brad's mother all right? She looks lovely, but she seems a little, well, shaky."

Marcie's gaze roamed the room until it

settled on Isabel. "She hasn't been feeling well, Mrs. Fletcher, hasn't for days. Brad and I tried to convince her to stay home this evening, but she wouldn't hear of it. There was no way that she'd miss the opening." She looked at me and smiled. "It's because of her that we're even here. Of course, if I can just convince her to ditch those high heels, she'll be a lot steadier on her feet."

"That must be it," I said. "I was just concerned, that's all. She looks beautiful. As do you. You both look terrific."

"Marcie Fowler says that Isabel hasn't been feeling well," I told Seth when I rejoined him.

"Ayuh. She's supposed to see me tomorrow. I hope she keeps her appointment. The lady has some problems that need addressing. Not sure she should be prancing around in those stilettos."

"They aren't stilettos," I corrected, "just higher heels than I think she's used to."

"Tell that to a podiatrist."

I knew better than to press for further details about Isabel's state of health. Seth Hazlitt was a stickler about respecting the sacred rules of doctor-patient confidentiality.

When our drinks were served, we clinked

glasses and perused the menu. My mind wandered to what my agent, Matt Miller, had said about Gérard Leboeuf being investigated, but that thought was interrupted when Brad came from the kitchen to see how things were progressing in the dining room. I waved, but he ignored me and disappeared back through the swinging doors. My brief glance told me that he was a young man with a weight on his shoulders.

A party atmosphere had developed in the room, people leaving their tables to chat with friends at other tables, their conversations overriding the smooth Frank Sinatra recordings that came through the restaurant's sound system. At the same time a certain tension had developed when it came to the staff. The waiters seemed to circle the room aimlessly, going empty-handed as they paced back and forth and went in and out of the kitchen. I heard one couple who'd arrived early complain at how long it was taking for their dinners to be served. I mentioned it to Seth.

"It does seem that way," he said, "but you know as well as I do that a new restaurant needs time to get its act together. Always best to give it a few weeks to work out the kinks."

Seth was right, of course. Restaurant

reviewers usually afford a new place a shakedown phase before judging the food and service.

The hefty menu contained many pages. "Feels like a novella," Seth commented. Two pages were devoted to dishes created by Isabel Fowler. Her picture appeared along with the items, and Brad had included a tribute to his mom: *My mother, Isabel Fowler, is the best cook in the world. These dishes were created by her, and I invite you to enjoy them as much as I have over the years. Because we live in Maine, the lobster capital of the world, my mom has spent a lifetime researching and creating different recipes to go with lobster. Of course, if you like yours plain — steamed, boiled, baked, stuffed, or cold — no matter what your preference, you'll find what you're looking for at the Fin & Claw. Enjoy!*

"Isabel must be thrilled," I commented as I continued to thumb through the pages. The list of lobster dishes from Isabel's recipe book was extensive. Apart from basic entrées that you would expect in a seafood restaurant, there was lobster with Asian vegetables; braised lobster with black truffle risotto cake and crème fraîche; Brazilian-style lobster with sea scallops; quesadilla with grilled lobster; and even a Cuban dish, "Mango Tango" lobster with mojo Cubaneau sauce.

"It all looks yummy," I said. "Does anything appeal to you?"

"None of these fancy ones," he replied, as I'd expected he would. "This menu is a little overwhelming," Seth said under his breath. "Too many dishes. You can't do justice to that many. Besides, lobster is best boiled or steamed, with melted butter."

I agreed that the menu was ambitious. In addition to the pages devoted to lobster, there were other seafood entrées, meat dishes, and a strange pairing, at least for me: lobster with butternut squash. How could Brad and his kitchen crew possibly deal with so many choices? But I'd often felt that way in the local diner outside town, where the menu also went on for pages, and they managed to keep their customers satisfied. I was eager to give Brad's kitchen the benefit of the doubt.

Leboeuf's party, however, was not so generous. They mocked the extensive menu and were loud in voicing it. There was a hearty laugh as Leboeuf proclaimed loudly, "Look at this! Black truffle cake and crème fraîche. How to ruin a lobster in one easy lesson."

"What do you expect from a housewife playing around in her kitchen?" the chef,

Chang, added, which elicited more guffaws.

I looked for Isabel to see if she'd overheard Chang's nasty remark, but she was far enough away not to be privy to it.

Their snide comments continued as they ordered their meals, and I became increasingly uneasy. Leboeuf may not have liked what he saw on the menu or what he was served, but common courtesy should have precluded voicing his harsh opinions for all to hear. Although Seth said little, I sensed that he shared the discomfort I was feeling at that moment. What had begun as a festive opening of Brad and Marcie's restaurant was rapidly deteriorating into a negative atmosphere, compliments of Gérard Leboeuf and his arrogant party. I kept glancing at their table in expectation of the next cutting remark. Leboeuf's wife, Eva, looked bored, as though she would gladly pay anything to be somewhere else. Her son, Wylie, shared his mother's ennui, conveying his disinterest in what was going on around him by staring into his cell phone. I was sure that it was galling to have his father's celebrity status thrust him into the spotlight. A popular tabloid magazine had once reported that Wylie had had a serious drug problem when in his teens and had spent time in an expensive rehab center.

Was it true? I trust little that appears in such publications, although there had been major stories broken by their editors from time to time. Regardless, it must have been difficult for the young man to find himself a focus of media attention. When most teenagers make their mistakes — and hopefully learn from them — it's out of the glare of the public eye. Perhaps that was why he had cultivated a rigid expression, devoid of emotion.

"What will it be this evening?" Seth asked, snapping me out of my focus on the next table.

"I'm going to have that lobster with butternut squash," I said. "I've never tried that combination."

Seth opted for the more conservative boiled lobster, and we both ordered salads to start. When our dishes arrived, we were delighted to see that our lobsters were of the new-shell variety, which made access to the sweet and tender meat easier.

"This is wonderful," I told Seth, breathing in the enticing aroma of the perfectly cooked lobster perched on a puff-pastry cushion over a rich butternut sauce. I dipped my fork into sautéed spinach, which offered a sharp contrast to the buttery main ingredient.

"Not bad. Not bad," was Seth's assessment as he dipped a luscious claw into a bowl of clarified butter.

As we enjoyed our meal, Leboeuf's table continued to poke fun at their dishes.

"He obviously has no idea how to properly cook trout," someone said.

"If you think the trout is bad," Leboeuf said, "you should try the baked stuffed clams. All bread, no clams."

"Why don't you tell him where he can find good clams," Chang said.

Another round of sarcastic mirth.

Our waiter was also serving the Leboeuf table. As they expressed their complaints to him, his face mirrored his confusion and unhappiness. His only retort was to head for the kitchen to relay the complaint and then return with, "The chef is sorry that the meal isn't to your liking. Would you like to order something else?"

I felt sorry for him. Whether or not the Leboeuf party's choice of appetizers and entrées had pleased them, it seemed to me that they were making much too much of a public display of it. I even considered turning to Leboeuf and suggesting that he take into consideration that it was opening night, with the kitchen and staff getting their footing, and to tone down the spiteful remarks. But as that possibility ran through my mind,

Isabel approached the Leboeuf table. "Good evening," she said brightly, enhancing her greeting with a smile. "I'm so glad you came to help us celebrate the opening. I'm sure that when your restaurant opens, we'll all be there to help you —"

"You're the owner's mother," Leboeuf said through a Cheshire-cat smile. "You look just like your picture in the menu."

"Oh, I was a little younger then," Isabel said, her hand creeping up to touch her coiffure, "not quite as many gray hairs. I'm looking forward to having dinner in your place, Mr. Leboeuf. I hear that the food in your other restaurants is always wonderful."

Leboeuf looked at his companions as he said, "Well, compared to here, I suppose it always is."

It took Isabel a moment to grasp what he was saying. She started to reply, didn't find the words, pursed her lips to keep them from trembling, turned, and walked to the kitchen, almost tripping on her heels, which caused giggles at Leboeuf's table.

I was furious. I'm not a violent person, but I wanted to slap Gérard Leboeuf's face.

"Of all the nerve," I said to Seth.

With that the kitchen door swung open. Brad Fowler came through it and headed straight for Leboeuf. His mother stood in

89

the open doorway.

"Uh-oh," I said.

"You have a problem, Mr. Leboeuf?" he said, his face red, hands clenched into fists at his sides.

"Your food is second-rate," Leboeuf said, "and the service is pitiful."

Brad looked around the room. "Everyone else seems to be pleased."

"Maybe their standards are lower than mine," Leboeuf said, which elicited titters from his dining companions.

"What did you say to upset my mother?"

"Nothing at all! I told her she looks like her picture in this — in this tome you call a menu."

"If you're not pleased with your dinner — why don't you and your gang just get out of here before I punch your lights out?" Brad's voice was loud enough that other diners turned to see what was going on.

"So, you're not only the owner of a lousy restaurant," Leboeuf said as he stood, "you're a tough guy."

"I'll show you how tough I am," Brad said, making a move toward Leboeuf. He hadn't taken two steps before the two young men at the table sprang to their feet and stood between them.

"Get out of my way," Brad commanded.

One of the young men pushed Brad, causing him to stumble back. Marcie, who saw what was happening, ran through the dining room to her husband's side. "Stop it," she said.

"Your husband has a big mouth, sweetheart," Leboeuf said, patting her on the cheek.

Eva grabbed his arm. "Gérard? What are you doing?"

"Keep your hands off my wife," Brad said, unable to move around the blockade formed by Leboeuf's men.

"Please go," Marcie said, fighting to hold back tears. "There's no charge."

"With pleasure," Leboeuf said, taking out a wad of bills and throwing a few on the table. "For the waiter." To his entourage: "Let's get out of this dump. This place doesn't deserve our patronage."

Everyone in the dining room watched as they huffily abandoned their table and strode through the room, Leboeuf muttering under his breath on the way. Eva turned to look back at Marcie, her gaze cold. Wylie never took his eyes from his cell phone's screen as he walked with them.

Brad glared after them. Marcie rubbed her hand over his back and whispered something in an attempt to calm him down.

He breathed heavily, and his hands clenched and unclenched. He suddenly lurched away from her and disappeared into the kitchen, where his mother had also retreated.

Marcie looked at me and Seth and shook her head. She instructed the waiter to clear Leboeuf's table before pasting a tight smile on her face and returning to the dais at the front.

"What a shame," I said to Seth, who'd taken in the incident without commenting.

"There was no need for Mr. Leboeuf to act the way he did," Seth said, "no need at all. Downright rude and arrogant."

"I feel terrible for Marcie and Brad," I said. "It was supposed to be a festive, special night, and it ends up in an ugly confrontation. I feel saddest for Isabel. Her dream was to make their dream come true. She must be so upset."

From the buzz, I guessed that everyone in the restaurant was discussing what had just transpired. Seth and I picked at what was left of our lobster dinners, our appetites flown. "What a shame that Isabel had to see Brad treated with such disrespect," I said.

"He'll have to put it behind him," Seth commented. "He's got a business to run and —" He looked up to see Brad walking swiftly toward our table.

"Dr. Hazlitt," he said. "Come quick. Please. It's my mother."

Seth dropped his napkin, got up, and followed Brad to the kitchen. I waited a few moments to avoid making it appear as if a parade of people were heading into the kitchen, then followed. Seth was on his cell phone, standing next to Isabel, who sat in a chair, her face ashen. He pressed the cell phone to his ear, a frown creasing his face. "Right," he said. "Ayuh. Get some EMTs and an ambulance here yesterday, back door of the new restaurant on the pier, the Fin and Claw. Pull up Isabel Fowler's records in the computer. Have a stroke team waiting. I'll be there as soon as I can."

"Isabel's had a stroke?" I asked.

Seth nodded, his eyes grave. "I'll ride with her to the hospital. Sorry to abandon you."

"Don't give it a moment's thought."

The ambulance arrived within minutes, and two EMTs, carrying a wheeled gurney, entered the kitchen. A few minutes later they wheeled Isabel Fowler out, covered by a sheet up to her chin.

Seth fished in his wallet.

"You go ahead, Seth. I'll get the check. Plenty of friends here to give me a lift home."

I returned to the dining room and sank

back into my chair at the table. I looked at the half-consumed lobster on my plate and willed myself to not cry. Instead of a night of celebrating the grand opening of the Fin & Claw, the evening had turned into one of rancor and sorrow.

CHAPTER SEVEN

Marcie came to my table. "Will she be all right?" she asked.

"I hope so." It was the only thing I could think of at the moment. I walked her back to the entrance to keep our conversation private.

Mort Metzger joined us. "What's going on, Mrs. F.?" he asked.

"Isabel Fowler has been taken to the hospital. Seth says she's had a stroke."

"So that's why the doc hightailed it outta here."

"Yes. He's accompanying her."

"If you need a lift home, Maureen and I will take you."

Brad emerged from the kitchen. He'd shucked his white chef's garb and wore a sweater, jeans, and a tan Windbreaker. "I'm going to the hospital," he told Marcie.

"Do you want me to come with you?"

"You can't, sweetheart. Customers are still

95

coming in. I need you to take over here."

"Who'll run the kitchen?" she protested. "I'm not sure I know what to do."

"Jake can handle the kitchen. You'll be fine with the rest. Get a ride home from somebody when you close up," he said. "I'll call you later."

With that he was gone.

Marcie slumped on the stool behind the dais and rubbed her forehead. "What else can possibly happen?" she said, struggling to maintain her composure.

"If it's any comfort, you must know that Isabel is in competent hands," I said. I took in the dining room, which was filled with customers in various stages of enjoying their meals, some of them aware that something was wrong, others oblivious to the drama behind the scenes.

"Do you think you should announce that there's been a family emergency and close up?" I suggested to Marcie.

"No!" She wiped her eyes and stood. "Brad is trusting me to stay." She addressed a couple who had come to the podium to express their concern. "We've had a family emergency," she said, "but please don't let that spoil your evening."

I had to admire her fortitude.

"I'm going to see if Jake needs any help

on the cook line," she said. "Excuse me. I'll get to the hospital as soon as everyone is gone." She assigned one of the waitresses to cover the podium and went into the kitchen.

"We've already paid our bill," Mort said to me. "Maureen and I can take you home."

"Thank you, Mort, but I'd like to swing by the hospital on the way."

"No problem, Mrs. F."

I bade good-bye to friends at various tables — the Shevlins and Wilsons, Tim Purdy, photographer Richard Koser and his wife, Mary-Jane, and others. They had questions, which I managed to deflect, telling them that I'd talk to them the following day. I used a credit card to pay for our dinner and followed Mort and Maureen to their car. Fifteen minutes later we pulled up in front of the Cabot Cove General Hospital.

"Thanks for the lift," I said.

"Want us to come in with you?" Maureen asked.

"No, thank you. I'll see how Seth is doing. He'll drive me home."

When I entered the hospital's lobby, I saw Seth sitting with Brad Fowler on a bench in the far corner of the room. Seth waved me over.

"How is Isabel?" I asked.

Seth just shook his head, a somber expression on his face.

"Is she — ?"

"She's alive, but it was a massive stroke, intracerebral if I'm not mistaken. She's undergoing a CAT scan as we speak."

Brad, who was fighting back tears, asked, "Is she going to make it, Doctor?"

"We have to give it some time, Brad. We generally do pretty well with stroke victims who are treated within three or four hours of the onset, depending upon the sort of stroke it is. We've got a few good drugs that really help early on."

Brad stood and paced the lobby.

"Quite a night for him," I said to Seth.

"One he'd just as soon forget. What happened at the restaurant after I left?"

"Marcie took charge, and there's a sous chef named Jake who was taking over in the kitchen."

"Good. I keep thinking about that arrogant son-of-a-gun Leboeuf and the way he acted."

"He's the least of Brad's worries at this moment," I said.

Seth was paged and told me to wait for him. Brad slumped into the seat next to mine. "She was so happy today," he said. "She was smiling and trying to cheer me up, while I was a nervous wreck." He looked at me sadly. "I don't want to disappoint her, Mrs. Fletcher. She's invested all she could to make our dream come true — Marcie's and mine — even though we're not exactly experts in this business. She never held it over us. She spent hours in the kitchen, patiently showing me everything she knew. 'It's my pleasure,' she kept saying when I told her she needed to rest. Do you think that's what made her sick?"

"I'm sure Isabel was telling you the truth when she said it was her pleasure, Brad. And I don't see how that could have made her sick. Whatever health problems she has are not because she spent too much time teaching you to cook."

"She's the best mother a guy could ever ask for." He shook his head. "I haven't been the best son, I know. I was a terrible student. Got in trouble in school. I'm short-tempered and stubborn. I can't seem to help it. She says I'm just like my dad, but I think she just says that to give me an excuse." He sat back and closed his eyes, a tear escaping and rolling down his cheek. "At least I did one thing right."

"What's that?"

"I married her favorite person. She loves my wife like a daughter. And Marcie loves her right back."

"You're a lucky man to have two such beautiful women in your life."

Brad swiped under his eyes with his fingers and smiled. It was the first smile I'd seen on his face that evening, but it didn't last. "We'll take care of her no matter what. But what'll I do if I lose her, Mrs. Fletcher?" He shook his head and knocked a fist against his skull. "I can't even think like that."

"It's better not to anyway," I said. "Dr. Hazlitt and the other medical personnel will do everything in their power to keep her with us. We can't ask for more than that."

We said little more to each other until Seth returned twenty minutes later, his face etched with apprehension. He sighed as he sat next to Brad.

"It's not good news, son," he said. "I'm afraid she's sustained a lot of cranial bleeding. There is a strong possibility of permanent damage. All we can do is wait and see if the drugs will get her through."

"Can I see her?"

"Not right now. They've taken her up to intensive care. The specialists are working with her."

"How long will it take before we know?" Brad asked, his voice cracking.

Seth shrugged. "Certainly hours, perhaps

days. Sorry to have to be the one to tell you, Brad. If she survives the night, she might not be right. She might be . . ." He looked away.

"A vegetable?" Brad filled in. His head dropped into his hands and he moaned. "Nooo! She would hate that, absolutely hate that."

"Let's not think the worst," Seth said. He squeezed Brad's shoulder. "My suggestion is that you go back to the restaurant and take care of business there. I think Isabel would want you to do that. Don't you? I promise that I'll call you if there's any change."

"He's right," I told Brad. "There's nothing you can do for your mother here except worry. But I'm sure that Marcie needs your help right now."

Brad glanced at his watch and heaved a sigh. "Maybe you're right," he said. "She'll want to know what's going on. I'll check on things at the restaurant and we'll come back as soon as we close. Do you think we'd be able to see Mom then?"

"There's a much better chance once they've got her settled in and had an opportunity to monitor her response to the medication."

"Okay."

Seth and I watched the young man cross the lobby and disappear through the doors.

"I ache for him," I said. "The ugly scene with Leboeuf and now this. If trouble *does* come in threes, Seth, I dread to think what's next for Brad Fowler."

CHAPTER EIGHT

I waited while Seth looked in on his patient, consulted with his colleagues, and gave the hospital staff directions. Mort had kindly retrieved Seth's car and had a deputy park it at the hospital. Eventually we drove to my house, where I put up a kettle of water for tea for myself and my exhausted friend.

"Quite a night," Seth said as he pulled a teacup from my kitchen cabinet.

"So much has happened," I said, "that I'm having trouble wrapping my brain around it, from the opening of the Fin and Claw, the episode with Leboeuf and his party, and now the situation with Isabel. Will she make it, Seth?"

"We'll know soon enough," he said as he plopped a tea bag into boiling water. "Dr. Kloss is an expert on treating stroke patients, had plenty of experience at Mass General before settling here."

"I wonder how things ended up at the

restaurant," I mused, sipping my tea. "I hope that Brad's sous chef and Marcie were able to handle all the orders in the kitchen. More customers were arriving as I left with Mort and Maureen, so things must have gotten especially hard without Brad. The whole evening has been so upsetting."

"I'm sure they got through it okay, Jessica. Drink your tea. It'll calm you down."

Seth's assurances about the tea's soothing qualities didn't make them real. After he left I stayed up far past my usual bedtime, the night's events tumbling in my mind like a cement mixer on steroids. What was supposed to be a joyous evening had turned into something far removed from that. Was it John Lennon who said, "Life is what happens while you're making other plans?" I knew that he'd used it as a line in a song he wrote for his son, Sean, but it had appeared earlier than that in a number of places. Its genesis didn't matter. There was solid truth behind it, and this evening proved how accurate it really was.

I slept fitfully until the phone rang at seven the following morning. It was Seth.

"Sorry to start the day with bad news, Jessica," he said, "but we lost Isabel Fowler. She never recovered consciousness."

"Oh, Seth. I'm so sorry."

"Might be a blessing," he said. "If she'd survived . . . well, our stroke team said it was so severe, it wouldn't have left her with much of a life."

The rain of the previous night offered a surprise the next morning. It had turned into a wet snow, and there was lots of it. Maine is infamous for April snowstorms. Everyone in town hunkered down, as people in the snowbelt always do, this Maine resident included. I called the man who usually shovels me out but was informed by his wife that he'd taken a job at Gérard Leboeuf's restaurant and wouldn't be available any longer for shoveling duties. Fortunately, a young fellow who lived up the road knocked on the door to see if I needed help, and I was grateful to pay him to create a pathway from my front door to the road. A food store truck managed to traverse the slippery roads and delivered some groceries that I was running low on. With my cupboard full, I resigned myself to a long day at home.

News of Isabel Fowler's death spread quickly, and I received a number of calls from mutual friends. Mostly they wanted to express their shock at Isabel's untimely demise and to ask if I had any information about funeral arrangements — which I didn't. But some callers who hadn't attended the opening had also heard about what happened at the Fin & Claw and knew that I'd been present. I tried to make light of the event, pass it off as a simple misunderstanding. They seemed to accept that, although others, like Tim Purdy, Richard Koser, and Tobé Wilson, who'd also witnessed it, pressed me on whether I knew anything further about the dustup between Brad Fowler and Gérard Leboeuf. I downplayed it, and they were easily satisfied — or at least said that they were — but Evelyn Phillips of the *Cabot Cove Gazette* didn't even pretend to be content with my offhand dismissal of the confrontation.

"I was surprised you weren't there," I told her.

"Marcie Fowler invited me, but I had another engagement. Just my luck to have missed a doozy of a brawl."

"Oh, Evelyn, it was anything but a brawl, just a few words exchanged between Brad and Gérard Leboeuf."

She ignored my characterization and said, "On top of that, poor Isabel Fowler fell ill and had to be carried out on a stretcher. You heard, of course, that she died at the hospital."

"Yes, I did. I'm finding it hard to believe. I've known Isabel for so many years. Cabot Cove won't be the same without her."

"I didn't realize you knew her so well. I'm sorry for your loss, Jessica."

"Thank you. I do feel like I've lost a good friend. We were together over Thanksgiving when she shared the news that Brad and Marcie were opening a restaurant. And last night she was in such good spirits and proud of what they had accomplished."

"What do you think will happen to the restaurant?" Evelyn asked.

"Happen to it? What do you mean?"

"You saw the menu, Jessica. Isabel's photo is there and a list of all her recipes. Now that she's gone, I —"

"I assume that Brad and Marcie will forge ahead, Evelyn. They have a lot invested in this business. Not only because it's the right thing to do, but because it's a way to honor Isabel's memory."

"That's what Brad says."

I paused. "You've spoken to Brad?"

"No. I called the house to issue my condolences and got Marcie. Strong lady, that one, even in the face of a family calamity. Naturally she was very upset."

"Naturally."

"Brad wasn't there. He was at the funeral

107

home, making arrangements for his mother's wake. I asked Marcie about plans for the restaurant."

"And what did she say?"

"She wanted to close it down tonight as a tribute to Isabel, but Brad wouldn't hear of it. They evidently have a slew of reservations, and he doesn't want to lose the business, especially since they must be deep in debt."

"I can understand that. Closing temporarily, while a nice gesture, isn't what Isabel would have wanted."

"I suppose you're right, Jessica. Now, about the fight between Brad Fowler and Gérard Leboeuf. I'm told that the Leboeuf party was asked to leave in the middle of their dinners."

I glanced at my watch. It was time to end the conversation. I understood Evelyn's need as a newspaper editor to find out everything she could about what was going on in town, but I didn't want to be put in the position of analyzing for her what had occurred between other people. It would be thirdhand hearsay, and I wasn't about to sensationalize an unfortunate confrontation between a pair of excitable restaurateurs. "You'll have to ask Brad and Leboeuf," I said.

"But you were there, Jessica."

"Yes, I was, eating my dinner — the food was excellent — and not really paying attention to them. You'll have to excuse me, Evelyn, but I really have to run."

"Run *where*? With all this snow?"

"Lots to do around the house."

"I'm just asking you on background, Jessica. I won't quote what you say."

"You're a good reporter, Evelyn. You don't need me."

I heard a big sigh on the line. "Okay, but I may call you again later."

After spending the better part of the day housebound and on the phone, I decided to venture out with the help of my friendly taxi company, whose owners had the good sense to include four-wheel-drive vehicles in their small fleet. The driver dropped me off in front of Charles Department Store, where I sipped the latest coffee blend they were providing their customers and perused their assortment of winter boots on sale.

"That must have been quite a tussle at Brad Fowler's restaurant last night," the clerk, who'd been working at the store for a long time, said as she rang up my purchase.

"How did you hear about that?"

"That's all everyone is talking about today," she said. "I had a customer who was

109

seated near to Gérard Leboeuf and his party. She said that he was pretty obnoxious."

I didn't respond.

"It's too awful about Isabel Fowler, isn't it?" she said. "Dr. Hazlitt's nurse was in earlier and told me. Nice lady. Must have come as a shock to everyone. One minute she's enjoying her son's restaurant opening, and the next minute she's dead."

"A terrible tragedy," I said.

"What do you think is going to happen with the Fowlers' restaurant, Mrs. Fletcher?"

"I hope it will be a huge success."

"It won't be, according to Mr. Leboeuf."

"Oh?"

"He came in to buy a strainer. For his new kitchen, he said, but I think he just wanted to be seen around town."

"And what did he say?"

"When I asked him if Brad and Marcie's restaurant would make it tough for him to open his new place, he laughed and said something like, 'I never have a problem with amateurs. I give them a month before they fold.' "

"Not an especially generous comment," I said. "Most important is that he be proved wrong, which I'm sure will be the case."

"Of course, I hope so, too. Well, enjoy your new boots, Jessica."

"I'm sure I will. Thanks for your help."

A call to the taxi company brought the same driver who'd delivered me downtown, and I was ensconced in my study a half hour later with a steaming cup of tea on my desk and a pile of correspondence I'd retrieved from my mailbox. In a velvety cream-colored envelope was an invitation from Gérard Leboeuf to be his guest at the grand opening of his new restaurant the following weekend.

I debated whether to accept. I'd developed a sour taste in my mouth about Gérard Leboeuf. He was a self-centered man to begin with, and his behavior at the Fin & Claw had been atrocious. Every time I thought about it, I got angry on behalf of the Fowlers. My heart went out to Marcie and Brad. It's difficult enough to go into debt to launch a new business, with all the stress that it involves, but then to lose the one person who shared their commitment to the dream both emotionally and financially must be unbearable. That was a lot for a young couple to face without having someone make a show of trashing their efforts in public. Tapping the envelope on my desk, I decided to call Seth to see if he, too, had received the invitation.

"Ayuh," he said. "Arrived in today's mail."

"Are you planning to go?"

"Been thinkin' about it. You?"

"I've been — thinking about it."

"I talked to a new patient of mine who works in Leboeuf's kitchen. He says that Leboeuf is picking up the tab for everyone on opening night."

"No such thing as a free meal, Seth," I reminded him.

"Not always true, Jessica. Sampling what comes out of his kitchen doesn't carry with it an obligation to like the man. Hopefully, his opening night won't end up the way the Fowlers' did. I think we should accept Mr. Leboeuf's hospitality. It's not as though he doesn't have the money to put on a spread. Besides, I happen to like French food, especially onion soup prepared the right way, and steak frites."

Seth's reasoning didn't surprise me. He's the ultimate pragmatist, although he can project an ornery side if someone rubs him the wrong way.

"You'll be my date for the evening?" he asked, a hint of mirth in his voice. "I know that your Inspector Sutherland isn't here to escort you, but I'll do my best to fill in for him."

112

The sentiment behind his comment wasn't lost on me. My friend George Sutherland was a senior investigator for Scotland Yard in London, and we'd struck up a "relationship" after first meeting years ago. Seth was well aware of the fondness that had developed between George and me, and enjoyed teasing me about it from time to time. Close friends speculated that Seth might be jealous of the handsome, dashing Scotland Yard inspector, which I always dismissed. If anything, I considered Seth to be a good friend and adviser of sorts, not a potential paramour. The truth was that as much as I adored George Sutherland, I wasn't looking for a romantic relationship with anyone.

So Seth and I accepted the invitation to be Gérard Leboeuf's guests at the opening of his French bistro, and I hoped that Brad and Marcie Fowler wouldn't view it as an act of disloyalty.

The week leading up to Leboeuf's grand opening was eventful and sad. I attended Isabel Fowler's funeral with a large number of men and women who knew and loved her, and the eulogy given by her son, Brad, emptied everyone's tear ducts. Isabel had been on view in her casket at the funeral home prior to the church service, and a succession of mourners passed to issue their final good-byes. Quite a few people spoke — Isabel had many friends in Cabot Cove — and it was a lovely tribute to a lovely woman who had been a valued member of our community. At one point I found myself talking with Brad, who'd retreated to a secluded corner of the large room.

"Mom looks beautiful, doesn't she?" he said.

"She was always a beautiful woman, Brad. I feel privileged to have been her friend. How are you and Marcie holding up?"

"We're all right. Thank goodness for the restaurant. It was Mom's dream for us, and now we get to carry on her dream. I'm glad we've been real busy, because it leaves less time to feel sorry for ourselves."

"I understand the Fin and Claw is doing splendidly," I said.

"I don't know about splendid, but yeah, business is good. Did you see the review Ms. Phillips gave us in the *Gazette*?"

"I certainly did," I said, smiling. "And well deserved."

"I'm sorry about the way things turned out on opening night when you and Dr. Hazlitt were there."

"It couldn't be helped, Brad. Besides, it certainly wasn't your fault."

"It was that nasty b—" He paused. "That louse, Leboeuf," he said, venom in his voice.

I didn't want to get into that sort of discussion but wasn't sure how to smoothly transition to something else. "Now is not the time to talk about him," I finally said. "I'm just glad that your mom was around long enough to see her picture and recipes in the menu."

"He insulted her," Brad said flatly. "She was shaking when she came into the kitchen after she talked to him." Tears filled his eyes. "She was so upset. That's probably what caused her stroke. As far as I'm concerned, he's responsible for my mother's death."

I looked beyond him and saw Marcie talking with a small group of visitors.

"I think Marcie wants you, Brad."

"She does?" He looked back, took a deep breath, and let it out. "Okay. Thanks for being here, Mrs. Fletcher. Mom would have been pleased that you came."

I was disappointed at how our conversation had ended. The resentment Brad harbored toward Gérard Leboeuf was not going to go away, and I was afraid it would have ramifications as time progressed. We were going to have two new restaurants competing with each other, and that could have been positive for Cabot Cove. But negative feelings were running deep in both men. Combine Brad's rage with Leboeuf's arrogance and I could see only further unpleasantness down the road.

CHAPTER NINE

"Jessica, I have a favor to ask." Maureen's voice sounded urgent.

"Of course, Maureen. Is something wrong?"

"Oh, gee, I hope not."

Mort's redheaded wife was prone to theatrics, but now she had me thoroughly confused. "Well, what can I do for you?"

"I sent a sample in with Mort this morning, and before I send it over, I just wanted you to tell me if it's okay."

"You sent a sample of what with Mort? And you're sending something over where? And what am I supposed to tell you is okay?"

"Really, Jessica. I thought you'd understand. Didn't you hear what I said?"

"Why don't you slow down and start over, Maureen. I'm listening."

"Okay. I gave Mort two of my pies to bring into the station-house. He's supposed to drop one off with Marcie Fowler. She said she'd buy pies from me, but only if I used Isabel's recipe, which I did. I made two pies using fresh strawberries; they're exactly the same."

"All right. Now I think I see. And the favor you're requesting? Did you want me to taste one of the pies before he brings the other one to Marcie?"

"Yes," she said on a long sigh. "My reputation is at stake here, Jessica. If Marcie refuses to accept my pie, I'll never be able to hold my head up in this town again."

"I don't think Marcie would spread nasty rumors about your pie, but I'm not certain my skills as a pastry taster are enough to get you hired."

"Well, even if I don't get hired, if you taste one of the pies and say it's okay, then whether she accepts the other one or not, at least I'll know I made it right."

We agreed that I would stop in at the sheriff's office and offer my considered opinion on the quality of his wife's strawberry pie. Maureen said she'd call ahead so Mort would expect me. Unfortunately, pie was the last thing on Mort's mind when I pushed through the door that morning.

"I understand your concern, Mr. Souzy,

but we have procedures we have to follow, just like everyone else," he was telling a gentleman in a navy blue pinstripe suit.

"Don't give me your 'procedures' routine, Sheriff. You know as well as I that an immediate arraignment is not only acceptable under the law, but preferable. I have a note here from Judge Hastings that says he'll open his court for the boy if you'll have your deputies bring him over. We can even do a video arraignment if you don't have anyone available. You have the equipment, I assume?"

"We don't do video arraignments as a matter of course." Mort ran his fingers through his hair. "There's a long list of conditions that have to be met before that takes place."

"Look, I want this boy out of jail, and I want him out now. Give me a copy of the complaint and do whatever you have to do to make it happen!"

Music from the original *Dragnet* television program sounded from Mr. Souzy's pocket. He pulled out his phone and barked into it, "Hold on!" He aimed a raised eyebrow at Mort. "I have to take this call. When I get back, I want Wylie ready to go to court." He marched out of the station, yelling into his phone. "What? Speak up. I can't hear you."

Mort let out a big sigh and sank into his chair. He cocked his head at me.

"Was that Millard Souzy?" I asked. Souzy was a criminal defense lawyer with myriad connections in Maine's legal and legislative worlds, including close ties with some of the area's judges.

"The very same."

"And is the Wylie he's talking about Gérard Leboeuf's son?"

Mort nodded. "But you didn't hear it from me."

I took one of the chairs across from his desk. "What was he arrested for?"

"Possession of CDS — controlled dangerous substances — with intent to sell. We got a tip about him dealing, and when my men went to question him, he had enough marijuana and cocaine on his person to set up shop on the worst blocks of Alphabet City. I'd like to know who his supplier is, and it better not be anyone in town." He picked up his phone and dialed a number. "Chip, bring in the Leboeuf boy. You're going to take one of the cruisers and deliver him to Judge Hastings's court. Yeah, I know he plays golf on Tuesdays, but he's holding off to accommodate our celebrity boarder."

The sound of angry voices reached us from outside. Gérard Leboeuf stormed into the station house followed by a ruffled Millard Souzy.

"Where is he?" Leboeuf shouted at Mort.

"At the moment, he's in cell C, Mr. Leboeuf. One of my deputies is just bringing him here."

"What have you got him on?"

"Possession with intent to sell."

"Is that all?"

"It's more than enough to arrest him. He was carrying twenty packets of what we believe to be cocaine. More than fourteen grams makes it a felony. If any of those packets turns out to be heroin —"

Leboeuf cut him off with, "Spare me the details."

"Gérard, would you let me handle this, please?" Souzy said.

"You said you'd have him out in an hour, and he's still here."

"Like it or not, there are procedures to follow."

I saw Mort rub his jaw and was sure he was covering a smile.

The door leading to the jail cells swung open, and Chip led in a scruffy-looking Wylie. He didn't have enough of a beard to affect the stubble look so popular these days, but his hair was greasy, and he was wearing what I'd come to think of as the standard teenage uniform: ripped blue jeans and a puffy black ski jacket. When he caught sight of his father, he smirked.

"Get that nasty smile off your face," Leboeuf snarled, striding across the room. He stopped in front of his son and slapped him across the face.

Both Chip and Mort jumped to pull Leboeuf away. "I'll have none of that," Mort said, "or you'll end up occupying the cell we just took him out of." Mort glared at Souzy. "Get him out of here now. And there better not be any more violence at the courthouse."

Souzy tugged a furious Leboeuf toward the door. "Come on, Gérard. This is not the time or the place."

Wylie held a palm to his red cheek and sniffled. "Hey, he's not allowed to do that, is he? Don't I have any rights here? Why don't you arrest him?"

"I'll talk to you about rights, you mewling, cowardly spawn of Satan."

"You're talking about yourself, you know," Wylie yelled. "I'm your spawn. That makes you Satan." He forced a laugh, but it sounded as if he was closer to tears.

Leboeuf seemed to notice me for the first

time. "You!" He pointed at me. "I'd better not see any of this in the newspaper," he said.

"You're in no danger from me, Mr. Leboeuf. I'm not a reporter."

"That's okay. That's okay," Wylie said. "Tell everybody. Tell them the son of the great Chef Leboeuf is a criminal just like his dad."

"Wylie!" Leboeuf roared, but Souzy pushed him out the door.

Mort shook his head and looked at Chip. "I'll get someone to bring my cruiser around to the side entrance, and when you get to the court, don't let his father anywhere near him. I'll alert Judge Hastings."

While Mort made arrangements to transport Wylie to the courthouse, I pondered what had just taken place. In my estimation, Leboeuf's son was a little old to be exhibiting signs of teenage rebellion, but that appeared to be the case. If he was using drugs — and worse, selling them — as a way to gain his father's attention, he couldn't be pleased with the results. Then again, if he was trying to punish his father for whatever reason, he'd certainly found the ideal line of attack.

Once the prisoner was taken out, Mort offered me a cup of coffee, which I declined.

123

He poured a large mug for himself and sank down at his desk. "I never asked why you came in, Mrs. F. And then all this craziness took place."

"I don't suppose you want to talk about strawberry pies at this juncture, do you?"

Mort slapped his forehead and groaned. "Maureen's pies! Oh, no. I left them in the trunk of the cruiser. And now I just sent them over to the courthouse with the kid."

Leboeuf's Saturday-night grand opening was only a few days away. On the Thursday preceding it, I attended a morning meeting of the Cabot Cove Historical Society chaired by Tim Purdy. As the town grew, it had become increasingly difficult to keep progress from infringing upon our historic past. Tim and his crew of volunteers did a splendid job of fighting to preserve that past, and I was an enthusiastic member of the committee.

Evelyn Phillips attended the meeting, as she usually did, to report in her newspaper on its activities, and I sat next to her as the tall, erudite Tim ran down his ambitious agenda for the upcoming months. It was during a break for coffee and doughnuts that Evelyn took me aside.

"You've heard, of course," she said, "about

the Leboeuf boy."

"You shouldn't assume that I hear every rumor the moment it's launched," I said.

"Well, this isn't a rumor. He was arrested for drug possession."

"I'm sorry to hear that," I said, deciding not to admit I was already privy to the particulars.

"His father hired Millard Souzy to defend him. Souzy arranged for an arraignment, and the boy was released on bail," Evelyn further explained.

"Is he charged with selling drugs, or using them?"

"From the information I've gotten, he had enough with him to be charged with intent to sell, but I don't know whether he was charged with that. I'll have to go back and ask Mort; he didn't specify."

"I didn't know he made a public statement."

"Don't look so surprised, Jessica. Unlike our previous sheriff, Mort believes in transparency where the press is concerned. The public has a right to know."

"I'm well aware of that," I said, masking my annoyance at being lectured on civics.

She lowered her voice to a conspiratorial level. "I'm told that the boy had similar problems in New York."

"From good sources, I'm sure."

"Of course. I wouldn't put any faith in it if my sources weren't credible."

Now we were equally irritated with each other.

While I recognized that Evelyn Phillips was a dedicated and experienced newspaperwoman who was tenacious in bringing news of Cabot Cove to its citizens, she and I didn't always agree. She'd worked on big-city papers before settling in our town and had transformed the *Gazette* from a sloppily written and edited vehicle for press releases and publicity hounds eager to get their pictures on the front page into a paper with thorough coverage of Cabot Cove and its environs, and with integrity in its reporting. That kind of thoroughness, however, could approach impinging on people's privacy, on occasion mine. This wasn't the first time that Evelyn had gotten my hackles up, nor would it be the last. But my respect for her tempered my moments of pique.

"I'm sorry that Wylie is in this sort of trouble," I said. "It must be especially difficult to be a child of two well-known people and have a spotlight shone on you whenever you behave badly."

"Being charged with a crime is more than

misbehavior, Jessica."

"I agree, Evelyn. I was speaking in generalities. By the way, will you be at Leboeuf's opening Saturday night?" I asked, hoping the change in topic would smooth the waters between us.

"I wouldn't miss it. You?"

"Seth and I will be there," I said. "We're hoping it will be more peaceful than the Fin and Claw's grand opening."

Evelyn's laugh was ironic. "It'll make for a better story if it isn't. See you there, Jessica."

With the Fin & Claw in mind, I decided to drop in for lunch after the meeting. Marcie Fowler had taken an ad in the *Gazette* announcing their daily specials, which included Isabel Fowler's prize-winning chowder recipe. Although the snow had melted, the temperature outside was still nippy — the perfect chowder weather. The restaurant was half-empty when I arrived, and Marcie led me to a table. Although she flashed a smile, I could see signs of strain on her face.

"How are things?" I asked after I'd been seated and told her that I'd been enticed by Isabel's clam chowder recipe.

"Things are   well, to be honest, things aren't going all that well."

127

"I imagine it takes time to build up a crowd at lunchtime."

"It isn't that," she said, hesitating.

"Anything I can do to help?"

She drew a breath before leaning forward and whispering, "The inspector for the Maine Center for Disease Control and Prevention inspected us yesterday for sanitary violations."

"And?"

"And we failed on more than one count."

"Oh, my goodness. I'm sorry to hear that," I said. "Were they serious violations?"

"Any health violation for a restaurant is serious," she said. "The thing is, we've been meticulous about keeping the kitchen clean. I just don't know how . . ." Marcie spotted two customers coming through the front door and excused herself, leaving me to ponder what I'd just heard.

That Brad and Marcie Fowler would allow an unhealthy situation to exist in their restaurant was a surprise to me, and apparently to them. I suppose that it was possible they'd overlooked a regulation in dealing with the Fin & Claw's hectic opening and the events that followed.

"Tell me more about the inspection, Marcie," I said in a low voice after she had returned to my table.

"I'm sick over it. It'll be around town before the day is out." She looked around the restaurant. "Maybe it already is."

"How serious *were* the violations?" I asked.

She looked to the front of the restaurant, saw that no new customers were arriving, and took the chair across from me. "That miserable man Harold Greene came in here unannounced, flashed his stupid badge, and said he was here to inspect the premises. Brad told him he should have made an appointment, but Greene ignored that."

"Sorry to interrupt, Marcie," I said, "but it's routine for inspectors to arrive unannounced so the owner doesn't have advance notice and time to clean up."

She reared back and looked at me as though I were an enemy. I realized I probably shouldn't have defended Greene so abruptly.

"Maybe I'm wrong," I said.

"I don't know, Mrs. Fletcher. Maybe you're right. Anyway, Greene just marched into our kitchen, a clipboard and pen in his hand, and started looking around." She leaned forward again. "Mrs. Fletcher, I swear to you, the kitchen is pristine. Brad is a fussbudget about cleanliness. At home he rinses the dishes so thoroughly that by the

129

time he puts them in the dishwasher they're squeaky clean."

I smiled at her anecdote.

"Greene found some things that he said were violations, silly little things like whether certain cooking utensils were too close to one another, how we store mayonnaise — which, by the way, is the right way to store it. And then . . ."

I waited.

"He got down on his knees and started looking at the floor under the range. He looked up, a smug expression on his face, and said, 'mouse droppings.'"

"Oh, dear."

"Mrs. Fletcher, those mouse droppings weren't there when he arrived. He put them there. I know it. I just know he did."

"That's a serious charge, Marcie. What can you do about it?"

She stood, misery etched into her pretty face. "He gave us two days to correct the alleged violations, but even if we do — and how do you correct something that isn't there in the first place? — we've been fined four hundred dollars."

"That's a lot of money."

"Everything is a lot of money, Mrs. Fletcher. It seems that there's no end to what we have to lay out. It's a nightmare.

This whole experience of opening a restaurant has been one big, expensive headache."

I smiled and reached for her hand. "It's really early in the game," I said. "Starting something as ambitious as a restaurant always involves unexpected expenses and setbacks."

"Tell that to Brad," she said.

"Where is he?"

"In the kitchen. Please look in on him before you leave. I know he'll be glad to see you. He's beside himself."

After I'd finished my soup and paid the bill, I took her suggestion and pushed open the swinging door into the kitchen, then questioned whether I should have. Brad was in the midst of a rant against his sous chef, Jake, calling him names I'd just as soon not repeat. Jake responded by whipping off his white apron and throwing it at Brad, who caught it and flung it across the kitchen.

Jake pushed past me just as Marcie was coming into the kitchen. "Jake, where are you going?"

"I'm outta here."

"Oh, hi, Mrs. Fletcher," Brad said, breathing hard in an attempt to calm down.

"Hello, Brad. I'm sorry if I'm disturbing anything, but Marcie thought it would be a good idea for me to stop by to see you."

"Mrs. Fletcher has some good advice for us," Marcie put in.

I tried to remember the advice I was supposed to impart.

"Really? The only advice I need is how to get rid of that shark Leboeuf. I'd like to tear his heart out."

"You don't know for certain that he's behind Mr. Greene's findings during the inspection," Marcie said. "And why were you arguing with Jake again?"

"He's in Leboeuf's pocket. I'm sure of it! Who else? Mouse droppings? Either he or the inspector put them there. There are no mice in this kitchen, Marcie, and you know it."

"Brad, please calm down."

"Calm down? Leboeuf is opening his place in a couple of days. Do you know what's he's doing, Marcie? He sent Jed Richardson to Boston in his plane to bring a couple of celebrities to Cabot Cove for his opening."

"So he has more connections than we have. So what? The celebrities aren't going to stay around to keep eating at his restaurant."

"He and his gang have been bad-mouthing our food all over town."

I tried to smooth things over. "The people in Cabot Cove are more likely to place their faith in someone they've known all his life than in newcomers to town," I said. "You have to trust in people's good judgment, Brad."

"That's only the start of it, Mrs. Fletcher. He's scheduled full-page ads for almost a month in the *Gazette.* And look at this." He handed Marcie a receipt from a vendor. "Joey, who delivers our bread, says that he can't supply us anymore, because Leboeuf has put in a big order for his place here in Cabot Cove and for all his restaurants around the country."

"Why would he buy his bread for his other restaurants from a baker here in Maine?" I asked.

"To cut off our supplies."

"Can he do that?" Marcie asked.

"He can keep us from getting it at a decent price," Brad said, shaking his head sadly. "And what about Winston down at the dock?"

My quizzical expression prompted Brad to say, "Tell her, Marcie."

"Caleb Winston called to tell us that he wouldn't be able to provide us with fresh clams any longer."

"You don't have to ask why, Mrs. Fletcher.

I'll tell you. Because Leboeuf bought him out. He put in such a large standing order that Caleb said he can't ignore it."

"He was all apologetic, of course," Marcie said. "Brad and he went to high school together. But Caleb said that Leboeuf's order commits him to all the clams he can dig."

"There's no way that Leboeuf can use as many clams as he's ordered," Brad said, his voice rising. "He just wants to corner the market on them and keep us from another source."

"There must be other clam diggers in Cabot Cove," I said.

"But it's like starting all over again," Marcie said, "researching the quality of supplies and making deals with new vendors. We thought we already had those arrangements covered. That kind of planning takes time, and we'd already moved on to the next phase, until Leboeuf —"

"See?" Brad said. "It's Leboeuf, always Leboeuf." He slammed a spatula on the stainless steel countertop, causing the other three workers in the kitchen to jump and to look at one another.

Marcie tried to calm him down by saying, "Brad, you have to get ahold of yourself. I'm worried you're going to get sick. Mrs.

Fletcher told me that these sorts of problems are only natural when opening a new restaurant." She looked at me imploringly. "Isn't that right?"

Brad sighed. "What do you know about opening a restaurant?"

"Nothing, I'm afraid," I said, taken aback by his question. "I'm only trying to give you my support. I'm sorry that you had a problem with the inspector, but I'm sure it will work out all right." I made a show of looking at my watch. "I wish I could offer you something more concrete, but right now I have to leave."

"Thanks for trying to help, Mrs. Fletcher," Marcie said as we walked from the kitchen into the dining room. "Can I offer you some dessert? On the house. We have a new strawberry pie on the menu today."

"Another time," I said.

Across the way, at Leboeuf's restaurant, trucks were delivering produce, meat, and fish for the opening-night festivities. The thought of attending his opening wasn't especially appealing at that moment. While Gérard Leboeuf had every right to live in Cabot Cove and to open his French bistro, he was spreading rancor and bad feelings throughout the town I loved. I wished that he'd found another idyllic seaside spot in which to build a summer home and expand his restaurant empire.

Brad Fowler was justified in being upset. Leboeuf was up to his old tricks, putting pressure on his competitor by closing off his suppliers — pressure that the smaller business was not prepared to counter. There was nothing I could do to help. It was true that I didn't know anything about opening a restaurant. My fear was that Brad and Marcie didn't either. But they were learning, and learning fast, that all was not fair in love and war — and the restaurant business.

CHAPTER TEN

Despite my misgivings about attending the launch of Leboeuf's restaurant, it was only natural to be swept up in the anticipation of the opening. Although Seth was loath to exhibit his excitement — well, maybe "excitement" is too strong a word where Seth is concerned — he'd dressed for the occasion, just as I had. After he admired my outfit, we drove to the town dock, where uniformed valets parked his car.

The weather had cooperated, and it was a beautiful night. When we arrived, there was a vivid red carpet at the entranceway, and two video crews trained their cameras on arriving guests. It felt as though we were attending the Oscars. I spotted Evelyn Phillips, who was gussied up for the occasion after an afternoon at Loretta's Beauty Shop, where I'd also had my hair done. She was interviewing one of the celebrities who'd been flown from Boston for the occasion, a tall, striking redhead who regularly appeared on a TV reality show — which I'd never seen and didn't intend to, but knew about from Evelyn's write-up in the *Gazette*. The other celebrity attending tonight was a news anchor from a Boston television station, a familiar handsome man with a deep voice who delivered the day's grim news each night.

I knew that Seth was eager to try the food at Leboeuf's "authentic" French bistro. He loved steak frites and onion soup and was a real fan of crème brûlée, especially the vanilla variety, which he'd pointed out was on the menu and had been featured in an ad that Leboeuf had placed in the *Gazette*.

Across the street, the parking lot of the Fin & Claw was half-empty. That wasn't necessarily a bad sign for Brad and Marcie Fowler. It's hard to compete with a grand opening of any sort, and particularly one in which the dinner was being given away free. But it was only one night; their competitor would be charging for his dishes the next day.

The bistro was crowded with familiar faces from town and many that I didn't recognize. I glanced across the lobby and saw another cadre of friends. Spirits were high. The sound of a string trio playing spirited French tunes — I immediately thought of Édith Piaf — wafted through the restaurant's open door. No doubt about it — Gérard Leboeuf had gone all-out for his special night. He may not have had George Clooney and Meryl Streep in attendance, but the evening had all the trappings of a movie premiere.

I wondered what role Leboeuf's wife, Eva, played in the restaurants. She was a stunning woman who'd once graced the covers of leading magazines, and she would make a smashing hostess. But she wasn't at the reception desk. I also looked for their son, Wylie, but he wasn't in attendance either, at least as far as I could see. Evelyn's revelation about his arrest on drug charges may have prompted his parents to keep him away from an event that attracted news coverage. Those were my thoughts as I looped my arm in Seth's and we went inside, where Leboeuf himself greeted us.

"Ah, Mrs. Fletcher and Dr. Hazlitt. What a pleasure to see you again, and so glad you could come." He winked at me. "All is forgiven, eh?"

"Your restaurant is lovely," I said, avoiding his question as I took in the bistro's dining room. It was all glittering glass and chrome, reflecting lights from the crystal chandeliers in the mirrors that ringed the room. A wall of wine bottles nestled on curved steel mesh shelves. Crisp white tablecloths showed off sparkling place settings, and huge vases of fresh flowers in strategic spots softened the hard edges throughout the room. I thought of my favorite French restaurant in New York City, L'Absinthe, and how different Leboeuf's French Bistro was from Jean-Michel Bergougnoux's approach to establishing a Continental mood for his customers. Whether the food was as good as Jean-Michel's was yet to be determined.

Leboeuf's guests for the evening weren't immediately seated. Waiters passed trays of fancy hors d'oeuvres and glasses of champagne while Leboeuf made his way through the crowd, his face set in an expansive smile, shaking hands, slapping backs, and in general making everyone feel welcome.

Seth and I circulated among friends and ended up chatting with my dentist, Ed Filler, who'd recently repaired a cracked tooth for me. Ed's full name was Edward Zachary Filler, an apt name for his profession. The sign in front of the home he shared with his wife, Elaine, and where his office was located, read E.Z. FILLER,

DENTIST, and was regularly stolen as a souvenir. Ed and Elaine's waterfront home was one property removed from the summer mansion that Leboeuf had constructed. I was pleased to see that the restaurateur had invited the couple next door.

"Quite a shindig," Ed commented.

"Mr. Leboeuf has gone all out," I said.

"This is Cabot Cove's first and only French restaurant," Elaine said. "Don't you love the music? I can't wait to try the food."

"Well," Seth said, "your neighbor is putting on quite a show. I imagine that you and the Leboeuf family have become good friends, living near to each other as you do."

They looked at each other and grinned.

"Hard to be good friends with people who are seldom there," Elaine said, "although they have spent more time at the house since construction of the restaurant started."

Ed laughed. "We always know when they're in residence, however. Never a quiet moment."

Seth was not about to let that go. "Meaning what?"

Ed lowered his voice. "I shouldn't say this, since we're his guests tonight, but the Leboeufs tend to be loud when they're fighting."

"They do that often?" Seth pressed.

"Often enough," Elaine said. "When the police arrived . . ."

Her husband shook his head.

"Well, there's no need to go into that."

"Police?" Seth said.

I hadn't mentioned to him that the Leboeuf boy had been arrested on a drug charge.

"It's not important," Ed said as he reached out and plucked an hors d'oeuvre off a passing tray. "Don't bite down on anything hard," he told me through a laugh. "I'm off duty."

The cocktail hour at an end, waiters began leading guests to their tables. At each place was a small shopping bag with the name of the restaurant on its side. I saw Maureen Metzger draw out a card and smile.

While we waited our turn, Eva Leboeuf entered the room and walked up to her husband, who'd been chatting with customers. The look on her face indicated she was not especially pleased at the moment, and her stern expression was at odds with the perpetual grin Gérard had adopted for the evening. Seeing his wife, Leboeuf's smile dipped into a scowl. He started to say something, but she snarled at him, waving a long, manicured, crimson-tipped index finger in his face, and turned her back to

142

her husband, surveying the room.

Seth had noticed their exchange, too. "That's one angry lady. Do you know about this business of the police going to Leboeuf's home?"

I nodded. "His son was arrested for drug possession."

"And where did you learn that, Jessica?"

"I was at the sheriff's office when Mort released him."

Leboeuf, his lips once more set in an upward curve, invited stragglers to find their tables and announced that dinner would soon be served. Eva drifted away from him in our direction.

Settled in our seats, Seth and I peeked into our little shopping bags to find a lipstick sample — "Not my color," he said, handing it to me — and a tiny vial of men's cologne — "This will smell better on you," I said, dropping it in his bag. Also inside mine were a postcard advertising Eva's cosmetics website, a refrigerator magnet with the telephone number of Leboeuf's French Bistro in large numbers, and a small box covered in gold foil. I opened it to find a delicate glass with the Leboeuf logo embossed in gold on its side.

"This is stunning," I said, holding up the glass.

"Isn't it?" Eva said.

I hadn't seen her come up to our table.

She took the glass from my hand and held it up to the light.

"What's it for?" Seth asked.

She seemed startled by the question and handed the glass back to me. "It's a stemless wineglass, of course. We had them especially made for the opening by a glassblower in Murano. They used cotton gloves to pack them." She gave me a wan smile. "Sorry if I smudged yours."

"Not at all," I said. "It's very beautiful. I'll look forward to using it."

"You do that."

Seth waited until Eva stopped at another table before he handed me his box. "You take it. I'll only break it."

"Are you sure? It's a lovely memento."

"I'm sure." He folded up his bag and stuffed it in his jacket pocket. "The Leboeufs certainly know how to leverage their brand."

" 'Leverage their brand?' When did you become so knowledgeable about marketing?"

"You're not the only one who reads the business sections of the newspaper."

Our host interrupted our conversation by bringing Walter Chang from the kitchen and introducing him. "Can we assure these good people that you will see to it that every dish they order reflects the best in French cooking and is done to their liking?"

"Yes, Chef," Chang barked on cue. He seemed anxious to get back to the kitchen but dutifully thanked everyone for coming.

Leboeuf led a round of applause while Chang disappeared through the swinging doors. "And so, as proprietor of Leboeuf's French Bistro, I give you the classic gastronomic salutation: *Bon appétit!*"

Seth rubbed his palms together. "Well, I'm eager to sample some authentic French cooking. Haven't had it since the last time I was in Cuba, of all places."

"Good cooking crosses all borders," I commented as I opened the menu. "Where shall we start?"

As the evening progressed, I was taken with the smooth choreography of the dining room, in contrast to what had been more fitful service at the Fin & Claw's opening night. That reflection naturally morphed into thoughts of Brad and Marcie Fowler, and I wondered how they were doing that evening. Had Leboeuf invited them to the opening? That would have been a neighborly gesture, although given his crass behavior at their restaurant's debut, I doubted if they would have accepted any overtures of friendship from him. Then again, judging from the way Leboeuf had roped off his parking lot to keep opening-night patrons of the Fin & Claw from using it, it was unlikely he had been diplomatic enough to try to mend the breach he had created. What a shame that such bad feelings existed between them. Cabot Cove has always been a friendly place. Yes, there's competition between some business interests here, but they've always been played out with little ill will, with a few exceptions.

The food was superb. Around us, as waiters passed with trays of French specialties, we caught the delicious aromas, our anticipation rising. The meals did not disappoint. Once we were served, Seth took his time over onion soup, a crock of rich beef and onion broth with a crust of melted cheese on top, followed by steak frites, a French version of steak and fries that featured a robust sauce made from the pan juices. I enthusiastically dipped into my coq au vin, a classic Gallic stew of chicken cooked in red wine with mushrooms, onions, and garlic. If I closed my eyes, I could bring up visions of the French countryside where I'd sampled some of these dishes years ago.

We lingered over his dessert — I'd passed on ordering one, but enjoyed a few spoonfuls of Seth's vanilla crème brûlée — and strong coffee.

"I'd say that Mr. Leboeuf knows his way around a kitchen," Seth said after scraping the final dollop of crème brûlée from its scalloped ceramic shell and patting his lips with his napkin.

"Or Mr. Chang does," I inserted.

"All in all a delightful meal."

"If the food is any barometer, Leboeuf's French Bistro will be a rousing success."

Seth nodded. "Hope it is. Hope Isabel's son's venture does well, too. Hope they all succeed. Did you read what Leboeuf said in that feature on him in Evelyn's newspaper?"

"That he foresees Cabot Cove becoming an even greater tourist attraction in a few years?"

"Ayuh. Seems a bit over-the-top, wouldn't you say?"

I had to agree. While our idyllic seaside town in picturesque Maine had been growing — and our annual Lobsterfest drew big crowds — to envision Cabot Cove as a tourist mecca was a stretch. But I supposed that Leboeuf had to justify, at least in his own mind, his reason for committing so much money to opening a restaurant here.

Eva Leboeuf passed by our table a few more times, but she didn't stop again. She was tall and willowy and walked with the sort of self-assurance that beautiful women usually possess. I took note that she rarely spoke with anyone, simply made herself visible to the patrons, nodding and smiling as if she were a member of a royal family. She crossed the room several times as though on a mission, only to disappear outside, or into the kitchen, occasionally accompanied by one of the two grim young men who always seemed to be in attendance with the Leboeufs. Were they bodyguards? Why would the Leboeufs need bodyguards? The face of the young man trailing Eva was set in a stony expression, only his roving eyes testifying that he was constantly taking in his surroundings.

"Good-lookin' young fellow," Seth commented during one of their passes.

Seth was interrupted by Mayor Shevlin's wife coming to our table.

"Jessica, you look stunning."

"Thank you, Susan, and may I say the same about you."

"Isn't it fun to get dressed up for these wonderful evenings in Cabot Cove? Won't happen again, I'm sure, but I've loved being part of these restaurant openings in our little corner of the world. If this keeps up, I told Jim, I'll have to start booking the travel agency's clients for staycations instead of vacations."

With the dinner service complete, a festive party atmosphere prevailed, enhanced by the music and waiters delivering after-dinner drinks. We left our seat to do as others were doing, mingling with friends.

"Must have cost Leboeuf a fortune, picking up the tab for everyone," Tim Purdy said as he held her coat for his date.

"Chump change for him," Levon Walsh, a local attorney, chimed in.

Walsh's wife, Dora, said, "His wife used to be a model. She's beautiful, but she always looks as if she's posing for the camera."

Mort and Maureen Metzger also stopped to greet us on their way out.

"What's this I hear about Leboeuf's son bein' in some sort of trouble?" Seth asked Mort in his usual direct way.

The sheriff shook his head.

Seth got the message and didn't pursue it.

The evening had continued much later than I'd expected, extending well past my usual bedtime. But I was wide-awake. The lilting music was infectious, the conversation with so many friends stimulating, and the handsome surroundings created an atmosphere that I was reluctant to leave. But as the crowd dwindled, I noticed that Seth had sat in his chair again and was fighting to stay awake. Chances were that he'd have a waiting room full of patients first thing in the morning, and I decided it would be selfish to stay longer.

"Time to go home," I told him, jolting him awake.

Seth went to retrieve his car, instructing me to wait inside. "No use both of us shivering in the cold."

I looked through the window that flanked the front door. The valet-parking attendants were busy fetching cars for the many people leaving at the same time. I caught sight of Brad Fowler standing at the edge of his parking lot, the yellow light from a streetlamp casting an eerie glow on his face. *Oh, dear,* I thought. *Don't be discouraged. There will be plenty of business for both you and Leboeuf.*

By the time the parking attendant delivered Seth's car to the door, Brad was gone. A young man held the door for me, and I slid into the front passenger seat. As I buckled my seat belt, I looked across the pier to where Wylie Leboeuf stood at a railing, the red ember of his cigarette acting like a beacon directing attention to him.

"That's the Leboeufs' son," I told Seth as he settled in the driver's seat.

"I didn't see him inside. Wonder what he thinks of the evening," Seth muttered.

"I hope he's proud of what his father has accomplished," I said.

"You always look on the bright side," my curmudgeonly friend complained.

I smiled. "Someone has to."

As we pulled away, I took a look back at Wylie Leboeuf, who tossed his cigarette butt over the rail into the sea and walked in the direction of the rear of his father's restaurant complex, where a door led into the kitchen.

"Enjoy the evening?" Seth asked.

"Yes, very much." I held up my little shopping bag. "Everything was carried off well — don't you think?"

"Nothing to complain about. The food and service were good."

"Do you think Leboeuf's restaurant and Brad and Marcie's place will be able to coexist?" I asked.

Seth shrugged. "That remains to be seen, doesn't it?" he said with his characteristic bluntness.

As much as I'd been offended by Leboeuf's behavior at the Fin & Claw's opening night, I had to admit that *his* opening

151

night had been a delightful evening. I suppose the fact that he'd picked up the tab for everyone and had given all of us gift bags added to the celebratory spirit that permeated the restaurant, but along with that generosity, everything had been handled with class and professionalism. And, of course, the food had been excellent. Seth, who can find fault with half the dishes served to him in restaurants, had nothing but praise for his meal, and I mirrored his approval.

I quickly fell asleep that night, my concerns about Brad and Marcie Fowler getting lost in my pleasant reverie. Nor were they on my mind when the telephone on my nightstand rang, a jarring way to awaken from a deep sleep. I looked at the clock radio: six o'clock.

"Hello?"

"Jessica?"

I don't know who else you might have expected, I thought through the sleep that was still fogging my mind.

"Yes?"

"It's Seth."

I sat up in bed and blinked furiously to snap my eyes and brain into functionality.

"Did I wake you?"

"Of course, Seth, but that's all right. Is

something wrong?"

"I'd say so. Gérard Leboeuf is dead."

CHAPTER ELEVEN

"Say that again."

"Gérard Leboeuf has been murdered. Doc Whitson, the medical examiner, is out of town; they called me."

"Oh, my goodness," I said, hardly a comment with the gravitas to do the message justice. "Where? When? How did it happen?"

"In the kitchen of his new place. Sometime around three a.m., somebody stabbed him with a big knife."

"Good heavens! Are there any suspects? Do the police know who did it?"

"Not yet. None that I'm aware of, Jessica. Just thought you'd want to know before you start your day."

Some way to start a day.

"I wonder if this has anything to do with what Matt told me."

"Matt who?"

"My agent, Matt Miller. He said that

federal authorities were looking into Leboeuf's business practices to see whether he'd been laundering money for the mob."

"Well, aren't *you* full of surprises, Jessica."

"I forgot about it until this minute."

"Any more tidbits that you've *forgotten* to tell me?"

"I don't think so. What about you? Any 'tidbits' you haven't told me?"

"Only that I imagine I'll be asked to do a formal autopsy later today. I suspect he had a lacerated spleen and bled out. But you never know until you look into these things. Mort hasn't released the body yet. Not sure what he's waiting for, but I can give you more information later. Right now I'm thinking there's no question what killed him, and it wasn't a heart attack."

"What about his family?"

"What about them?"

"Have you spoken with any of them?"

"Not my job. I'm just the substitute ME."

"Who discovered the body?"

"You sound like a detective."

"Sorry. Natural instinct."

"The chef — Chang, isn't it? — found Leboeuf and called the police. Mort was still there when I left." He yawned. "Got to ring off, Jessica. I'm going to have patients backed up here at the office, and I need a little shut-eye before I greet them or I won't remember my own name, much less theirs."

I clicked off the phone, swung my legs off the bed, and drew a deep breath. What Seth had said seemed impossible. Less than twelve hours ago Leboeuf was shaking hands, smiling, and basking in the glory of his opening-night festivities. What could have caused the night to end in such a shocking, brutal way?

I showered, dressed, and made myself toast with raspberry jam and coffee. The phone started ringing again; I let the answering machine take the calls, although I could hear the callers' voices. Maureen Metzger was one of them, followed by Evelyn Phillips of the *Gazette,* Mayor Jim Shevlin, and three other friends, all asking whether I'd heard about Leboeuf's murder. I decided to return Maureen's call first.

"I can't believe it," were her first words.

"I know what you mean," I said. "I talked to Seth Hazlitt. Dr. Whitson is out of town."

"Mort told me. He was rousted out of bed at three this morning. He's still at the restaurant. Too bad about Leboeuf. He was such a wonderful cook. I was hoping he would give some classes here. You know I've never dared to try any of his recipes. They're so complicated. I saw him make that famous fish soup on TV, on *Kitchen Wars*. What's it called?"

"Bouillabaisse?"

"That's it. And . . ."

"Have any suspects been identified?" I asked, hoping to divert Maureen before she launched into a discussion of her cooking shows.

"Not that I know of. Of course, there's talk. Oops! Mort's just coming through the door. Don't want him to hear me discussing his case. Talk to you later. Bye."

After returning other calls, I retreated to my home office, sat in my leather swivel chair, and attempted to put my thoughts in order. The information that I'd received from Seth, and the reactions to the news by a half-dozen other people, had settled in on me.

Gérard Leboeuf's murder would impact Cabot Cove as though a hurricane had come ashore, turning this otherwise peaceful seaside town upside down. Because Leboeuf was an internationally known celebrity, if he died of anything other than natural causes — which appeared to be the case — the investigation would involve many more authorities besides Mort Metzger and his perpetually understaffed sheriff's department. Everyone who had had any contact with the victim — which certainly included me — would be questioned. The media would descend on us, generating myriad theories and rumors, and fingers would be pointed.

I looked up at the gift bag from the opening, which I'd left on a shelf and absently began jotting down notes on a lined yellow legal pad. What did I remember from the previous night? That expanded into observations about every time I'd had as much as a conversation with Gérard Leboeuf. Before I knew it — and despite the ringing telephone that never seemed to stop — I ended up with almost a dozen pages chronicling my recollections of the famous chef, going back to when I'd first interviewed him in New York for a novel I never finished.

Leboeuf's offices were located in the Flatiron District of the city. The reception area was handsomely decorated with expensive pieces of furniture, white carpeting into which I sank as I crossed the room, and colorful abstract art on the walls. Photos from Leboeuf's television show and guest appearances on the Cooking Channel lined the walls. A stunning brunette sitting behind a large desk gave me a warm smile as I approached.

"I'm Jessica Fletcher," I said. "My agent, Matt Miller, arranged for me to meet with Mr. Leboeuf this morning."

"Of course, Mrs. Fletcher," she said with a charming French accent. "Monsieur Leboeuf is expecting you."

A minute later I was face-to-face with the famous chef himself. "Please sit down," he said, indicating a pair of armchairs upholstered in a rich red and gold fabric. Despite his French name, there was no trace of an accent, which didn't surprise me. I knew from having done research on him before our meeting that he'd been born in St. Louis to American parents who originally came from French stock, which accounted for the name.

"I appreciate you giving me some time this morning," I said.

"I don't have a lot of it. I have another engagement."

"I'll try to be brief." I flipped to an empty page in my notebook and jotted down the date.

Leboeuf squinted at me. "Where are you from?"

"I live in a small town in Maine. You probably haven't heard of it. It's called Cabot Cove."

"I'm familiar with Cabot Cove."

"You are?"

"My wife and I have been looking at waterfront property in that area."

"Really? We'd be neighbors."

"Nothing definite," he said.

His receptionist entered the room carrying a tray on which coffee cups, spoons, a small, delicate sugar bowl, and a carafe sat. She placed it on Leboeuf's desk and, to my surprise, used a wooden tongue depressor to perfectly level the sugar in its bowl. I managed to suppress a smile; Leboeuf was obviously a man who liked things neat and precise.

His overall bearing was as carefully put together as the sugar in the bowl. He wasn't tall — we looked each other eye to eye — but he had the type of frame on which his obviously expensive clothing draped nicely. I wouldn't describe him as particularly handsome. He had a certain pugnacious look to him, his lips a little too large for his thin face and a nose that appeared to have been broken at one point in his life. What most struck me was that he carried himself the way self-assured, successful men usually do, on top of the world and not reticent to broadcast it.

Once our coffee was poured, he asked what sort of information I was looking for to use in my novel.

I explained the loose plot that I'd concocted and that I was hoping the research would help me further develop the story. I left out the details so as not to try Leboeuf's patience, which seemed in short supply. He listened impassively, saying nothing but occasionally nodding.

"That's it," I said when I'd finished my capsule explanation of the book.

"I hope you're not about to make me a murderer in this book," he said, not smiling.

"I can promise you I won't," I said. "What I'm hoping you'll do for me is take me backstage to give me the feel, the atmosphere, what goes on in a real restaurant."

"Backstage at a restaurant isn't a pretty place," he said.

"Certainly hectic."

"Have you ever been in a busy commercial kitchen?"

"A few times. I have friends who own restaurants."

"Then why are you wasting my time? Why don't you get the information you need from your friends?"

"I certainly could," I said, wondering whether he was about to blow me off, "but since I'm in the city, Matt Miller encouraged me to see you. If you'd rather not talk today —"

He waved my comment away. "No," he said. "I've already set aside the time. Besides, Matt's a good agent."

"One of the best."

"You want to spend a day or two in one of my restaurants?"

"If that wouldn't be too much trouble. I'd also like to gain some insight into the business end, how restaurants are financed, the relationship with suppliers, choosing the menu, the nitty-gritty of being a restaurateur."

"I assume you'll credit me in the finished book."

His premature concern over credit brought me up short.

"Certainly," I said. "I always acknowledge those who've helped with my research."

"All right," he said. "I'll have the manager of my midtown restaurant show you around. I have a half hour before I'm due at a meeting. Fire your questions at me about what you call the nitty-gritty."

That half hour extended into almost an hour. The chef seemed happy to talk about himself and his rise to fame, although he didn't provide much factual information

162

about running a restaurant. I would have to get those details from the manager of his midtown restaurant. When we said goodbye, I met up with Matt Miller for lunch.

"How did it go with Gérard?" Matt asked.

"Fine. I learned all about his career, but I'm not certain that I can use any of it in the novel. However, I have an appointment with one of his managers, and that should prove helpful."

"What did you think of Leboeuf personally?"

"He was pleasant enough, certainly sure of himself."

"That's an understatement, Jessica." Matt laughed. "His ego is the size of an aircraft carrier."

"Well, I didn't want to be so blunt. He may become a neighbor."

"Oh?"

"He said that he and his wife are looking at waterfront property in Cabot Cove."

Matt leaned back in his chair and gazed up at the ceiling. "I envy them that. I wouldn't mind having a summer place in Cabot Cove."

"We have more summer residents every year."

"Maybe Gérard will open a restaurant there."

163

"That would be interesting," I said, and turned my attention to the menu.

Little did I know at that juncture that when the dust settled and Leboeuf's murderer had been brought to justice, I would be sitting down, surrounded by piles of research materials, to finish the novel I had set aside two years earlier. Only this time the story would be about two competing chefs — and the title *Murder Flambéed* would become *Killer in the Kitchen.*

■ ■ ■ ■

PART TWO

■ ■ ■ ■

CHAPTER TWELVE

Sheriff Mort Metzger, the first law-enforcement official at the scene of Gérard Leboeuf's murder, and his deputies were joined the following afternoon by investigators from the Major Crime Units (MCU) of the Attorney General's Homicide Unit, who'd been dispatched overnight to Cabot Cove from Portland. At Jim Shevlin's urging, Mort held an impromptu press conference in the council chambers at town hall. I found out about it from the mayor himself and decided to attend.

Not only had the state investigators responded quickly, but members of the press had, too. Contingents from Augusta and Portland were joined by reporters from Bangor, Boston, and New York, as well as a writer-photographer team from a leading restaurant-industry trade magazine. Evelyn Phillips was there, of course, as were a few employees of Leboeuf's Cabot Cove restaurant. I looked for members of his family, but they weren't present. I was also surprised to see Marcie Fowler seated at the rear of the room. I started in her direction, but she looked as though she wouldn't welcome company; instead I chose a seat next to the reporter from the trade magazine.

"I sure don't like having to get up here and talk to you today about what happened last night," Mort said after he'd established quiet in the room, "but as you all know, one of our citizens — and a pretty famous one — died at the restaurant he'd just opened here in town." He consulted notes in his hand. "The deceased's name is Gérard Leboeuf, and he heads up — or I guess I should say *headed* up — a big restaurant chain in New York and other cities, including the new place he opened here, Leboeuf's French Bistro. This is an ongoing investigation, so there's not a lot I can tell you at this point about how he died, but I can say that we're considering his death a homicide unless the investigation turns up something different. Our ME, Doc Whitson, is on his way back and will be doing an autopsy this evening. He will be assisted by Dr. Seth Hazlitt, who filled in for Doc Whitson last night when the body was discovered."

"Where is Dr. Hazlitt now?" a reporter asked in a loud voice.

His intrusion flustered Mort for a moment. "He's not here because Doc Whitson will be taking over."

"But it was this Dr. Hazlitt who first saw the body," the reporter pressed.

"Was he invited to be here?" another reporter asked.

"Doc Hazlitt has a busy private practice," Mort said.

"Where can we reach him?" Mort was asked.

Jim Shevlin, who as mayor had opened the press conference and introduced Mort, said, "I'm sure that Dr. Hazlitt will be glad to speak with you at a later date."

I wasn't sure that the mayor was correct in that promise. Seth's disdain for the media was well-known in town, often to Evelyn Phillips's chagrin, and I wasn't at all surprised that he wasn't present at the press conference.

There were three other people standing with Mort and Jim at the front of the room: a handsome African-American man, a middle-aged woman with sharp features, and a young man wearing large horn-rimmed glasses who looked professorial. They were all immaculately dressed, and I suspected they were members of law enforcement. It's a look I recognize, although don't ask me to define what that is. It's just there, on their faces and in their body language.

Mort confirmed my suspicion when he introduced them as detectives who'd come to Cabot Cove to aid in the investigation.

"We're told that Mr. Leboeuf was stabbed to death," a reporter said.

"I'm not at liberty to discuss method of death," Mort said, "at least not yet."

"Ah, come on, Sheriff. It's all over town that he was found with a big kitchen knife sticking out of him."

As he said it, I looked to where Marcie sat with her arms tightly wound about her, as though she were seeking to collapse herself into invisibility.

"What about the bad blood between Leboeuf and the other restaurant owner next door?" The reporter also consulted notes. "Fowler. His name's Bradley Fowler, owner of the Fin and Claw."

"I don't know anything about bad blood," Mort said. "Everyone who knew the victim will be interviewed in due course."

As other reporters called out questions in a noisy chorus, Marcie abandoned her seat and slipped out of the room.

"That's all I have to say at the moment," Mort said. "We'll post a notice when the next press briefing will take place."

There were disgruntled comments from the reporters about how useless the press conference had been. "He said nothing," one growled to a colleague. "A waste of time," said another.

"Have you talked to this Fowler guy?" someone asked.

"That's what I intend to do next," was the reply.

"I talked to one of the kitchen help an hour ago."

"What'd he say?"

"Not much. He says that while he and others in the kitchen cleaned up at the end of the night, Leboeuf was still there," he said, "having a drink at the bar with his wife and his manager, Chang. Why don't you do some reporting of your own?"

"I've been working another angle. This guy Fowler's mother died in his restaurant on *his* opening night. That famous murder-mystery writer Jessica Fletcher lives here and was close with Fowler and his mother. Anyone talk to her yet?"

"Not yet, but I have her number."

One of the reporters turned to me. "Who are you representing?" she asked.

171

"Representing?" I replied, relieved that she hadn't read my books and didn't recognize me from my photo on the dust jackets. "No one. Just a curious citizen." I left quickly, hoping no other reporter would connect my face to my name.

Outside town hall, I looked for Marcie but didn't see her. I wanted to talk to Mort and Seth but knew it wasn't the time to contact either of them. But then Mort suddenly came through the door accompanied by one of the investigators.

"Mrs. F., got a minute?" Mort said.

"Yes, of course."

"Mrs. F., this is Detective Clifford Mason."

We shook hands.

"Detective Mason would like a few words with you," Mort said.

"Certainly."

"Buy you a cup of coffee?" Mason asked in a deep, gravelly voice.

"That sounds appealing," I said.

"Not you, Sheriff. You're not as pretty as she is."

Mort rolled his eyes. "I'll be in touch later," he said as he retreated back into the building.

I suggested to Detective Mason that we try a small coffee shop on the corner that had recently opened. The last thing I wanted to do was to walk into Mara's Luncheonette with a detective; it would be all over town in fifteen minutes, and I'd be peppered with more questions than were already being thrown at me. We ordered small lattes and took a table by the window. Thankfully, we were the only customers in the shop.

"I appreciate you taking time for me, Mrs. Fletcher," Mason said as he poured sugar into his cup.

"I don't mind at all, Detective, although I don't know how helpful I can be."

His smile was meant to assure. "Let me be the judge of that," he said thoughtfully while stirring. "Although I've just gotten here, I have been informed that you knew the victim quite well."

I shook my head. "I knew him, yes, but we certainly weren't close friends."

"But your acquaintance with him goes back to New York, what, three, four years ago?"

"True." I explained my interview with Leboeuf for the novel I'd been writing at the time.

"Mind if I refer to some notes?" he asked.

"By all means."

He pulled a small sheet of paper from his jacket pocket, placed a pair of half-glasses on his nose, and scanned what was on the paper. "You were Mr. Leboeuf's guest at his restaurant opening," he said flatly.

I laughed. "Along with half the town. Mr. Leboeuf generously picked up the tab for *everyone* at his opening night."

"And you were also at the opening of his competitor, the Fin and Claw."

"That's correct. Again, many in town attended both restaurant openings."

"At the first opening, that's when the owner of that restaurant, the Fin and Claw, got into an argument with Mr. Leboeuf? Is that correct?"

I was impressed at how much the detective had learned in the short time he'd been in town.

"That's right," I said.

"I understand that during this argument, Mr. Fowler — Bradley Fowler, the owner of the Fin and Claw — threatened Mr. Leboeuf."

"Did he?" I said. I tried to put my brain in reverse and go back to that opening night at the Fin & Claw. "Yes," I said once my memory had snapped into focus. "Brad Fowler did say something about — I'm not sure I remember exactly what he said — but he did say something to the effect that he would 'punch his lights out.' Yes, I think

174

those were the words he used."

Mason smiled. "I haven't heard that expression in a while."

"And it's just that, an expression, Detective Mason. That's all. Brad was upset that the Leboeuf table was making disparaging remarks about the food and service and that Leboeuf had insulted Brad's mother —"

"Brad's mother?"

"You don't know about that, Detective?"

He shook his head.

I told him about Isabel Fowler suffering a stroke and Brad being convinced that Leboeuf's callous remarks had precipitated her illness.

Mason's eyebrows went up. "That's a pretty serious accusation," he said.

"You know that in the heat of the moment people will say things they don't really mean." It occurred to me what the purpose of our chitchat was: Mason, and I assume the other investigators, including Mort Metzger, were zeroing in on Brad Fowler as their chief suspect in the murder of Gérard Leboeuf.

"Frankly, I don't believe that Brad Fowler is capable of killing Gérard Leboeuf," I said, the suddenness of my comment causing Mason to sit back, eyes open wider.

"I didn't say that he was," Mason said.

"But that's what you're working up to, isn't it?"

"We have to start somewhere, Mrs. Fletcher. I'm sure you're aware after having written so many bestselling murder-mystery novels that everyone is considered a suspect at the beginning of a murder investigation."

"Which is as it should be," I said, "and I understand why you're looking at Brad. It's just that I'm always uncomfortable when someone is viewed prematurely as a prime suspect. It's been my experience that too often that person had nothing to do with the crime."

"Then again," he said, "it's been my experience that first hunches often prove to be right."

There was nothing to be gained by arguing with the detective. I was not a trained investigator; nor was I in a position to defend Brad Fowler. I had no idea where he'd been at the time of the murder. While I found it hard to believe that the young man was capable of committing such a grievous act, Brad certainly appeared to have had a motive for killing his business rival, not to mention the fact that he had made his hair-trigger temper abundantly obvious in recent days.

"I'm afraid I don't have any more to offer

you," I said.

Detective Mason replaced the note in his pocket and sipped his coffee. "I'm not sure that's true, Mrs. Fletcher, but we can let it rest for the moment. I would appreciate having access to you from time to time as the investigation progresses. You have a reputation of possessing a particularly keen insight into crime, plus you're known to be on the inside track in this town."

I couldn't help but laugh. "I'm not sure that's an especially flattering trait," I said.

"But it could prove useful. After all, you're a respected long-time resident of Cabot Cove and know all the players. I'd like to arrange a time when I can do a more formal interview of you."

"I'm at your disposal anytime you wish."

"And my colleague, Ms. Lucas, will also want to talk to you. We work as a team."

"Who is the third person that Sheriff Metzger introduced as an investigator?" I asked.

"Him? He's FBI. He's interested in this case for a different reason. Thanks for your time. We'll be in touch."

We shook hands in front of the coffee shop, and I watched him walk back up the street toward the sheriff's office. FBI? Could his "different reason" for being interested in

Leboeuf's murder have to do with the rumor Matt Miller had passed along, that Leboeuf was being investigated for laundering mob money?

That thought remained with me on my way home. If it was true, my sleepy little town of Cabot Cove was about to become the epicenter of a massive investigation into the murder of a famous chef and restaurant owner and what role organized crime might have played in his success.

I felt like I was back in New York City.

CHAPTER THIRTEEN

There were a number of recorded messages on my answering machine at home, including one from Marcie Fowler, who sounded distraught. I recognized the number she left as the phone at the restaurant.

"It's Jessica Fletcher," I said when she answered.

"Oh, Mrs. Fletcher, thanks for getting back to me so quickly."

"Is everything okay?" I asked. "You sounded frazzled on your message."

"It's Brad."

"Is he ill?"

"No, he's — he's just been taken away by two of Sheriff Metzger's deputies for questioning about Leboeuf's murder."

"That isn't surprising, Marcie. Everyone with any connection to Leboeuf should expect to be questioned about the murder. I've just spoken with one of the detectives myself. I'm sure it's just routine."

179

"I don't think so, Mrs. Fletcher." I could tell that she was fighting to maintain her composure. "Everyone is pointing a finger at Brad because of the bad feelings he had about Leboeuf."

"Have people said anything about it?"

"They don't have to. I can just tell that they think Brad killed him," she said, her voice quavering. "I can see it in their eyes, those who don't turn their backs to me." Now her composure cracked, and she cried.

"I'm sympathetic, Marcie, believe me. But you'll be no help to Brad if you fall apart. He needs you to be on top of things right now," I said, knowing that self-control didn't seem to be a strong suit for either of the Fowlers.

"And I need him, too. We have a full house of reservations tonight and — I don't know what I'll do without Brad."

"Chances are he'll be back in time to take over the kitchen. And if he's a little late, what about his sous chef, that fellow Jake?"

Her tears turned to an angry snort. "Jake? That two-timing snake. You were here when he walked out. He's gone to work at Leboeuf's place, and Brad says he noticed some things have gone missing in the kitchen."

"What kinds of things?"

"A fancy Microplane grater that Isabel gave him last Christmas, mixing bowls, one of our new frying pans . . . Who knows what else? I never got around to doing an inventory of our tools. We've been too busy."

"Do you know if the bistro will be open tonight?" I asked. "I thought they might close in light of the events."

"Oh, they'll be open. You can bet on that. The police have taken down the yellow crime-scene tape and said that they could use the kitchen again. People will flock there to see where the famed Gérard Leboeuf was killed, and they'll come here to see Brad, the murderer."

I was out of positive things to say.

"One of the kitchen help, the salad maker, says he can help me handle the cooking," Marcie said.

"That's good."

"This is a nightmare, Mrs. Fletcher."

"Do you have room for one more reservation?"

"What?"

"I'd like to come to dinner tonight."

"Are you sure?"

"Absolutely sure, Marcie. Maybe we can find some time to chat."

"All right, Mrs. Fletcher. Just you?"

"Just me. Make the reservation at seven.

181

I'll see you then."

After hanging up, I thought about our conversation. *Strange that Leboeuf's restaurant would be open the night after its namesake was brutally murdered. I wonder whose decision that was.* As far as I knew, Leboeuf's wife, Eva, wasn't involved in the restaurant's operations, and I doubted that their son, Wylie, would be in a position to decide to open the doors the night after his father's death. Was it the chef who'd made the call? Chang ran the kitchen. What about the two young men always seen with the Leboeuf family? What part did they play?

My musing was interrupted by Detective Mason, who hadn't wasted any time in contacting me again. I hadn't been home an hour when he called.

"Sorry to bother you again, Mrs. Fletcher," he said, "but you did say that you'd make yourself available for an interview."

"Of course," I said. "I just didn't expect to hear from you again so soon."

He laughed. "I believe in speaking with people while recollections are fresh."

"That's understandable," I said. Detective Mason obviously knew that time has a habit of eroding even the best of memories. It was precisely for that reason that I'd made my series of notes about Gérard Leboeuf as soon as I'd learned of his murder.

"Would you like me to come to your home?" the detective asked.

"I don't want any special treatment," I said, thinking it would be better to have the interview in a more neutral, official setting. "I'd rather come to police headquarters. I assume that's where you're conducting other interviews."

"That's correct, Mrs. Fletcher. Sheriff Metzger has been extremely cooperative and accommodating. But he tells me that you don't drive."

"That's true. I don't suppose he mentioned that I fly — airplanes, that is."

Mason gave a hearty laugh. "I didn't think you flew on a broom."

"Just making sure we have the facts correct," I said, smiling. "Taking flying lessons was — well, it fulfilled a dream of mine. What time would you like to see me?"

"How about now?" he said. "The sheriff said he'll send a deputy to pick you up."

"That's very good of him."

"Shall we say a half hour?"

"That will be fine."

Before the deputy arrived, I took a few minutes to go over the notes I'd made about Leboeuf to refresh my memory. I considered taking them with me but decided against it. The detective would probably want to keep them, depriving me of access to my initial impressions.

Mort Metzger was in the reception area of the Sheriff's Department when I walked through the door.

"You're here to see Detective Mason," he said.

"Right, Mort. Thanks for arranging the ride."

Mort laughed. "Mason said he'd never met an adult who didn't drive."

"Well, he's met one now," I said. "Where is he?"

"I'll take you to him, Mrs. F., but I want you to know that even though the state sent these detectives, I'm in charge of the investigation. It happened on my turf."

"Of course," I said, recognizing the onset of a jurisdictional dispute, a frequent occurrence when law-enforcement authorities are forced to work together.

"Just didn't want to have any misunderstandings," Mort said.

He led me to one of the interrogation rooms at the rear of the building, where Mason and the other detective, who introduced herself as Anne Lucas, were seated at the table.

"We don't want to take any more of your time than necessary, Mrs. Fletcher," Mason said, "so I'll get right to the questions. The first one has to do with the night Mr. Leboeuf was killed. You were at the opening of his restaurant."

"That's right."

"Did you see anything unusual that night?"

"Many things," I said, "but nothing nefarious. Mr. Leboeuf picked up the tab for the entire evening, which I suppose was unusual. It was a festive, enjoyable evening."

"Did he have any confrontations with anyone?" Lucas asked.

"Not that I observed," I said. I thought of the brief, seemingly contentious moment between Leboeuf and his wife, Eva, but to say their conversation was as angry as their expressions would have been speculation on my part. Nevertheless, I mentioned it to Mason and Lucas with the caveat that I hadn't overheard what they'd said to each other.

After a series of questions about my interactions with Leboeuf over the years — which were few and far between — Lucas asked whether I saw Brad or Marcie Fowler the night of the murder. "Were they at the dinner?" Mason asked.

I was sure that the detectives had already asked the Fowlers whether they were there and were looking for someone to contradict them.

"They had their own restaurant to run," I said.

"You didn't see them that night?"

"No. Well, yes, I saw Brad as Seth — Dr. Seth Hazlitt — and I were leaving the bistro. I saw Brad standing at the edge of his restaurant's parking lot."

"What time was that?" Lucas asked, taking notes as the questioning continued.

"Close to midnight," I replied.

"What was he doing?"

"Just standing there. Only for a few seconds. I turned away. When I looked again, he was gone."

"You were present when the victim and Mr. Fowler had an altercation at Mr. Fowler's Fin and Claw."

That led to a lengthy series of questions about that evening and what I'd seen and overheard. I pointed out that Leboeuf and his party had behaved rudely and had insulted Brad's mother, who had given them a pleasant welcome. "I was offended by their attitude, and so was my dinner companion, Dr. Hazlitt. That's Seth Hazlitt." I spelled out his name.

"We'll be talking with Dr. Hazlitt later today, after his office hours."

"Is there anything else you'd like to know?" I asked.

"Not unless you remember something additional," Mason said.

"I did see the Leboeuf boy outside as we were leaving. I should say young man. Leboeuf's son must be in his twenties."

Mason consulted his notes. "Wylie Leboeuf," he said.

"Yes. He was having a cigarette by the seawall. He finished smoking, tossed the cigarette into the water, and walked toward his father's restaurant, in the direction of the back of the building."

"Where a door leads into the kitchen," Lucas said.

"You must be correct. I haven't been through that door," I said. "In fact, I've never been in the bistro kitchen."

"Did you ever hear Mr. Fowler threaten Mr. Leboeuf?" Lucas asked.

"Aside from hearing Brad say that he'd like to punch Leboeuf's lights out — just a heated expression, of course — I've never heard him issue a direct threat." Of course Brad had made harsh comments about Leboeuf in my presence, but I chalked them up to his frequent frustrated outbursts. They were not direct threats, and I decided not to add fuel to what could be a manufactured fire by trotting them out for the detectives.

"That'll do it," Mason said. "We really appreciate you giving us your time, Mrs. Fletcher."

"I'm available anytime," I said.

"Before you go," Mason said, "I have a favor to ask."

"Oh?"

"Detective Lucas and I know how wired in to the Cabot Cove community you are, and you might pick up information in your travels that would help in our investigation of Mr. Leboeuf's murder. All we ask is that you share anything you happen to hear."

I was a bit taken aback. What they were asking was exactly what I was trying to avoid. "If I think it's relevant, Detective Mason, I'll contact you, but I won't pass along any gossip or loose talk. It wouldn't be fair to you or to the victim of speculation."

"Can't ask for more than that," Mason said as he and Lucas stood. "Thanks again for coming in."

I left the room and wandered down the hall in the direction of Mort's office. His door was open and he was sitting back, feet up on his desk, reading something in a manila file folder. He looked up, saw me, stood, and waved at a chair. "Come and sit a few minutes, Mrs. F. How'd the interview go?"

I settled myself in the seat across from him. "It went well, I think. Detectives Mason and Lucas are very pleasant."

"I suppose they asked you to keep your eyes and ears open around town."

"As a matter of fact they did, Mort."

"Yeah, well, I told them how you know almost everybody in town."

"That was nice of you," I said, waiting for what I knew was coming next.

"The point is, Mrs. F., I'd really appreciate you running anything you come up with past me first."

My expression was quizzical.

"You know how it is. These out-of-town types come in and take over, grab all the credit, even when the local authorities do all the groundwork."

"Happy to do it," I said, "but turnaround is fair play."

He raised one eyebrow and cocked his head. "What do you mean?"

"May I ask *you* a question?"

"Shoot."

"Has the murder weapon been examined for prints?"

189

"It's at the lab for further analysis. They were able to pull one clear print from it, but no identification yet. But remember, Mrs. F., those kitchen guys wear gloves when they handle the food. I *can* tell you that it was a pretty fancy knife." He flipped open the manila folder and ran his index finger down the top page. "It was a Corkin, which I'm told costs as much as a suite for the night at the Waldorf Astoria Hotel." He looked up. "Are we agreed?"

I smiled and assured him that he would be the first to know if I came across any relevant evidence.

I realized at that moment, even though I was not involved in any way with the murder of Gérard Leboeuf and didn't have any official reason to delve into it, that people were expecting I would anyway because my natural curiosity would be running rampant. I'm ashamed to admit that it was. When that happened — and it happened too often as far as Seth Hazlitt was concerned — I was almost powerless to overcome it.

Not only that, but I don't like it when a murder takes place in my beloved Cabot Cove, and I was now determined to do whatever I could to shine light on whoever had killed Gerard Leboeuf and see that justice was served.

PART THREE

CHAPTER FOURTEEN

I knew that probing into the Leboeuf murder would have to be done tactfully, as always. When I become involved in a case — unofficially, of course — I have to be careful not to run the risk of alienating the authorities whose job it is to solve such crimes, especially Mort Metzger, our sheriff and my good friend. Although Mort and I have butted heads on several occasions, I always try to be sensitive to his feelings, and he's been gracious enough in previous cases to acknowledge my contribution to their resolution.

Before leaving the house for dinner at the Fin & Claw, I called my dentist, Ed Filler, and caught him as he was about to close his office for the evening.

"Trouble with that cracked tooth?" he asked.

"No. It's fine."

"Then you must be calling about Gérard

Leboeuf. You've heard, of course?"

"Impossible not to."

"Well, then, how can I help?"

"I've been spending some time with Sheriff Metzger and the investigators who've come in from out of town, but haven't had the opportunity to get out your way. Since the Leboeufs live next door, can you look out your window and tell me what it's like at the neighbor's property?"

"No need to look. I've been dealing with it all day. It's chaos, of course. The street has been roped off, and there is a uniformed chap standing sentry duty. I assume he's been hired by the family. It wasn't easy for my patients to get to the office this morning."

"I can imagine. Have you seen Mrs. Leboeuf or their son?"

"No. Why your interest in them?"

"I'm like everyone else in town, Ed. How often do we have a celebrity murdered here?"

He laughed. "Let's hope we never have another. By the way, I expect to see you again shortly; you're due for a cleaning."

"I haven't received your postcard reminding me."

"You will soon. Elaine just sent them out. Make sure you call for an appointment

194

when you get yours."

"Yes, sir."

I had debated asking Seth to accompany me to the Fin & Claw that night but decided against it. I wanted to be free to speak with Marcie without worrying that I was abandoning Seth at the table or making him feel that I was using him as a cover for my investigation, which would have been the truth. Besides, when there was only myself to be concerned with, I could come and go as I pleased and perhaps learn a little more.

Before leaving for the restaurant, I watched the news on a Portland TV channel. The Leboeuf murder was the lead story. Mort Metzger was interviewed, although he didn't say anything more than he had at the press conference. What was surprising was that Eva Leboeuf agreed to an interview. It lasted only thirty seconds, during which she said that the brutal murder of her husband was a terrible tragedy for the family, and that she and their son, Wylie, were urging the authorities to act swiftly and bring the murderer to justice. She handled herself the way you'd expect from a former top fashion model and businesswoman: poised, her voice well modulated, and just a hint of tears. Wylie wasn't with her, presumably not emotionally up to the task.

When I arrived at the Fin & Claw, I took note of the almost empty parking lot. Next door, diners were lining up to get into Leboeuf's French Bistro. While Marcie may have guessed correctly that people would flock to Leboeuf's restaurant in a macabre celebration of his newfound celebrity as the victim of a brutal murder, her expectation that they would also come to the Fowlers' restaurant to ogle the man who'd become the prime suspect was clearly wrong. Of course Brad hadn't been officially designated as a top-rung suspect, but based upon my conversations with Detective Mason, I silently agreed with Marcie that Brad was their number-one target. I winced as I thought of him being interrogated by the police. Had he cooperated? Had he kept his temper in check? Had he been released? Was he back at the restaurant, or would they hold him overnight for further questioning? I'd find out soon enough.

As the line entering Leboeuf's place moved forward, I was surprised to see detectives Mason and Lucas. What they might come away with while sitting at a table was pure conjecture, but who was I to question the actions of seasoned homicide investigators? Maybe they simply needed to eat and figured a visit to the bistro was in order. That they chose to dine where the murder had taken place might also justify putting their pricy dinners on the expense account. I, on the other hand, had no expense account, but I never planned on ordering an elaborate meal anyway.

When I walked into the Fin & Claw, Marcie wasn't at the dais to welcome customers, nor was anyone else. Only three tables were occupied in a room that could easily accommodate ten times that number. A tuxedoed waiter, a familiar face to me, approached from the kitchen. "Ah, Mrs. Fletcher, it is so good to see you."

His name was Fritz Boering, known around town as "Fritzi." He'd been a waiter for years at the famed Sardi's in New York City before retiring to Maine with his wife, and I remembered him from his days and nights serving New York's theater-loving crowds when I lived in Manhattan. I'd also seen him around Cabot Cove and was surprised that he was waiting tables at the Fin & Claw. He hadn't been there on opening night.

"I didn't realize that you were working here," I said.

He grinned. "Retirement is boring for someone used to plenty of action. I heard that the Fowlers were looking for a waiter with experience and decided, *Why not?* Helping my wife in the garden isn't my thing. Besides, my pension from the waiter's union doesn't go very far. It's my first night on the job. The staff here is young, and the Fowlers wanted a seasoned veteran to help train them. You'd like a table?"

"Eventually," I said, "but I was hoping to talk to Mrs. Fowler before being seated."

"Marcie — Mrs. Fowler — isn't here," he said. "She's —"

"She's not ill, is she?"

"No, just busy with other things. She'll be in later. Would you like to take your table and wait for her, or would you prefer the bar?"

"The table will be fine."

"Has Mr. Fowler been in?" I asked after I'd been seated.

"He was, but he — well, he had to leave."

I knew, of course, that he'd left in the company of sheriff's deputies.

"You heard about what happened next door," he said.

"Yes. Quite a shock."

He looked around before leaning closer and saying, "I wouldn't be surprised if it was the wife."

My startled expression mirrored my reaction. "Mr. Leboeuf's wife? Why?"

His bushy eyebrows went up and down. "You write murder mysteries, Mrs. Fletcher. As they say — and I read a lot of mysteries — when you're looking for a murderer, *cherchez la femme*. Always look first for the woman."

"Ah. I must admit that I've heard that advice before, but I don't necessarily follow it in my novels, and I don't know that it has any relevance in real-life crime."

He shrugged. "Just trying to be helpful."

"Have you told the police about your theory?" I asked, thinking that I'd find the conversation amusing were it not for the grim subject matter.

"They would never listen to me. But I've heard from many sources that the Leboeuf family fought all the time. There was always lots of scuttlebutt about it back in New York. The staff at Sardi's would gossip about how indiscreet Leboeuf was. Quite the ladies' man, as I understand it, which is not destined to please a wife."

"Many couples argue and most don't end up killing each other."

"Oh, of course. I know that. But everybody in town has an opinion about who did it." Again leaning closer, he added, "People are also talking about Brad Fowler.

199

There was no love lost between him and Leboeuf."

"I hope you're not suggesting that — ?"

"That he did such a thing? No, no, of course not. Brad is a wonderful young man, and I feel privileged to be working for him. But people who were at the opening here saw the argument they had, and — well, he is known for having a short temper."

"A short temper doesn't always accompany a violent personality," I said, feeling my own temper begin to rise. "Do you mind if I offer you some advice, Fritzi?"

"Please do."

"You keep saying that 'people' are talking about who killed Mr. Leboeuf and that Brad and he didn't get along. But this kind of loose talk could damage an innocent man's reputation."

"Well, I'm only repeating what I heard."

"That's just it. Nothing can be gained by idle speculation. If I were you, I'd let the authorities do their job. In my experience, they're usually pretty well-informed."

"You're right, Mrs. Fletcher." He smiled. "I suppose I just miss all the juicy stories that were always floating around at Sardi's about the celebrities who came there, some almost every night. Those were wonderful days. Can I get you a drink?"

"A glass of Chablis, please."

I browsed the menu he'd left on the table, and a wave of sadness came over me when I saw Isabel Fowler's lovely face peering up from the page devoted to her recipes. She would have been appalled at what had transpired since Brad and Marcie's opening night, when she'd proudly pranced around the room in her brand-new high heels, greeting customers, her pride in what her son and daughter-in-law had accomplished embedded in her smile.

Fritzi delivered my wine, and I'd just taken a sip when the front door opened and the Fin & Claw proprietor came through. Brad saw me, hesitated as though debating whether to come to my table, decided to, and dropped onto a chair across from me.

"It's good to see you," I said.

"I've been through some grilling by those clowns from out of town."

I let his characterization of the visiting detectives go and said, "It's only natural that they want to talk to everyone who —"

"Everyone who had a reason to kill Leboeuf?" he said, nervously wringing his hands.

"Not only a motive," I said, "but who was in the vicinity when he was killed. I realize that it's painful to go through a police interrogation, but I'm glad to see that you've survived it."

"That's what I did, Mrs. Fletcher, survived it." He let out a breath with a whoosh. "And I'm sure they're not through with me." He glanced sadly around the restaurant. "I guess nobody wants to eat dinner at a place owned by a suspected murderer."

I instinctively placed my hand on his.

"Brad," I said, "you and Marcie have been under a significant strain lately, opening the restaurant, your mother dying so unexpectedly, and now Leboeuf's murder and the police asking you about it. You have to keep a level head about you. I know that's cheap advice, but you must do it for Marcie's sake and to make a success of the Fin and Claw."

"In other words, I'd better keep my temper under control."

"It would be a good place to start — don't you think?"

He took in the empty tables again and shook his head. "One of the detectives, the woman, said that they'd interviewed you and that you told them about my fight with Leboeuf."

"That isn't exactly true, Brad. They were well aware of the altercation before they ever talked to me. I simply confirmed that I had witnessed an argument, which is the truth."

"But you think I killed him, don't you?"

"I don't," I said. "But you've made it easy for a spotlight to be shone in your direction, and you need to understand why."

"Just because a guy gets hot once in a while doesn't mean he would kill anyone."

"True. However, you can understand why some people might be suspicious, Brad."

"I'm not a criminal, Mrs. Fletcher."

"I didn't say you were, but it's natural that the police will want to know where you were the night Leboeuf was killed. I'm curious, too. Where were you?"

"I wasn't in the bistro kitchen. I can tell you that," he said, rearing back. "What gives you the right to demand answers?"

"I'm not demanding anything. I'm just asking. I don't know who murdered Gérard Leboeuf. Do you?"

"No idea."

"Well, then, we're in the same boat."

"And I don't care."

"I'm sorry to hear that. However, unlike you, I do care, and I hope that Leboeuf's killer is identified and brought to justice — whoever that might be."

"I didn't mean that," he said, shaking his head. "Sometimes I just can't keep my big mouth shut." He stood and said, "Thanks for patronizing the Fin and Claw, Mrs.

Fletcher. Looks like you didn't have any problem getting a reservation."

As he started to walk away, I asked, "Will Marcie be coming in this evening?"

He looked around as if just realizing that his wife was not there. "I have no idea. I hope so."

I ordered a bowl of Isabel Fowler's clam chowder for starters and was pleased to see other customers trickling in, greeted at the door by Fritzi. I'd almost finished my soup when Marcie arrived. She came directly to my table.

"Thanks so much for being here, Mrs. Fletcher. It's nice to know we have some loyal friends."

I didn't point out that my presence had nothing to do with loyalty. Instead I told her I'd just spoken with Brad.

She took the same chair her husband had recently occupied. "He said the investigators were mean when they questioned him."

"I don't know about 'mean,' " I said, "but I'm sure they were direct. That's their job. They have a murder to solve. Marcie, I realize that I don't have any official reason to talk with you about the night Leboeuf was killed, but I am curious where you and Brad were when it happened."

She stared at me blankly.

"I ask because sometimes things get out of hand when someone is suspected of having committed a serious crime. There's little doubt that the authorities are especially interested in Brad because of the angry exchange between him and Leboeuf. Sometimes — and I'm not being disparaging of the authorities — sometimes law-enforcement people focus in too quickly on a prime suspect. They jump to conclusions, and innocent people can become ensnared by their drive to wrap up a case."

She looked down and played with her fingers as she said, "Do you think that's what's happening to Brad?"

"Let's make sure it doesn't. I can try to help you, but I need you to tell me the truth. Where were you and Brad at the time Gérard Leboeuf was murdered?"

"Brad was — I was home. I'd left the restaurant about midnight. We didn't have a lot of customers. The whole town was over there." She gestured in the direction of the bistro. "I'm sure the talk about the mouse droppings didn't help things. Anyway, all the craziness was catching up to me. The opening. Isabel." Her eyes filled with tears. "Just everything. I was exhausted."

"I'm sure you were. What about Brad?"

"He, ah — well, he came home later than

that. I'd fallen asleep and didn't wake up until morning. I asked him what time he'd gotten in and he said around one. I think it might have been later though, because the last time I remember looking at the clock, it was one thirty."

"Where had he been?" I asked.

"Right here. I asked him where he'd gone after the restaurant closed, and he said he stayed around for a while before coming home, just trying to unwind after a difficult night. He was so depressed about Leboeuf's opening. It's hard to compete with a free dinner. He worries so much, Mrs. Fletcher. People don't realize that he's a sensitive guy. Sure, he has a rough edge, but underneath he's just a frightened little boy."

I nodded before asking, "So he said he got home at one?" I decided to leave her overly sympathetic assessment of her husband for another time.

"Maybe it was a little bit later. I already told you, it was after I'd gone to sleep. Why are you asking me this, Mrs. Fletcher? I'm sure the police already asked Brad the same questions."

"I'm just trying to get a sense of what happened that night," I said, although I could see that my questions were not being received well.

"Well, I don't have an answer to that, Mrs. Fletcher, and neither does Brad. We were here and then we went home. You'll have to get your 'sense of what happened' from someone else. Excuse me. I'd better get to work."

It was obvious that my inquiries into the Fowlers' whereabouts the night of the murder hadn't gone down well with them. I supposed I could understand their reactions. They'd both turned cold, and I'd had the impression that they were reconsidering their relationship with me. Was I now an enemy, an arm of the law who was narrowing in on Brad as the prime suspect? The truth was that I wanted very much to help them through the ordeal they were experiencing, although they weren't making it easy. It was hard to believe that Brad, with all his negativity, was the son of a woman beloved by all who knew her. I couldn't blame his temper on the loss of his mother, since his reputation for hotheadedness preceded her death. Marcie claimed Brad was a sensitive soul beneath what she called a "rough edge," but I would have to be convinced. His cold attitude toward Leboeuf's death seemed to contradict her assessment and did not endear him to me, even after he regretted his words.

I finished up dinner with a lobster cocktail. My appetite had waned during my brief confrontations with Brad and Marcie. I kept hoping they would talk with me again, but I was disappointed. My opportunity to have a longer conversation with Marcie hadn't materialized. Perhaps trying to see them at work was the wrong approach. In the restaurant, their attention was on other things. They couldn't understand my reasons for prying and just became frustrated that I was yet another person who suspected the worst. Maybe it was presumptuous of me to look into matters that were none of my concern. But I'd promised myself that I would do what I could to unravel what had happened to Gérard Leboeuf and see the guilty party pay the price.

I paid Fritzi for dinner and the wine and headed for the door, where Marcie had taken up her position at the dais.

"Good night, Marcie," I said. "Dinner was delicious. I'm sorry if I've upset you. I hope you know I only want what's best for you and Brad. I owe that much to Isabel. If she were still with us, she would be counting on me."

"Brad didn't kill Leboeuf, Mrs. Fletcher," she said flatly.

"Of course he didn't. That's why I'm trying to help."

There were other things I wanted to say, but clearly this wasn't the right time. I wished her a good evening and stepped outside, enjoying the fresh air that seemed to have been sucked from the atmosphere in the restaurant's interior. I went to the seawall and looked out over the water. It was a clear evening, white stars poking holes in the progressively darkening sky, the almost full moon illuminating the ripples and waves. I was deep in thought when noise from the direction of Leboeuf's bistro diverted my attention. A man was being dragged from behind the building and tossed like a sack of grain onto the front walkway by two other men, the same two who seemed always to be hovering over Leboeuf and his family. They laughed and disappeared back behind the restaurant.

I ran over to where they had dumped the man on the pavement. Dressed in a suit and tie, he looked like a respectable older gentleman. Blood was smeared on one cheek and had intruded into his hairline. He struggled to get up but fell back against the sidewalk. My questions of him were met with groans.

"Don't move," I said. "I'll call an ambulance."

I took my cell phone from my purse and dialed 911. "There's an injured man in front of Leboeuf's French Bistro," I told the dispatcher. "We need an ambulance right away."

A crowd gathered as I hovered over the injured man and waited for the ambulance to arrive. It pulled up a few minutes later, and two EMTs emerged.

"Anybody know this man?" one asked as the other knelt beside him and checked his pulse.

"I was the person who called," I said. "I don't know who he is. Two men from the restaurant dragged him here. Perhaps he has identification on him."

The EMT groped for the victim's wallet, managed to pull it from his back pants pocket, and said to no one in particular, "His name's Shulte. Warren Shulte."

They loaded him on a gurney, slid it into the rear of their vehicle, and drove off. I walked away from the knot of curious people and called for a taxi to pick me up. As I waited, I looked to the rear of Leboeuf's restaurant. The two young men who'd so callously deposited the man on the pier stood laughing. I was tempted to confront them, but decided a more appropriate move was to report what I'd seen to Mort

Metzger. I called him at home.

"What's up, Mrs. F.?" he asked.

"I just witnessed an assault on a man in front of Gérard Leboeuf's restaurant."

"I heard about it. Somebody called it in to nine-one-one."

"I called it in."

"It was *you*?"

"Yes. I saw the poor man dragged from behind the restaurant by those two men who are part of the Leboeuf staff."

"I didn't hear that part of it," he said.

"I think you should confront them about it."

"Whoa, slow down, Mrs. F. Does the victim want to press charges?"

"I don't know. I just assumed he would. He was badly beaten and was incapable of talking."

"Do you know him? Who is he?" Mort asked.

"I heard one of the EMTs identify him as Warren Shulte."

"I'll check it out," Mort said. "Thanks for your call."

"I thought you'd want to know."

"By the way, Mrs. F., how come you were there when it happened?"

His question surprised me. "I had dinner at the Fin and Claw and had just left the restaurant."

There was a hint of amusement in his voice. "Were you there asking questions about the Leboeuf murder?"

I ignored the question, apologized for calling him at home, and after we hung up, dialed Seth Hazlitt's number.

"Am I taking you from dinner?" I asked.

"Just finished up, Jessica. Where are you?"

"On the pier by the French bistro. I just witnessed an assault on a gentleman by two men who work for Leboeuf. I called an ambulance for him. The EMTs just took him to the hospital."

"Who is it?"

"His name is Warren Shulte."

"Doesn't sound familiar. Do you know him?"

"I don't, but I called Mort Metzger and reported it."

"How badly was this fellow hurt?"

"He looked pretty beaten up, but I don't think he suffered critical injuries. Then again, I'm not a doctor."

"You would have made a good one."

"Not sure that's true. I was wondering if you would be good enough to call the hospital and find out what you can about him."

"I guess I can do that. You heading home?"

"As soon as the taxi arrives."

"I'll call you there if I find out anything of interest."

The cab arrived as I clicked off my call to Seth.

"Home, Mrs. Fletcher?" the driver asked.

"Yes. Wait. No. Take me to the hospital. There's someone there I need to visit."

CHAPTER FIFTEEN

The emergency room at Cabot Cove General Hospital was quiet when I arrived. The woman at the admitting desk recognized me and expressed surprise that I was there. I explained that I was the one who'd called 911 about the man who'd been deposited on the pier, and asked how he was. "His name, I believe, is Warren Shulte."

"I'll check with Dr. Keane," she said. When she returned, the doctor was with her.

"Hello, Mrs. Fletcher," he said. Joseph Keane had moved to Cabot Cove two years earlier. He'd been an ER physician at New York Presbyterian; I'd met him through Seth Hazlitt.

"Hello, Dr. Keane. Busy night?"

"To the contrary. I understand you're the one who called for the ambulance for Mr. Shulte."

"That's right. How is he?"

"Better, although you'd never know it from his face. Whoever mugged him did a pretty good job of roughing him up."

"He wasn't mugged," I said.

Keane's eyebrows went up. "What happened to him, then?"

I started to explain what I'd seen when Mort Metzger, wearing his sheriff's uniform, came through the door.

"Hello, Sheriff," Keane said.

"Doc," Mort said. "Hello, Mrs. F. Thought you'd be home. Didn't know you were coming here."

"I didn't know that you'd be coming here either," I said.

"I thought I'd best follow up." Then he turned to Keane and said, "Can he talk?"

"He's pretty groggy, Sheriff. We've given him painkillers, but you can speak with him as long as you make it short. I've ordered X-rays and a CAT scan. He'll be admitted."

Because no one told me that I wasn't invited, I followed Dr. Keane and Mort back into the treatment area, where the man lay on a bed, its head slightly elevated. He was covered by a sheet, and a nurse checked his vital signs. Shulte's eyes went from face to face, finally settling on the doctor's. "Who are they?" he asked, his voice weak and raspy.

"Our sheriff," Keane said, "and the woman who found you and called for help, Jessica Fletcher."

Shulte closed his eyes and groaned.

"Just want to ask you a few questions," Mort said, coming to the side of the bed.

"What?" Shulte said, opening his eyes.

"Mrs. Fletcher here says she saw the two men who attacked you."

Shulte's attention shifted to me, but he said nothing.

"Can you name them?" Mort asked.

He started to respond but swallowed the words before they emerged.

Mort looked at me.

"As I told you when I phoned, Mort, it was the two men who work for Leboeuf."

"You're sure about that, Mrs. F.?"

"I didn't see them hit him. I only saw them carry him to the curb and drop him on the ground. They seemed to think it was amusing."

Shulte said what sounded like, "They owe me."

"They owe you?" I asked. "Who owes you?"

"Leboeuf."

"What does he owe you? Money?" Mort asked. "Did you work for him?"

Shulte groaned again and nodded.

"Where did you work for them?" I asked.

"New York."

"Doing what? In what capacity?"

He mumbled something and closed his eyes.

"I think that's enough," said Keane.

Mort and I went from the ER to the lobby.

"Wonder what this is all about," Mort muttered.

"You'll be able to ask more questions when he's up to it," I said. "I think I'd better call a cab and go home."

"No need. I'll drop you off, Mrs. F."

We were almost to the door when a young man in horn-rimmed glasses walked in. I recognized him as one of the investigators who'd been on the dais with Mort and detectives Mason and Lucas during the press conference.

"Good evening, Sheriff," he said.

"Hello, Agent Cale," Mort said. "Have you met Mrs. Fletcher?"

"No, I haven't." He extended his hand. "Special Agent Anthony Cale."

He turned to Mort. "Where is Mr. Shulte?"

Mort inclined his head toward the emergency room. "Back there. I just tried to question him, but he's pretty well out of it."

How does Special Agent Cale know the victim's name?

"Detective Mason called me right after you called him to report the incident," Cale told Mort.

"Thought I should fill Mason in, considering that it might involve Leboeuf and his people. Mrs. Fletcher says he was probably assaulted by two of Leboeuf's men," said Mort.

Another question came to mind. *Why did an FBI special agent consider it important enough to show up at the hospital?*

"I appreciate being informed of this," Cale said. "I'll take over from here."

Take over what? Why would the FBI be interested in what happened to a stranger who got himself beaten up?

Seth called shortly after I'd arrived home.

"I called the hospital to check on your Mr. Shulte," he said. "Tried you earlier but got your infernal answering machine."

"I was at the hospital," I said.

"Why?"

"Well, I was the one who called for help for him. I thought I should check up on the patient."

"So I wasted my time calling on your behalf," he said, but I could sense the smile on his face. "Let's see who found out more information. What did *you* learn?"

"Nothing, really." I told him about Mort and the FBI special agent arriving.

"Well, I know a bit more than you, then. Seems he's a VIP of some sort," Seth said.

"Oh? Why do you say that?"

"They've got him in a private room, no visitors, no information given out to anyone who calls. That's the order. Of course, the nurses talked some to me. He's stable, a couple of broken ribs and a possible broken nose, but nothing life threatening. So, Dr. Fletcher, your earlier assessment was pretty close to the mark."

"Since they talked to you, Seth, did you find out why he's getting the VIP treatment?"

"Nope. Didn't apply my investigative powers any further."

"Strange," I said. "Well, I appreciate your checking on it."

"Happy to oblige. Mind a word of advice, Jessica?"

"Have I ever minded, Seth?"

"Just don't want to see you get yourself all wrapped up in what happened to Mr. Leboeuf. We've got Mort, those investigators from out of town, and an FBI agent on the case. Best you spend your time writing your books and leave solving Leboeuf's murder to others."

"I'll take it under advisement, Seth. Thank you."

Now his smile turned into a chuckle. "Which means you haven't heard a word I've said."

CHAPTER SIXTEEN

Marcie Fowler had gotten over her pique at my questioning of the previous night and phoned me the following morning to apologize.

"No apology needed," I said. "I can only imagine the strain you've been under."

"But that's no excuse for being rude to you. It was good of you to come to dinner."

"Not another word about it, Marcie. Have you heard anything new about the investigation?"

"Only that Jake Trotter spent hours being questioned by the police."

"Your former sous chef."

"Yes, the one who quit on us to work for the enemy. He and Brad never got along. Brad confronted him about the missing items in the kitchen, and Jake denied it, but I still believe he took them. Jake is a very stubborn man. Leboeuf's opening night was the first night that Jake worked there. One of the kitchen help told the police that Jake got into a heated argument with a co-worker. So Brad isn't the only one he irritated."

A stubborn man like your husband, I thought. "Is Jake still working there?" I asked.

"I don't know, Mrs. Fletcher, but have you heard about Wylie Leboeuf?"

Was she referring to his arrest for drug possession? If so, I didn't want to indicate that I was already aware of it and have to identify my source.

"What about him?" I asked, hoping that she would elaborate.

"After the Leboeuf party left our restaurant on opening night, we heard that Wylie not only argued with his father, but he physically attacked him — punched him, is what I'm told."

Another Cabot Cove rumor raising its ugly head.

"I hadn't heard that," I said, relieved that it didn't have to do with his drug arrest. "Who told you that?"

"A member of Leboeuf's staff told one of our kitchen workers, who told Brad. I just thought you might have heard it, too."

"Afraid not, Marcie."

"I won't keep you. I know you have a lot

222

to do. I hope you'll come back soon for dinner."

"You can count on it. Please give my best to your husband."

After ending my call with Marcie, I gathered up some paid bills and other correspondence, one of which required overseas postage, and rode my bicycle over to the Cabot Cove Post Office. There was a line waiting to see Debbie, one of the two clerks who regularly staffed the desk there. I grabbed a copy of the *Gazette* from a pile left on the windowsill and took my place behind the last person.

I was perusing Evelyn's coverage of the Leboeuf case, even though I'd already read this issue at home, when someone whispered in my ear.

"Did you solve the crime yet?"

I turned to see the proprietor of Mara's Luncheonette. "Mara! What are you doing here?"

She held up a box. "I'm sending a birthday gift to my sister in Grand Lake Stream. Is that so shocking?"

"Not at all." I laughed. "I guess I'm just accustomed to seeing you at the restaurant and don't expect to find you anywhere else."

Mara rolled her eyes. "I know I work long hours, but believe it or not, I do have a life."

"Of course you do. I didn't mean to offend you."

"No offense taken." She nodded at the newspaper I held. "I was kidding about solving the murder, of course."

"Of course." I smiled, refolded the paper, and put it back on the stack by the window.

"I know you may not believe this since I was so snippy about all the attention going to Brad Fowler and his new restaurant, but I was sorry to hear about the health inspection finding."

"How did you learn about it?" I asked on a sigh.

"Are you kidding me? Kitchen workers are the worst gossips out there. And you'd better not tee them off. They have ways of getting even you wouldn't believe."

"I think I'd rather not hear about those," I said.

"Never in my kitchen," she said. "I keep a sharp eye on my staff, and I'll tell you something else. I also keep a sharp eye on that health inspector. Harold Greene always has his hand out."

"What do you mean? Does he ask you for bribes?"

"Not me. Never me. I wouldn't give him the time of day. But I've heard about others who paid their way out of a failing grade."

"Oh, dear. That's not good news."

"They're probably not the places you patronize anyway. But when that guy comes walking through the door, I follow him around like a bird dog. I don't let him do a thing unless I'm watching closely. He hasn't pulled any fast ones on me, but I'm not so sure Brad and Marcie were as careful around him as I am."

"What are you saying, Mara?"

"Just that you can't always believe the health inspector's report. They might not have had any mice at all. He could have been testing them. And when they didn't offer him any shut-up money, he made them regret it."

"That's awful! Have you ever reported this inspector to the proper authorities?"

"No." She laughed. "First of all, I'm no whistle-blower. I don't want to rock the boat. You don't know how high up the corruption goes. Second, I'm not Jessica Fletcher. I may suspect this guy is a crook, but I can't prove it, and I don't have the time to try."

"Next!" Debbie called out, and I realized it was my turn at the counter.

"Nice to see you, Mara."

"You, too, Jessica." She lowered her voice. "Tell Brad and Marcie I said to keep their

225

heads up. It'll blow over."

"I'll do that," I said, but I wasn't certain if Mara was talking about the health inspection or the rumors about who committed the murder.

When I got home, I called Seth Hazlitt.

"Caught me on the way out," he said. "I've got a couple of patients in the hospital I need to check on, including that fellow who was attacked. He doesn't have a local doctor. The hospital wants me to take on his case."

"Mind if I tag along?"

"No, but why?"

"I'd like to see how he is."

"You can always call the nurses' station."

"I'd like to see him for myself. Of course, if you'd rather I didn't —"

"I don't mind taking you, Jessica, but I can't guarantee you'll be able to see him."

"I'll take my chances."

"Okay. I'll swing by and pick you up in ten minutes."

Seth reminded me during the short drive to the hospital that the man who'd been beaten, Warren Shulte, had been placed in a private room, with an order that no one aside from medical personnel or law enforcement were to be granted access to him.

"Why do you think that is?" I asked.

"Your guess is as good as mine," he said as he turned into a parking lot reserved for hospital staff. "You were there when the agent from the FBI arrived. What did he say — something like 'he'll take over?' "

"Or words to that effect. Who is this Mr. Shulte who demands such secrecy and protection?"

Seth pulled into a space reserved for physicians and shut off the ignition. He turned to me and said, "You didn't want to come here today to see how this Shulte character is doing medically. You wanted to come with me because you're determined to get an answer to your questions about him and why he's being given special treatment. Am I right?"

I held up my right hand. "Guilty as charged," I said.

"And," he said, "to continue my hypothesis, you thought that you could use my credentials at the hospital to wheedle some information out of somebody, maybe even Mr. Shulte himself."

"You know me too well, Doctor."

"Considering how difficult it is to know the *real* Jessica Fletcher, I take that as a supreme compliment."

Seth asked me to wait in the lobby while

he went to the physicians' locker room and slipped a white coat over his shirt and tie. When he returned he said, "You go get yourself a cup of tea at the canteen while I check in on my patients. I'll collect you there and we'll go up to see how Mr. Shulte is doing. If they let you in, fine. But you can't pretend to be my nurse."

"Would I do that?"

Seth raised one eyebrow at me. "Wouldn't put it past you."

I had just sipped my last drop of tea when he returned and joined me at the small table. "I spoke with Dr. Keane, who examined Shulte in the ER. He says aside from two cracked ribs and a broken nose, he'll live."

"That's good to hear. Did Dr. Keane say anything else about him?"

"Only that there's a deputy from the sheriff's department sitting outside the room to keep people away."

"With the exception of medical personnel," I offered.

Seth narrowed his eyes as he looked at me. "I can see where this is going," he said. "I already told you no medical disguises. I'm not about to jeopardize my standing in this hospital to help you satisfy your insatiable curiosity."

"You have such a warped view of me," I said.

Seth coughed and grumbled, "I hope I won't regret this. Well, come on. Let's see if Mort's deputy can be manipulated. But if he balks, you leave. Right?"

"Right you are, sir."

Seth repeated his instruction on our way to the elevator, "If Mort's deputy gives you a hard time about accompanying me into the patient's room, you'll have to accept that. I don't want to cause a scene."

"I understand perfectly, Seth. I'll be the model of discretion."

I couldn't read his expression, whether he believed me or found my assurance amusing. But he didn't say anything as the elevator doors opened and we walked down a quiet hallway in a secluded wing of the hospital. At the end sat Mort's uniformed deputy, Chip, a familiar face around town, who was engrossed in his cell phone. He looked up as we approached, stood, and said, "Good morning, Dr. Hazlitt."

"Good morning."

"And to you, too, Mrs. Fletcher."

"It's a lovely morning," I said, and waited for Seth to make the next move.

Seth headed for the door to Shulte's room. "I'm going in to see my patient."

I followed, but the deputy stopped me with, "Ah, Mrs. Fletcher, I'm not sure you're supposed to go in there."

"It's all right," I said. "I'm going on rounds with Dr. Hazlitt this morning. Isn't that right, Seth?"

Seth mumbled something and pushed open the door.

A puzzled expression crossed Chip's face. I smiled broadly at him and said, "Only be a few minutes."

The deputy watched us enter without saying anything else.

The room was cool and serene. Sunlight filtered through a partially open blind. A nurse, who had just finished taking the patient's blood pressure and temperature, greeted us as she noted the results on the chart and then left.

"Good morning, sir," Seth said.

Shulte was propped up in bed on pillows. His face was gray, his eyes sunken. Stubble on his cheeks and chin added to his pale look. Bruises testified to the thrashing he'd endured.

"I'm Dr. Hazlitt. I've been assigned to care for you as your physician. Feel free to ask any questions."

Shulte shifted in bed, which caused him pain. He moaned.

"You just relax," Seth said as he checked what was written on the chart. "Those broken ribs are bound to cause you a lot of discomfort. Expect it'll take several weeks before the pain is gone completely."

Shulte looked at me.

"I'm Jessica Fletcher," I said. "I was the one who found you and called nine-one-one."

"Thank you," he said softly, as though it hurt to speak.

"I'm glad I was there at the time," I said. I glanced at Seth before saying, "I also saw the two men who I believe attacked you."

His eyes widened and he licked his lips. "Punks!" he said in a stronger voice.

"They were dragging you from the back of the restaurant owned by Gerard Leboeuf," I said.

"Punks!" he repeated. "Mobsters." His face twisted into a snarl. "Leboeuf! He's another one. I'm glad he got his."

The vehemence in his tone struck me as though it were physical.

I checked Seth for a reaction to see whether he disapproved of my continuing to question Shulte, but he had his head buried in the chart, which said all I needed to know.

"Mr. Shulte," I said. "Mr. Shulte?"

The patient's eyes were fixed on a scene only he could see.

"Mr. Shulte?"

"Huh?"

"That's not your name, is it?" I asked.

"What's not my name?"

"Your name isn't Shulte, is it?"

"Who told you?"

"You didn't seem to recognize it when I called it."

Shulte or whoever he was sighed. "I knew I'd never remember that name. Never been good with names."

"Why would you need another name?"

The patient waved his hand in disgust.

Seth's eyes moved up from the chart and he speared whoever-he-was with a look.

"That's just the name I used when I got out of New York." The weakness he'd displayed when we'd first arrived was now replaced with resolve. He struggled to straighten up despite the pain and pointed a finger at me as though to make sure that I was listening closely. "I had to leave New York to save my life, you understand."

"For heaven's sake, why?"

"The wiseguys who bankrolled Leboeuf, that's why. I knew everything. I was the great man's accountant for years, since he opened his first restaurant — with money from 'investors,' he called them."

"Then you're aware of the rumors about Mr. Leboeuf's using his restaurants to launder illegal money."

"Of course I know about it, but I'll deny it if I have to testify."

"Hate to interrupt," Seth said, "but if your name isn't Shulte, what would you like me to call you?"

"Name's Compton, Charles Compton, CPA."

I thought of Special Agent Anthony Cale. Had Mr. Compton changed his name because he'd entered the Witness Protection Program? I asked.

He managed his first smile since we'd arrived. "Heck no," he said, shaking his head. "The Bureau wanted me to be a witness against Leboeuf, but I wasn't about to bite the hand that fed me. But when the goons behind Leboeuf got wind that the FBI was *talking* to me, I figured I'd better make tracks. That's what I did."

"Using an assumed name," I said.

"Just a precaution."

"Where have you been living?" Seth asked.

"Different places. I was with a daughter for a while, but I didn't like putting her in jeopardy, so I moved here, there, and ended up out on the east end of Cape Cod."

"You left New York because you were afraid for your life?" I asked.

"Right."

"And you felt safe there?"

"Safe as anywhere. Had a little place I rented. Good view of the road, although I always looked over my shoulder whenever I ventured outside."

"But the FBI would have protected you in its Witness Protection Program," I offered.

His guffaw morphed into a cough and became a groan. "Look," he said, after catching his breath, "I may not be the brightest bulb in the socket, but I don't trust the Feds any more than I trusted Leboeuf."

"You don't have to worry about him any longer," Seth grunted. He looked at his watch and raised his eyebrows.

I got the message and quickly asked, "If you wanted to get away from Leboeuf and his men, why did you come here to Cabot Cove and go to his restaurant?"

"I'm wondering that myself right now," Compton said. "When I heard that the big-shot chef had been killed — and I sure as shootin' wasn't sad about that — I decided to confront his wife for the money I was owed. I've been living hand-to-mouth and figured I had nothing to lose by seeing if Evie would make it right. I helped set her up in business. We used to be good buddies." He leaned back against the pillow and sighed. "I've made a lot of bad decisions in my life, and this was another one. When I told her why I was there, she told those two jerks who keep an eye on things for the 'investors' to get rid of me."

"They could have killed you," I said.

"They wouldn't do that. At least not as long as I have the goods on Leboeuf and the funny money that's behind him. That's why they're afraid of me."

"Not so afraid that they hesitated to tear the stuffing out of you," Seth said. "Have you given that information to the FBI?"

He shook his head. "The way I figure it, that information is my life preserver. It stays with me." He pointed at his head.

"If that's the only place your evidence is," I said, "it only gives them more of a motive to get rid of you."

"Look, I'm not that stupid, sweetheart. It's all written down in the safe in my attorney's office. If I die, he knows what to do. That's my ace in the hole. Leboeuf's goons know that, but what they don't know is who my attorney is."

As I pondered the wisdom of what

Compton considered his "ace in the hole," the door opened and FBI Special Agent Cale entered.

"What's going on here?" he demanded.

"I'm checking on my patient," Seth said mildly. He plugged his stethoscope into his ears and placed the chest piece over Compton's heart.

"What are *you* doing here?" Cale asked me.

"I saved this gentleman's life. I wanted to make sure he was okay."

"Well, now that you've seen for yourself that he'll live, you can leave."

Mort's deputy poked his head in the open doorway. "Everything okay here?"

Cale speared him with a frosty look. "I thought I told you no one was to visit him. Why did you let *her* in?"

"It's Mrs. Fletcher," Chip replied. "Everybody knows her, and she was making rounds with the doctor."

"You can wait for me outside, Jessica," Seth said. "I need a little time with my patient." He directed that last comment at Cale.

Several minutes later Seth joined me where I'd lingered in the hallway outside the door. The FBI agent had spent the time dressing down the deputy. I felt sorry for the young man whom I knew I had tricked into letting me go where I wasn't supposed to be.

Cale broke away from the deputy. "What did he tell you?" he asked Seth, pointing at the door.

"Can't reveal what we discussed," Seth said. "Doctor-patient privilege."

"I don't mean what you talked about medically. What else did you talk about?"

"Coming, Jessica?" Seth asked.

"Yes," I said. "Good seeing you again, Agent Cale."

I could feel Cale's eyes boring into our backs as we walked down the hall and waited for the elevator.

Seth returned his white lab coat, and we left the hospital and got in his car.

"Satisfied?" he asked as we pulled from the lot.

"It was an eye-opener," I said. "If I understood him correctly, according to Shulte — I mean Compton — those two young men who work for Leboeuf are members of organized crime."

"Ayuh."

"Either one of them might have killed him."

"Possible."

As we pulled into my driveway, Seth said,

"You heard Compton say that he's been looking over his shoulder everywhere he goes."

"Yes, I heard that."

"My advice to you, Jessica Fletcher, is that you do the same."

CHAPTER SEVENTEEN

As soon as I walked in the house, I went to my desk and made notes about everything Compton had said about Leboeuf and their former relationship. I had no idea at that juncture, of course, that one day I would be writing a book about the murder and would find these notes helpful. For the moment I was concerned only that I not forget things in the event they proved useful to the authorities in solving the Leboeuf murder.

Once I'd recalled what had transpired in the hospital room and got it down on paper, I sat back and thought about what it all might mean.

From what I knew of the man, Gérard Leboeuf had made plenty of enemies over the course of his career. According to Mr. Compton, Leboeuf owed him money. I wondered how many others the chef may have taken advantage of — even defrauded — not to mention those he had forced out

239

of business with his tough tactics. Notwithstanding his denials, Compton feared for his life to the extent that he had bolted from New York and had been living a low-profile existence ever since, constantly looking over his shoulder. From what he'd told Seth and me, as Leboeuf's accountant he'd been in a position to know everything about the restaurateur's fiscal dealings, including the source of the financing with which he'd launched his dining empire, as well as the allegation that he'd used his restaurants to launder money. Compton understood that such inside information could get a man killed, which motivated his skipping town. Perhaps he'd figured with Leboeuf dead, he was safe in confronting Eva over the money owed him. What he hadn't counted on were the two bodyguards, if that's what they were, who seemed to be tickled to have the opportunity to exercise their muscles against an aging man.

Evidently, the FBI had been looking for Compton, and I made a note to try to confirm how Special Agent Cale had learned of Compton's new identity as Shulte. He'd come to the hospital the night of the attack and had already known the man's assumed name. He'd said Detective

Mason had called him. But how did he know Shulte was the man he was seeking? Could he have suspected the accountant would come looking for money? Learning his quarry was in the hospital had spurred the FBI special agent into action. How the FBI knew Compton's assumed name was one of many unanswered questions, but Leboeuf's former financial manager clearly was not skilled at maintaining an alternate identity. I had quickly picked up that Shulte wasn't his real name.

I made a note on my lined yellow pad to find out when Compton had arrived in Cabot Cove. He claimed to have gone to the restaurant to find Eva Leboeuf and ask about the money owed him. But had he been in town earlier, early enough to have confronted Leboeuf himself and take action against him if his pleas fell on deaf ears? His hatred of the man was palpable, perhaps enough so to prompt such a drastic step.

That Eva had allowed the opening of the restaurant following her husband's murder felt strange to me, but perhaps she felt that he would have wanted her to carry on in his absence. How people respond when someone near to them has died is often confusing, complying with a logic only the bereaved can explain — and sometimes can't.

The Leboeuf neighbors, Ed and Elaine Filler, mentioned that the couple often fought. I had only encountered Eva socially a limited number of times, and truthfully, she'd never come across as a doting wife. The waiter Fritzi said that Leboeuf was known as a ladies' man back in New York, and Fritzi was right: A husband with multiple affairs wasn't destined to engender tender feelings in his spouse. However, few high-profile couples ever reveal the truth of their relationships in public, despite what the tabloids blare in their headlines. Eva ran a successful business that hinged on how beautiful she was. If I put myself in her place, I would have wanted people to comment on my products, not on my family. So it wasn't surprising to me that she worked to keep her private life just that — private. As a result, I had no idea how she really felt about her husband's death, much less about the fact that he'd been murdered.

It was also hard to eliminate their son, Wylie, from the equation. With a history of drug use and possibly violent behavior, he hadn't demonstrated any ambition or goals of his own, presenting himself as the opposite of his hard-driving father. And I'd

242

seen for myself the nature of the prickly relationship between father and son. Leboeuf was demanding — there was no doubt about that — and from what I'd seen of his son, Wylie seemed to be a disaffected young man with little interest in anything other than what was on the screen of his cell phone. Marcie claimed to have heard that the young man had struck his father the night of the murder, but if her "facts" came from the Cabot Cove rumor mill, they could hardly be relied upon as the truth. Someone working in Leboeuf's kitchen telling someone working in Brad's kitchen was not exactly firm evidence that such an assault had taken place. I would need to find someone who'd actually witnessed the two together before I believed such an aggressive encounter had taken place.

And speaking of those who worked in Leboeuf's kitchen, who there might have had reason or incentive to silence the chef? Could any of them have taken exception to being browbeaten by the boss? Jake Trotter, the sous chef, who moved from the Fin & Claw to Leboeuf's French Bistro, seemed to pick fights with everyone for whom he worked. I knew nothing about him except that he had a volcanic temper, and people with so much rage in them are capable of doing irrational things.

And what of Walter Chang, who'd been brought to Cabot Cove to manage the restaurant? According to Mort Metzger, Chang was the person who'd discovered Leboeuf's lifeless body in the kitchen. What was the tenor of *their* relationship?

When I thought of the kitchen staff at Leboeuf's, an image of the two young men dragging Compton from behind the restaurant blazed across my mental screen. Who were they? Were they connected to criminal elements? Compton indicated that they were. Maybe the two had taken out the famous chef, perhaps on instructions from a criminal organization that allegedly had financed him to begin with. But why would they want to eliminate the famous figurehead of Gérard Leboeuf's restaurant empire, the cash cow that must have made continuous contributions to their coffers — unless the chef was cheating them, skimming off money right under their noses. Had Leboeuf sufficiently angered his "partners" for them to call for his execution?

Thinking about all of these potential suspects kept pushing me away from facing the possibility that the police might already be investigating the right man. Could it be

Brad Fowler?

No matter how much I rail against authorities coming to hasty conclusions when investigating a murder, focusing on Brad could hardly be dismissed as a knee-jerk response. If I could weigh Jake's volcanic temper and imagine that his rage might lead to violence, I could hardly make excuses for Brad's anger at his competitor. Leboeuf opening his bistro next door to the Fin & Claw had threatened to destroy Brad and Marcie's dream. The snide comments from Leboeuf and his party at opening night were not only crude and uncalled for, but they bordered on a challenge to Brad to defend what was near and dear to him. And then there was Leboeuf's nasty comment to Isabel Fowler minutes before she suffered a fatal stroke. That could well have tipped Brad into a murderous mode when coupled with his well-known short fuse. Of everyone, he seemed to have the strongest motive, although I wanted desperately for Brad not to have been the murderer.

I'd known Isabel for many years. To suspect that her son and only child might be capable of such drastic action was unthinkable. Yet was it my sentimental attachment to his mother that made me willing to defend Brad, to believe that while he still had a lot of growing up to do, he was not the out-of-control teenager he had once been? If nothing else, Brad had matured into a man who loved his mother, adored his wife, and was willing to work long and hard to achieve a goal he'd held for many years. I prayed that that man had not betrayed the trust so many had invested in him to become a coldhearted killer.

Taking a break from the depressing work of analyzing motives for murder, I wandered outside and down the front path to the mailbox. Correspondence, whether paper or e-mail, could always be counted on to force me to abandon such thoughts in favor of catching up with friends, answering business queries, even dealing with household bills. Sorting through the envelopes I retrieved from my mailbox, I turned over a postcard with a cartoon drawing of a tooth on it. It was a notice from Ed Filler that I was due for a cleaning. Ed had said I would receive his reminder soon, and his postcard couldn't have come at a better time. Back at my desk, I picked up the telephone. Ed's wife, Elaine, answered my call.

"Hi, Elaine. It's Jessica Fletcher."

"Hello, Jessica. Ed ran out for a few minutes and I'm covering the phones for him. Need an appointment?"

"As a matter of fact, I do. I see I'm due for a cleaning."

"Oh, good. You got my card. Let me check the appointment book for you. Ooh, he's booked solid. Nothing open for a few weeks."

"I was hoping to get there sooner."

"Are you having problems with your tooth?"

"No. No. Ed fixed it perfectly."

"It can't be that you're that eager for a cleaning."

"Not exactly."

"Oh, yes, the neighbors," Elaine said. "Had a feeling you'd want to look in on them. I have an idea."

"I'm listening."

"Our niece Melinda is here visiting from California, just an overnight on her way to Boston. She's about to have her first novel published, a YA I think she calls it."

"Young adult, a popular category of books these days."

"Melinda knows that we live in the same town as Jessica Fletcher and would love to meet you."

"It'd be my pleasure."

"Let me see. I think I can fit you in as the last patient, six o'clock. Ed's hygienist is home sick, but Ed hasn't lost his cleaning touch. Are you free this evening?"

"As a matter of fact, I am."

"How about combining your cleaning with an impromptu cookout? Ed is a whiz at barbecuing ribs, almost as good as at putting in a crown. You can get your teeth cleaned by the man himself and enjoy good ribs with a heavenly barbecue sauce that Ed whipped up last night."

"How could I possibly say no?" I said. "Clean teeth and first-rate barbecued ribs? Pencil me in. I'll be there at six on the button."

Until that call, I had planned a quiet night at home, a simple dinner, a good book, and early to bed. But two things had changed my mind.

First, I thoroughly enjoyed being with the Fillers, and I would be fulfilling my dental obligations. Second, the Fillers' property was adjacent to the Leboeufs' summer home. Some tasty ribs, good conversation, and a chance to see close-up what was going on with the neighbors next door — a win-win situation.

I'd no sooner hung up when the phone rang. I looked at the readout; it was Mort Metzger. I was certain that he was calling about my conversation with Compton earlier that day and was undoubtedly irate.

248

I could envision Agent Cole chastising him about untrained deputies and poor police practices. I was tempted to not pick up and let the answering machine take the call, but I realized that would be cowardly on my part. Time to face the music.

"Hello, Mort," I said cheerfully.

"Hello, Mrs. F." He didn't sound cheery at all.

"How are you today?" I asked, knowing his reply would match the tone of his greeting.

"I could be a lot better, Mrs. F."

"Oh? A problem?"

"You know why I'm calling."

"No, I don't."

But I did, of course. Word had obviously gotten back to him about my accompanying Seth to see Mr. Compton despite Mort's deputy's orders to keep everyone out except medical personnel and the authorities.

"I heard you went to see the man who got beaten up, the one you called in to nine-one-one."

"I wanted to see how he was doing."

"Doc Hazlitt could have told you how he was doing. There was no need for you to show up there in person."

"I'm sorry if it has upset you, Mort."

"I'm a bit more than upset, Mrs. F. You

humiliated me in front of the FBI."

"Oh, dear. I didn't mean to do that."

"Agent Cale reamed me out, and you better believe I did the same to my deputy. I was going to suspend Chip, but he swore he now understands the meaning of 'no visitors.' "

"Please don't be hard on Chip, Mort. He meant well, didn't see anything wrong with allowing me to accompany Seth into the room."

"He had his orders. Makes me and the department look like a bunch of clowns."

"My apologies."

"Made us look like third graders in the schoolyard, like tourists losing their way in Times Square."

"I get the picture, Mort. I'm truly sorry to have embarrassed you."

"Now that I've gotten that off my chest, Mrs. F., maybe you'd be good enough to tell me what Compton told you."

"You know his real name."

"Of course I do. Just because the FBI has him under wraps — or so they think — doesn't mean that I shouldn't be in the loop."

"Of course not."

"So?"

"So — what?"

"We have a deal, don't we? I told you about the knife. Now you tell me about what Compton told you."

"I'm sure that I learned nothing you haven't heard from Special Agent Cale. Compton was once Gérard Leboeuf's accountant, which meant he was privy to Leboeuf's financial situation. Some of his financial dealings were evidently illegal, and Compton knew that being in possession of such information might put him in danger. That's why he left New York and has been living under the assumed name Shulte."

"Yeah, I know all that."

"Well, then, you know what I know. What else are you asking me?"

"I want to know what else you found out, Mrs. F., because I've seen how you get people to open up, spill their inner thoughts, things they seem to 'forget' when they're talking to law-enforcement professionals."

"That's very flattering, Mort."

"That's not why I'm saying it, Mrs. F. The FBI has its own agenda where Leboeuf is concerned, but I've got a murder to solve. Those two detectives from the state, Mason and Lucas, mean well, but all they've been doing is getting in my way. Let me ask you this. Do you think this guy Compton, or Shulte, or whatever name he uses, should

251

be viewed a suspect in the murder?"

I paused before replying. "Isn't it standard operating procedure that every person with a possible motive and access to the victim be included on the suspect list?"

"Sure. That's right. But I'm trying to narrow down the field. Did Compton say anything to you and to the doc that would lead you to think he might be the killer?"

"He certainly wasn't a fan of Gérard Leboeuf," I said.

"But he worked for him."

"That's true, but he claims that Leboeuf owed him money. He went to the restaurant after it had closed to confront Mrs. Leboeuf about it."

"When did he arrive in Cabot Cove?" Mort asked.

That was one of the questions I'd noted on my pad.

"He says he arrived the day after Leboeuf was killed, although I don't know that for certain."

"Maybe somebody saw him around town the day before," Mort offered.

"That would certainly be helpful," I said. "If I learn of anyone, you'll be the first to know."

"That's the way it should be, Mrs. F."

"I wouldn't have it any other way," I said.

"Oh, Mort, before you go. Please apologize to your deputy, Chip, for me. I didn't mean to get him into trouble."

"He needs to learn not to be manipulated, even by someone as charming as the famous J. B. Fletcher."

"I didn't —"

"You don't have to worry about Chip. He's not at the hospital anymore, but I've got him stationed out in front of the Leboeuf house to keep out the curious, especially those press people who are always trying to sneak in."

"I'm sure he'll do a great job," I said, relieved that my actions hadn't caused the young man any further reprimand.

During our conversation, I'd considered telling Mort that I'd be at the Fillers' house that evening, hoping to see for myself what was going on at the Leboeuf residence. But chances were that I'd learn nothing along those lines and would be content with a teeth cleaning and a lovely evening with good friends.

Unless, of course, I got lucky and picked up on something that would be useful to Mort.

We'd see.

Chapter Eighteen

Mort Metzger's deputy, Chip, was sitting in a marked sheriff's department car in front of the Leboeuf residence when my cabdriver pulled up next door. I paid him, got out, and walked over to the young deputy. He saw me coming in his side-view mirror, jumped out, and said, "Hello, Mrs. Fletcher."

"Hello, Chip. I see that you're on duty."

"Yes, ma'am."

"Keeping people from bothering the Leboeuf family?"

"Keeping away the press and the curious," he answered. "That's my orders."

"I'm sure the Leboeuf family appreciates what you're doing," I said.

He swallowed audibly. "You wouldn't be trying to get in to see them, would you, Mrs. Fletcher?"

"Oh, no. I'm going next door. I'm having dinner with the Fillers. I'm sorry for the trouble I caused you at the hospital, Chip. Sheriff Metzger told me he was not pleased."

He grinned. "That's okay, Mrs. Fletcher. The sheriff likes to blow off steam, but he gets over it pretty fast."

"An admirable trait," I said. "Have a nice evening."

Ed Filler greeted me as I walked through the side door to his office, which is attached to the house. "Glad you could make it," he said.

"I appreciate your fitting me into your schedule, Ed," I said. "Besides, I'm looking forward to that special barbecue sauce I keep hearing about. I hope it won't undo all the good work you're about to undertake."

"Nothing in it will stain your teeth, and I promise it will be the best barbecue sauce you ever ate."

"Even if you say so yourself," I said, smiling.

"Especially since I say so myself. Elaine says that I should bottle and sell it. Sounds like a great retirement business. But while I'm still working, Jessica, let's get those pearly whites sparkling clean. Then we can fire up the grill."

A half hour later we were seated on the Fillers' patio, glasses of wine in hand, an outdoor fireplace warming the space, and the aroma from the heating grill whetting appetites. Their niece, Melinda, visiting from San Francisco, was a pretty, ebullient young woman whose excitement about having sold her first YA novel to a publisher was palpable.

"I've been working at a restaurant in the Bay Area," she told me, "to pay the rent while I wrote my novel. A regular customer is an editor at a publishing house, a really nice guy. I told him about the novel and he asked to see it. Voila! He bought it. It's being published in six months."

"Makes you sound like an overnight success," Ed said, "but I know better."

Melinda blushed. "It's true. What I didn't tell you about were the four books I wrote that got rejected everywhere."

"That's part of the learning curve for most writers," I said.

"Well, they don't matter now. I finally got an acceptance, and I'm over the moon."

"That deserves a toast," I said, raising my glass. "To Melinda and her success as a writer."

"Would you read it, Mrs. Fletcher?" Melinda asked. "I'd really be honored. It does have a murder in it."

"Even if it didn't, I'm flattered that you

want me to read it," I said, which prompted her to run into the house, returning seconds later with a box containing the manuscript, which I put next to my purse.

While I was very much in the moment with my host and hostess and their niece, my attention occasionally wandered to the broad expanse of acreage next door, which sloped down to the water and a dock where the Leboeufs' boat, a moderately sized yacht, was tethered. In what my neighbors would call their "yahd," the Leboeufs had installed a putting green, tennis courts, a large free-form swimming pool, and a separate guest cottage, all of which had been commented upon during construction and none of which was visible from the Fillers' patio. However, because the Leboeuf deck was elevated, I could see it from where I sat despite a solid white board fence and tall hedgerow that defined the property line. Eva Leboeuf came in and out of a rear door. Obviously for tonight, at least, she was leaving the running of the bistro to the staff. The two brooding young men who'd beaten Compton also made appearances from time to time, including ten minutes tossing a football between them. I hadn't seen her son, Wylie, and wondered whether he was also at the house.

Ed Filler fiddled with his grill, which he said was called a Big Green Egg. He was a purist when it came to barbecuing, using a special brand of charcoal and tending it with loving care. When Elaine and Melinda declined my offer of assistance and went inside to put finishing touches on the evening's meal, I stood, stretched, and casually strolled down the hill to where a breakwater separated the two properties. I looked back. From this vantage point I had a better view of the goings-on at the Leboeuf house. Eva had returned to the deck. She wore sunglasses and a shawl around her shoulders and sat in a teak armchair, reading a magazine. One of the young protectors sat at the opposite side of the deck, lost in what I assumed was a smartphone. Today's technology is sometimes baffling to me, surefire evidence that I'm on the wrong side of fifty. But I have learned my way around my cell phone as well as my computer.

I was about to turn back to the Fillers' patio when something caught my attention on the Leboeuf boat. Someone was moving about.

I walked closer to the fence and shielded my eyes from the setting sun. The figure that I'd seen now came into view on the boat's aft deck. It was the Leboeufs' son, Wylie.

"Hello," I called, waving.

My greeting startled him. He looked left and right before focusing on me.

"Hello," I repeated. "It's Jessica Fletcher."

He appeared to be uncertain how to respond. Finally, he gave me a halfhearted wave and said, "Hi."

"It's a beautiful boat," I said. "Do you get to go cruising on it often?"

"No."

"That's a shame. You have such a picturesque spot here."

"It's nice," he mumbled; I had trouble hearing him.

"I wanted to let you know that I'm so very sorry about what happened to your father," I said.

Wylie's head bounced up and down, but he didn't respond.

I glanced back to see whether Eva and her watchdogs were aware of our conversation. They didn't seem to be.

"Do you mind if I talk with you?" I asked.

"Huh?"

"May I come aboard?"

When he didn't respond, I wedged through an opening at the end of the fence and hedgerow and walked out on the dock.

Wylie's expression was pure confusion.

"It's a lovely evening, isn't it?" I said as I stepped onto the boat's deck.

"I don't know if you should be here," he said, looking back to where his mother had dozed off. "I'm not supposed to talk to the press or anyone." Her two bodyguards — I suppose that was the proper description of them — had disappeared inside the house.

I held my hands up to show that I wasn't hiding anything. "I'm not the press," I said. "I just wanted to extend my condolences to you and your family. How are you and your mother holding up? Your father's death was such a terrible, unexpected tragedy."

He stared at me in wary silence.

An unexpected response to be sure; I didn't pursue it.

He walked toward the bow and I followed.

"Do you know how to pilot this boat, Wylie?"

"No. He never taught me — wouldn't ever let me touch the controls — but I think I could do it anyway. I watched how he did it, and sometimes when we had guests he hired a captain to do the piloting." He smiled softly. "*He* used to show me what everything was for."

"Maybe you can learn now. Your mother might like that."

"I don't think so. You're that writer, aren't you?"

"Yes. Jessica Fletcher."

"You're not a cop."

"No. I promise I'm not."

"Then why are you asking questions about my family?"

"Did you know your father and I were colleagues of sorts? We share the same agent in New York. I once interviewed your father for a book I was writing. He was very helpful to me."

Wylie gave a soft snort. "You must have been one of the few, but that doesn't explain why you're here."

"It's a terrible blow when someone is murdered, Wylie. I'm sure this is a painful time for you. And like you, I want to see your father's killer brought to justice."

He turned to face me, and I saw in his large brown eyes torment and hurt, anger and resentment. In the few times I'd seen him before, he'd never had that youthful glow that most young people have, and I wondered whether his use of drugs had dulled his expression, dulled every aspect of his life.

He stared at me. His lips moved, but no words came from them. Then he said, "It

261

was that guy Fowler who killed him, wasn't it?"

"I don't know," I said. "Is that what you and your family think?"

He nodded and mumbled, "Yeah. My mother said that's who did it. Rico said so, too."

"Rico? Is he one of the men on your father's staff?"

He nodded, his gaze going up to the deck of the house.

"I'm sure the police will determine who's responsible for your father's death," I said. "But it's a mistake to jump to conclusions until all the facts are in." I glanced back to the Fillers' patio, where Ed was fussing with his prized barbecue. "I think it's time I rejoined my hosts. It was good to talk with you, Wylie."

"What are you doing here, Jessica?" a harsh female voice asked.

It was Eva Leboeuf. She stood on the pier with hands on her hips, an angry expression on her fine-boned face.

"I'm having dinner with your neighbors," I said, gesturing up the hill. "I saw Wylie here and walked down to offer my sympathies to your son."

"Do you really think that's necessary?"

"He's suffered a tragic loss. I don't see

anything wrong in acknowledging that."

"You've been here longer than that. What else did you talk about?"

"About Dad's murder," Wylie said harshly.

Eve kept her eyes on me. "He doesn't know anything about it."

"As I said, Eva, I simply came to offer condolences. To you as well as Wylie."

Behind her, the two men had left the house and were heading downhill toward us. Max, the German shepherd, was with them, thankfully on a leash. "Is she bothering you, Mrs. Leboeuf?" one of them called out, as Max let out a series of sharp barks.

She didn't answer.

"I feel sad about your husband's death, Eva," I said. "I know we don't know each other very well, but in my few encounters with Gérard, he always spoke so proudly about you and —"

I started to retreat from the boat when Eva said, "Maybe it's time you and I had a talk, Jessica."

Her protectors flanked her, arms crossed, their faces stony, while Max growled at me.

"I'd like that," I said.

"I know that you're some sort of a celebrity in this wretched town and that you enjoy poking your nose into other people's business."

I was startled by her aggressive tone, but waited for her to continue.

"I also know that you're a friend of the Fowler family and that you questioned that imbecile, Compton, in the hospital."

"That's all true," I said.

"Gérard may have been helpful to you in business, but that does not give you the right to meddle in our lives."

"A vicious murder has been committed in Cabot Cove, and that impacts everyone who lives here. I would think that you, above all, would want the killer arrested and prosecuted as swiftly as possible."

"There are professionals investigating my husband's murder. We don't need amateurs analyzing us or thinking they know more than the police."

"I agree. However, I have been helpful to the authorities in the past, and I hope to be again."

"All they have to do is arrest Brad Fowler and charge him with the murder. You certainly can't think that he's innocent."

"Jessica, soup's on!" Ed Filler yelled from his patio.

Eva seemed to be trying to push me into concurring with her conclusion. But I didn't agree and wasn't about to be pressured to say something she could — and likely would

264

— use against me. "I'd like very much to continue this conversation, Eva, but it will have to be at another time. My host is calling. Please excuse me."

I could feel their eyes boring into me as I retraced my steps through the gap in the fence and up to the Fillers' yard, where I joined my friends at a nicely set table near the barbecue.

"Have a productive conversation with our neighbor?" Ed asked, grinning.

"I suppose you could call it that," I said. "It wasn't especially friendly, but considering what they're going through, I can hardly fault them for being reluctant to speak with me."

"They've never been friendly," Elaine put in, lowering her voice, although it was doubtful anyone next door could overhear our conversation. "She's always been a cold fish, and the son — well, you've heard the rumors about him."

"I feel sorry for him," I said.

"He's a loner. No telling what's on his mind," Ed said. "What did you talk about?"

"I mentioned the murder. He said that he and his family believe that Brad Fowler killed his father."

"Well, they're only saying what everyone else in Cabot Cove is," Ed said, "at least that's what I hear from my patients."

Elaine spooned homemade potato salad onto our plates. "I just wish it was over," she said. "Gérard Leboeuf's murder has the whole town on edge."

I silently agreed. Knowing that a murderer was wandering around Cabot Cove had created a pervasive tension among townspeople, me included. But I forced that thought from my consciousness. I chose to sit with my back to the Leboeuf estate next door as I dug into the meal in front of me. Elaine was right; the barbecue sauce that her husband had created was superb, the ribs tender and falling off the bone. There was, of course, lots of conversation with Melinda about her young-adult novel and her plans for the future. Such youthful enthusiasm was contagious, and her exuberance brought back memories of when I was her age and viewing the future with wide eyes and an equal amount of awe.

The setting had become still and serene after darkness had fallen. Patio lights, augmented by flickering lanterns, cast a soft glow over everything. Elaine brought out a key lime pie as special as her husband's barbecue sauce. I asked for the recipe.

"It's so easy, Jessica. Even Maureen Metzger couldn't mess up this pie."

After a cup of strong and flavorful coffee, I stifled a yawn and glanced at my watch. "I think it's time for this lady to head home and to bed," I said. "It's been a wonderful evening — good food, good friends, and spending time with a future National Book Award winner."

Melinda beamed as I picked up her manuscript and my purse and stood.

"I'll drive you home," Ed said.

"I can call a cab," I protested.

"Nonsense," Ed said. "Just give me a minute to carry some things inside."

"I'll help," I said.

With the table cleared, and after hugs to the ladies, I walked with Ed to his car in the driveway. As I was about to get in, my cell phone sounded.

"I wonder who that is," I said, rummaging through my purse in search of the phone. "Hello?"

"Oh, Mrs. Fletcher," a female voice managed between sobs.

"Who is this?" I asked.

"It's me — it's Marcie Fowler."

"What's wrong, Marcie?"

"You have to come. It's Brad. They took him away." The rest of her words were drowned in her tears.

"Please, Marcie, try to get ahold of

yourself. Where are you?"

"At the restaurant."

"What's happened to Brad?"

"Sheriff Metzger and his deputies arrested him for Gérard Leboeuf's murder."

"I'll be right there."

CHAPTER NINETEEN

Ed Filler said that he would be glad to come with me into the Fin & Claw, but I told him it wasn't necessary. During our drive there, I had filled him in about Marcie's call.

"The police must have the goods against him if they've made the arrest," he said.

It was a reasonable assumption on Ed's part. Brad Fowler's very public dispute with Gérard Leboeuf placed him at the top of the suspect list, and the authorities had focused their attention on him from the beginning. His arrest had begun to feel inevitable. Despite my hopes for Brad's innocence, I had to acknowledge that if someone was arrested and charged, there must be enough evidence to justify such action. Mort Metzger and the other investigators might well have uncovered tangible evidence that incriminated Brad beyond a reasonable doubt. If so, they were to be congratulated for solid police work.

However, knowing as I do that the police want to solve a crime as quickly as possible and that there have been times when they take the easiest path, I had to hope that this was one of those occasions.

I thanked Ed for the lift to the restaurant and for the lovely evening, got out of his car, and approached the Fin & Claw's entrance. There were quite a few cars in the parking lot, as there were in the parking lot for Leboeuf's bistro. It appeared as if Leboeuf's murder hadn't hurt either business, whether thanks to the food on the menus or the notoriety of both owners, one the victim of a brutal killing and the other suspected of the crime. Either way, both establishments were making money.

As I entered the Fin & Claw, I was greeted by Fritzi, who had abandoned his waiter's uniform for a suit and tie, befitting his role that evening as substitute host. I wasn't surprised. Marcie had been emotionally distraught when she'd called, hardly conducive to presenting a smiling, welcoming face to customers.

Fritzi's greeting was nonverbal. He raised his eyebrows and slowly shook his head.

I looked past him at the full dining room. "Where's Marcie?" I asked.

"In the kitchen or the back office," he

said. "You missed all the excitement."

"She told me that Brad has been arrested."

"That's right. Sheriff Metzger and two deputies hauled him off in handcuffs. Terrible!"

"Did they do it in front of the customers?"

He cocked his head toward the kitchen. "You'd better talk to her, Mrs. Fletcher — provided you can get her to calm down."

A number of familiar faces greeted me, and the conversational buzz grew as I passed by their tables on my way to the swinging doors leading into the kitchen. I drew a deep breath and stepped through them.

"Where's Mrs. Fowler?" I asked.

A young man at the salad-making station said, "In the office." He pointed to a door almost hidden by a massive stainless steel refrigerator. I went to it and knocked.

"Who is it?" Marcie's voice asked.

"It's Jessica Fletcher," I said.

Marcie was huddled behind a small desk piled high with papers. I could see from the doorway that her face was red and blotchy; her mascara had run down from her eyes over her cheeks, giving her a tragic-comic look. I closed the door behind me and approached the desk. There was one other chair, a red-and-white striped director's chair in a corner, which I pulled close to her.

"I came as quickly as I could," I said.

"Thank you," she said weakly. "I shouldn't have bothered you, but I didn't know who else to call. Isabel isn't —"

"Your timing was perfect, Marcie. I was just leaving Dr. Filler's house. I'm glad you reached out to me."

I thought she was about to cry again, but her reservoir of tears was empty. All that emerged from her were dry gasps. I waited until that spasm had passed before saying, "Do you want to tell me what happened tonight?"

"It was awful, Mrs. Fletcher, a nightmare."

"Sheriff Metzger arrested Brad here at the restaurant?"

"Yes. They must have gone to the house first. I got a call from my neighbor, who was there watering my plants. She said the sheriff and two other officers arrived in a pair of police cars and asked where Brad was. My neighbor told them that he was working. Where else would he be? We're here day and night, keeping the restaurant going."

"Brad knew they were coming? I mean,

you told him about your neighbor's call, didn't you?"

"Not right away. I was busy with two couples who wanted to change their table. No drafts. Not near the kitchen. Away from any children. I finally got them seated and went into the kitchen to tell Brad. I had just gotten his attention when the sheriff and his men came through the back door."

"And they arrested Brad right there in the kitchen?"

"No. I wish they had. The sheriff and his men came through the door that leads into the kitchen. Brad and his sous chef were cooking. Some of the waitstaff were picking up orders from the hot shelf, and —"

I waited for her to regain control of her voice.

"Brad saw them and panicked. He glanced at me and ran into the dining room."

I drew a deep breath. Running was the worst thing he could have done.

"What happened then?"

"Oh, God, it was terrible. The sheriff and his men raced after Brad. It happened right there in the middle of the dinner service; people were eating their meals, and the sheriff comes bursting through the kitchen doors."

"They subdued Brad in the dining room?"

She nodded, her sobs coming out in hic-
cups.

At least Mort Metzger had tried to be
tactful, to arrest Brad in the kitchen, out of
sight of the Fin & Claw's customers.
Although Mort and I had had our disagree-
ments over the years, I respected his
integrity and sensitivity and wasn't surprised
that he'd tried to take Brad into custody
out of public view.

*What had prompted Brad to run? Running
from the law is almost always viewed as an
indication of guilt.*

I put that thought aside and asked Marcie,
"Did Brad say anything to you when they
arrested him?"

"He was beside himself, Jessica. He was
trembling. He cursed at the police, which is
so unlike him. He never uses four-letter
words, at least not around me."

"Did Sheriff Metzger say anything about
why they were arresting him?" I asked.

She squeezed her eyes tightly shut, either
because her thoughts were painful, or
because she was trying to recall what had
been said. She opened them and said,
"They . . . they had him on his stomach on
the floor with his hands behind his back."
Newfound tears flowed.

"It must have been a terrible shock to

274

people at the tables."

"I was so humiliated," Marcie said, "not for me, but for Brad."

"Of course you were."

"The last thing Brad told me as they were taking him away was to stay here and take care of the customers. And then he —"

I cocked my head.

"Oh, Mrs. Fletcher, I wish he hadn't."

"What did he do?"

"He swore he didn't do it, but he also yelled out that he was glad that Leboeuf was dead."

Brad Fowler was obviously his own worst enemy. He not only ran from the authorities, but he fed into his motive for having killed Leboeuf.

"I followed them outside," Marcie said, mopping her eyes with a napkin. "I asked the sheriff if I could come. He said no. He said I should get a lawyer for Brad."

"Good advice," I said. "Do you have one you can call?"

"Only the lawyer who drew up the papers for the restaurant, but I don't think he handles criminal cases. Besides, Mrs. Fletcher, where will we get the money for a lawyer? We're broke. Every cent has gone into the Fin and Claw. Our last four hundred dollars went to pay the fine from the health inspector."

"The court will assign a public defender,"
I said. "There are some very good ones in
the area."

"I'm doing as Brad asked. I'm staying
here, but for what? I'm sure all the customers are leaving left and right without waiting for their dinners to come out. I don't
blame them."

"Well, actually, when I came through the
dining room, it appeared to me as if every
table was full."

"They are? I can't go out there looking
like this."

Fritzi interrupted us. "Sorry to bother
you," he said, "but customers are still coming in. Would you like me to put a 'closed'
sign on the door?"

"What should I do, Mrs. Fletcher?"
Marcie asked. "I want to get out of here
and see Brad."

"Can you cook?"

"Of course."

"Why don't you let Fritzi handle the front
of the house and you keep things going in
the kitchen," I said. "I doubt that they'll allow you to see Brad tonight. The best thing
you can do is take care of your customers
and then go home and try to get some sleep.
I'm sure Sheriff Metzger can arrange for

you to visit him tomorrow."

"I can't bear the thought of going home without Brad there."

"What about your folks?"

"They're down in Florida."

"Would you like to spend the night at my house?"

"Oh, Mrs. Fletcher, are you sure?"

"Of course I'm sure. I have a guest room that's always made up and ready for visitors."

A great sigh escaped her. "I'd be so grateful," she said. "I think what I need most is someone I can talk to, someone who understands."

"I'm flattered if you think I'm that person, Marcie. Go take care of your diners. You want them to keep coming back, don't you? I'll find a quiet corner of the dining room and wait for you."

Two hours later I got out of Marcie's car in my driveway. We entered the house and I offered to brew tea, but she asked if I had anything stronger. I poured her a snifter of brandy and made the tea for myself. We sat in my living room, each immersed in our own thoughts, until she said, "I never thought I'd say this, but maybe Brad *did* kill Leboeuf."

CHAPTER TWENTY

Marcie and I sat up talking until two in the morning. To be more accurate, Marcie talked and I listened, a role I was perfectly willing to assume. She needed to vent, to empty herself of all her conflicting feelings and thoughts about Brad, the Fin & Claw, and her life in general. She told stories of her childhood, of vacations with her parents, silly things she did as a teenager, and spoke in detail of how she met Brad, their courtship, marriage, and life together.

"I think what attracted me most to Brad," she said, "was how sure he was of things. I mean, when he made up his mind about something, or to do something, he did it. Nothing was going to stop him."

"That is an admirable trait," I agreed, "but sometimes we can be too sure of ourselves."

She looked at me, puzzled.

"This sure-mindedness you speak of, Marcie — I just wonder if he forged ahead with opening the restaurant without having benefited from what others might know about the business."

"We talked about that," she said, "and I urged Brad to seek advice from other people. He did. He studied and he read, but he also had his own way of doing things, and as I said, once he'd made up his mind, there was no stopping him."

Her conversation flowed easily. She seemed to be on automatic pilot, one recollection melding into another, the words sometimes coming so fast that I had to ask her to repeat what she'd said. Her nerves were exposed; she constantly ran her fingers through her hair as though to confirm that it was still there, and she had a habit of chewing her cheek between tales. Her stories didn't seem to follow any sort of chronological order.

But I kept thinking of what she'd said earlier, that she wondered whether Brad *had* killed Gérard Leboeuf. I wanted to pick my spot to raise that with her and found it when she said, "I'd never known Brad to take immediate offense with anyone until Leboeuf came into our lives. God, how he hated that man."

"Why do you think Brad disliked Leboeuf so much?" I asked. "Was it just the competition, or was it because you disliked him, too?"

"Me? I didn't have anything against the man."

"Now, Marcie, when I met you at the press conference when Leboeuf announced his new restaurant, you were upset."

"Of course I was upset, but it was because Leboeuf was such a big shot and he was going into competition with us."

"At the time, you told me you hated Leboeuf."

"I don't remember that. You must have misunderstood. I just didn't want our place to go up against a famous chef with loads of money behind him, that's all."

I decided not to pursue Marcie's faulty memory or my possible misunderstanding and asked about what had been nagging at me since we walked in the door. "When we first got home tonight, you said that you thought that maybe Brad *had* killed Leboeuf. That comment shocked me."

"I didn't really mean it," she said. "It's just that —" She took a deep breath and let it out.

"Just that what? Did something happen? Did Brad say or do anything to lead you to doubt his innocence?"

She shifted her position on the couch,

diverting her eyes from mine. I waited for her to reply. When she did, she said it flatly, without looking at me. "Brad wanted me to tell the police that he'd come home the night of the murder hours before it happened."

"But he hadn't?"

A slow shaking of her head was her response.

She turned to me. "Brad knew that he'd be the prime suspect because of the angry exchanges he'd had with Leboeuf. He was sure that what Leboeuf had said to his mother had triggered her stroke. There was also the threat to the Fin and Claw that Leboeuf and all his money represented."

"I think Brad was right in assuming that those things would cause the authorities to point a finger at him," I said. "It's only natural to first look at those who had a motive to kill. But motive alone doesn't prove guilt. Did Sheriff Metzger say anything when he arrested Brad to indicate that he had sufficient evidence to take such a step?"

"Not in front of me. No."

"Have you told the police what Brad asked you to do?"

"Oh, no, of course not."

"They have questioned you, though, haven't they?"

"Not for very long. I told them I was at home asleep. The kitchen workers could verify the time I left the restaurant. I guess that's my alibi."

Did she have a legal obligation to tell the authorities what Brad had requested of her? Did I? Because Marcie was Brad's wife, she was not legally obligated to say anything that would be injurious to her spouse. Morally? The line between moral obligations and legal requirements has always been gray. But what of *my* moral obligation?

A series of yawns preceded a lull in the conversation, during which Marcie's eyes closed and her head nodded.

"Time for bed," I said.

"Can't I sleep right here?" she asked, dropping her shoes to the floor.

"Wouldn't you be more comfortable in a bed in the guest room?"

She answered with another yawn. "I'm fine here, if you don't mind." She stretched out.

"The bed upstairs is made. You could just climb in."

But she'd already rested her head on a brown leather pillow on the couch. Within seconds her breathing told me that she was sound asleep. I pulled a throw from a chair and gently covered her with it.

Poor thing, I thought. *To be so young and to have to suffer through such a horrible experience.*

I left her sleeping, went upstairs, and ten minutes later I, too, was gone.

Four hours later I awakened to a noise from another part of the house. Groggily, I got out of bed, slipped on my robe and slippers, and ventured from the bedroom. Marcie was in the kitchen, looking out at my backyard.

"It's so pretty here," she said absently when I came into the room. "I'm sorry if I woke you."

"I'm just sorry that you had so little sleep."

She raised her arms overhead and stretched. "I'm fine. I used to get by on four hours when I was in school. Besides, your couch is more comfortable than our bed at home."

"What would you like for breakfast, Marcie?"

"Nothing, thanks. I'd better go home and change and then get down to police headquarters to find out what's happened to Brad. I'll also be needed at the restaurant to get ready for the lunch crowd. Hopefully there will be a crowd." She gave me a wan smile.

"I understand," I said. "Some coffee in a

traveling cup?"

She shook her head. "You were so sweet to let me ramble on last night."

"You needed to unburden yourself. And please call on me if there's anything more I can do to help."

I watched her pull away from the driveway, sighed, and headed back to the kitchen, where I made myself a cup of coffee and an English muffin with cherry preserves I'd recently bought. I debated going back to bed but decided that since I was up I might as well get an early start to the day. Dressed and ready for action, I settled in my home office and waded through e-mails that had accumulated and gone unanswered and tackled my least favorite office chore, filing. I was in the midst of creating multiple piles of paper on my desk when the phone rang.

"Hi, Jessica. Maureen here."

"Hello, Maureen. I understand your husband had a busy night."

"You've heard about Brad Fowler."

"Yes. His wife, Marcie, spent last night here."

"She did? Why didn't she go home?"

"I guess she felt the need for a little company. We sat up talking until the wee hours. She didn't get much sleep — and neither did I," I said, stifling a yawn.

"I feel bad for her, and for her husband."

"So do I."

"But I'm not calling about that, Jessica. Just want to make sure that you remember tonight."

"Tonight?"

"My dinner party. Don't tell me you've forgotten?"

There goes my early-to-bed night, I thought.

The truth was that in the flurry of events of the past few days, I *had* forgotten to put Maureen's dinner party on my calendar. I confessed to her that it had slipped my mind, but since my schedule for that evening was open, I assured her that I'd be there.

"I'm glad I called," she said. "It wouldn't be the same without you. By the way, I've made a wonderful dessert based upon Isabel Fowler's recipe."

"Looking forward to it, Maureen. I'd better get my calendar up to date."

I was thankful that Maureen had reminded me of her dinner party. It was uncharacteristic of me to have forgotten about it, and I would have felt terrible had I not shown up. Maureen's dinner parties were always pleasant occasions, although you could never be sure that the dishes she created would turn out the way she intended. But the food wasn't as important as the conversation that always sparkled when this group of friends gathered, and I'd be less than honest if I didn't say I was looking forward to a chance to talk with Mort Metzger about Brad Fowler's arrest.

Mort wasn't like many other lawmen with whom I'd interacted over the years. While he was always professional, he was more willing to confide things in me that those others wouldn't, never breaching the rules of confidentiality, of course, but taking me into his confidence after I'd shared something with him that aided his investigation. That he trusted me and occasionally sought my counsel was flattering. Nevertheless, I couldn't be sure he would share information with me this night about Brad's incarceration and the charges against him. I'd have to see how the evening progressed and whether I could find an opportune time to ask about the case.

As I prepared lunch for myself, the small knife I was using to slice a tomato triggered thoughts of how Gérard Leboeuf had been killed and what I'd learned about the knife his assailant had used. I left my half-prepared lunch to go to my computer, where I Googled *Corkin Knives*. The

Japanese company's website proudly pointed out that it took four separate craftsmen and two weeks to create one of their signature knives, and it involved fifty different steps — forging, edge crafting, handle making, and assembling. No wonder they were so expensive. Sharpening them was also an art, according to what I read, and testimonials from leading chefs were many: "There is nothing of greater value in my kitchens than a Corkin knife," one celebrity chef wrote.

Had a Corkin knife ever been used before to kill someone? If so, I wouldn't expect to see it on their website. Some of the articles written about Leboeuf's murder had mentioned a Corkin knife as the murder weapon — not the sort of PR the company would welcome, although the fatal use one of their knives had been put to certainly wasn't the company's fault. I printed out what I'd read, put the printout with the other notes I'd been keeping since the murder, and returned to the kitchen, where I finished making my sandwich and concentrated on eating it slowly even though my thoughts were in overdrive.

Brad and Marcie had alleged that kitchen items had been stolen, but they'd never reported the theft to police. Was a knife among the missing tools? They'd accused Jake Trotter of stealing, which he'd vehemently denied. Could it have been Brad's knife that had been used as the murder weapon? I jotted a note to follow up on the question and added a few more questions to pose to Mort Metzger, provided the opportunity presented itself that evening.

The previous night's abbreviated sleep caught up with me, and I napped that afternoon, which was unusual for me. By five thirty I was showered and dressed, and at six my taxi driver dropped me at Mort and Maureen's house.

I was among the earlier arrivals, but a half hour later all the guests had arrived, ten in all, including me. Mort and Maureen made twelve. It was a beautiful evening, unusually warm for the time of year, and with a gentle breeze that made having cocktails and hors d'oeuvres on their patio comfortable. Maureen was cooking in her kitchen, leaving it to Mort to entertain guests outdoors. He'd recently purchased a weatherproof bamboo bar, which he manned with obvious pride, pointing out its features to anyone who would listen. It was a theme party, judging from the mariachi band playing Mexican music through a boom box on the bar top, although Maureen hadn't specified that in her invitation. Another hint at the evening's motif was the sombrero Mort wore. I could only assume that the dinner Maureen had concocted would feature Mexican food, a first for her as far as I knew. I was glad that Seth Hazlitt was there. He could always be counted on to have a roll of Tums with him.

As the predinner festivities wound down, I found time at the bar with Mort, out of earshot from others. It was no surprise that much of the guests' chitchat had revolved around the Leboeuf murder and Brad Fowler's arrest, although I hadn't heard Mort join in any of those conversations.

"When will Brad Fowler be arraigned?" I asked casually, as though I really didn't care.

"Tomorrow," Mort said. "Refill on your margarita?"

"No, thank you. Marcie Fowler stayed at my house last night."

"How come?"

"She needed to talk, and I was a willing listener. You can imagine how upset she is that her husband has been arrested for murder."

"No more upset than Leboeuf's family is," Mort countered.

I let his comment pass and said, "I assume you and the other investigators have unearthed some damning evidence against Brad."

Mort's Cheshire-cat smile said a lot. "You don't think I'd arrest somebody and accuse them of being a murderer if I didn't have proof, do you?"

"Of course not. It's just that Gérard Leboeuf seemed to have alienated many people aside from Brad Fowler."

"That's true, Mrs. F., but it doesn't mean that any of them would stick a knife in him."

"Which also goes for Brad Fowler," I said, aware that the conversation was becoming slightly contentious.

Mort looked around before leaning closer to me. He removed his hat — "Maureen insisted that I wear this stupid thing" — and said, "Look, Mrs. F., I know that you're friends with the Fowlers and don't like seeing Brad in this pickle. I don't either. Truth is that I really liked his mother, Isabel, and I like his wife, too. He's not a bad sort. But I've got a job to do, and I'm doing it the best way I know how. Brad Fowler killed Gérard Leboeuf. Case closed."

Maureen came to the kitchen door. "Mort, come in, sweetheart. Dinner's being served."

"Hope you like Mexican food, Mrs. F.," Mort said to me. "Not my favorite thing, but I made the mistake of buying Maureen a membership in a cookbook-of-the-month club for Christmas, and the latest one was Mexican."

I laughed. "That's what called being 'hoisted by your own petard.' "

"What's that mean?"

"It was a phrase used in *Hamlet,* and it literally means you were blown up by your own bomb, but more casually it means you were undone by your own action."

"Undone, huh? I can buy that. Maureen's been trying out these exotic recipes for a week now. I've been the official taster of whatever she concocts." He made a face.

"That bad?"

"I have to admit that some of it tastes pretty good, but it smells up the kitchen something awful. It's okay. I'm getting used to it. Come on, Mrs. F. Time for Maureen's Mexican fiesta."

Mort's wife had set her buffet with a colorful serape as a tablecloth, on which she placed a variety of south-of-the-border dishes. I carefully chose which ones to taste, knowing that my tolerance for extraspicy was limited, and joined everyone at the table in praising what she'd created in her kitchen. Even Seth Hazlitt, whose dislike for most ethnic foods is well-known, agreed that some of the dishes were to his liking.

Maureen did a running commentary on what she served: "The chile verde is mostly green chiles and deep-fried pork," she proudly proclaimed. "The chilaquiles are tortilla chips with green sauce made with tomatoes, and this is my favorite, pollo pibil. It's a Yucatecan recipe — chicken wrapped in banana leaves with lots of spices added."

We gave her a round of applause after everyone had dined on her latest culinary creations, which delighted her. "Of course, you didn't have to taste the dishes I dumped in the garbage," she admitted, smiling at her husband. "Mort is such a good sport when it comes to my cooking."

"Helps to have a cast-iron stomach," her husband replied to a round of laughter, but he gave Maureen a big hug as we carried our plates into the kitchen.

"Still a beautiful night," Mort announced. "We'll have dessert and Spirit of Aztec coffee outside. The coffee comes direct from Mexico."

"Don't forget your sombrero, dear," Maureen reminded her husband. "You look so handsome in it, like a real caballero."

I've tasted strong coffee before, but nothing like the brew Mort served up from behind his bamboo bar. My occasional sweet tooth was satisfied with a layered lemon cake Maureen had whipped up, smothered with thick, sweet dulce de leche and topped with white chocolate curls. While my craving for sweets is a sometime occurrence, Seth's is seldom absent, and he opted for a second slice of the sinfully rich cake. Maureen had outdone herself; my appreciation for her efforts in the kitchen grew considerably that night.

With so many guests, it was difficult to corner my host again, but I waited until I found an opportunity to chat alone with Mort.

"You say that the Leboeuf case is closed," I said.

"That's right, Mrs. F."

"Everyone else who might have killed Leboeuf has been ruled out?"

"You know as well as I do that everyone is a suspect at first. I interviewed everybody. So did those detectives from the state, Mason and Lucas. Of course I took the lead and asked the toughest questions." He leaned closer and spoke in conspiratorial tones, "At first Mason and Lucas focused in on Leboeuf's son, Wylie. I went along with them, but there was something stuck in my craw, Mrs. F. The kid may be a foul ball, a druggie with a chip on his shoulder, but something didn't ring true to me.

Anyway, long story short, the techs think they have a match to Fowler's fingerprint on the kitchen door, and here's the kicker — I came up with an eyewitness who saw the murder go down."

I suppose my face reflected my surprise at what he'd just said. He smiled and nodded. "Can't do better than an eyewitness," he said.

"Who is — ?"

Mort held up his hand. "Don't even ask, Mrs. F. You'll find out soon enough, after Bradley Fowler has been arraigned."

I knew better than to probe and dropped the subject.

Later, after Seth had delivered me home, I pondered what Mort had said. He was right, of course. There was nothing more solid for a murder investigator than an eyewitness to the crime.

Provided, of course, that the eyewitness was both credible — and honest.

Who was this eyewitness?

As Mort had said, I'd know soon enough.

CHAPTER TWENTY-ONE

"Soon enough" happened at two o'clock the next afternoon.

I'd called the courthouse in the morning and learned that Brad Fowler's arraignment would be at two. It was open to the public, of course, and I decided that I'd be part of that public to witness the proceeding.

Most arraignments attract few people other than family members of the accused. Others might include retired folks who view the court's goings-on as a form of free entertainment. But this was the arraignment of the famed restaurateur Gérard Leboeuf's alleged murderer, and when I walked into the court building at one forty-five, I was among a throng of onlookers, including a few members of the press who'd returned to Cabot Cove when they got wind of the court date. I found a seat against a wall in the courtroom and waited along with everyone else for the judge to make her entrance and for Brad Fowler to be led in to enter his plea. I scanned the crowd for Marcie and saw her seated with her parents, who must have flown up from Florida to support their daughter. Eva Leboeuf was also there, accompanied by the PR woman who'd been part of the press conference Leboeuf had held when he'd announced his new restaurant. Walter Chang, the bistro's manager, was with her, along with the two sullen young men who were never far away. Although the capacity crowd tried to be discreet, their eyes kept wandering to Eva. She was dressed immaculately in a black silk sheath with matching hat and veil and looked as though she were about to pose for a *Vanity Fair* photo shoot.

Our attention was directed to the front of the room when the clerk announced that court was in session and instructed us to rise. When we did, the judge, her customary black robe floating behind her, entered, took her seat behind the bench, and instructed us to sit. Moments later, another door opened and Brad Fowler was led in by two bailiffs. A flash went off, and a number of people raised their cell phones to capture an image of the prisoner. Brad's ankles and wrists were shackled, and he wore a pale green prison uniform that was too tight for his muscular build. He looked frazzled. He needed a shave, and his eyes darted about the room as though seeking an escape hatch. It broke my heart to see him in that situation. Not long ago he and his ebullient wife had been basking in the excitement and promise of opening the Fin & Claw. Now their restaurant was in danger of becoming a losing venture, and he was an accused murderer. I was secretly grateful Isabel was not around to see how quickly her son's and daughter-in-law's fortunes had changed.

Brad was accompanied by the attorney assigned by the court to defend him, Kristen Syms. Kristen had settled in Cabot Cove after having practiced law in Augusta for ten years, and I'd met her through our memberships in various organizations. When I needed clarification of a legal term or process for one of my novels, she was always there with the right answer. Kristen was smart and dedicated, and I was pleased — and not a little relieved — to see that Brad would have good legal representation.

After some preliminary housekeeping between the judge and her clerk, Brad and Kristen stood, and the prosecutor read the charges against Brad. I had assumed that the charge would be first-degree murder, but instead it was murder in the second degree. The judge asked how Brad pled to the charges. When he didn't respond, Kristen nudged him with her elbow and said something in his ear.

"Not guilty," he said in a faltering voice.

The judge announced the schedule for an evidentiary hearing and court was dismissed.

When Kristen saw me, she waved and left Brad's side.

"Jessica, I'm so glad you're here," she said. "I have a favor to ask."

"Certainly. What can I do to help?"

"As soon as we leave here, I'm going to spend time with Brad in one of the holding cells, and I'd like you to join us. Would you mind?"

"I don't mind, but I'm curious as to why."

"Brad has told me repeatedly that you're on his side. He wants to meet with you. I could arrange for a separate meeting, but I think it would be better if I was present."

I hadn't prepared for this turn of events and tried to gather my thoughts. It wouldn't be the first time that I'd been involved in an interview of an alleged criminal, but I couldn't help wondering why Brad had had what seemed to be a change of heart. I'd become convinced that he viewed me as being one of "them," the people who automatically assumed that he'd killed Leboeuf. That he now considered me "on his side" was unexpected, and I had to do some mental shuffling.

"If you think it's appropriate," I told Kristen.

"No problem at all, Jessica. Give me ten minutes, and I'll meet you where they're holding Brad. The clerk will escort you."

As the courtroom emptied out, I sat quietly, trying to be as inconspicuous as possible. Unfortunately, I was approached by several members of the press who'd been informed of who I was and who demanded a comment from me about the case. I adamantly refused to say anything except to state the obvious, that the Leboeuf murder and its aftermath were sad days for Cabot Cove, but two of the reporters took seats on either side of me and continued to pepper me with questions. I was immensely grateful when the court clerk, whom I knew, summoned me to follow him.

Kristen and Brad sat in a sparsely furnished holding cell at the rear of the courthouse. Two bright overhead lights above a Formica table provided glary, unflattering illumination. Brad and Kristen sat opposite each other on uncomfortable folding gray metal chairs. Kristen indicated that I should take the one next to her. Brad stood when I entered, but I asked him not to. The loud "clang" of the heavy metal door being closed caused me to flinch.

"Thanks for coming, Mrs. Fletcher," Brad said.

"You're welcome," I said, "although I'm not sure why you wanted me here."

Kristen said, "Brad feels that you might have something to offer that would help his defense."

Because I couldn't think of anything at the moment, I simply said, "I'll do anything I can," not adding that while I was loath to believe that he had murdered Leboeuf, I couldn't be certain he was innocent. The jury, literally and figuratively, was still out.

I sat and listened while Kristen reviewed every event that had occurred since Leboeuf had arrived in Cabot Cove and announced that he was opening his bistro next door to the Fin & Claw. She'd obviously been thoroughly briefed by the prosecutor regarding the evidence he and his office had amassed to implicate Brad in the murder and included incidents Brad or Marcie must have told her about as well.

She brought up the threat to the restaurant's financial success; the regrettable confrontation between Leboeuf and

Brad on the Fin & Claw's opening night; the exchange between Isabel Fowler and Leboeuf on that same night, which immediately preceded her fatal stroke; Leboeuf's manipulation of local baked goods and seafood purveyors to cut the Fin & Claw out of the supply chain; the sanitary violations that Brad and Marcie were convinced had been planted by someone, possibly even the health inspector, perhaps at Leboeuf's request; and Brad's frequent — and public — harsh comments about Leboeuf.

While Kristen went over what the prosecution considered justification for bringing charges against Brad, none of it proof of his guilt in my view, two things continued to worry me: Brad asking Marcie to lie about what time he'd returned home the night of the murder and Mort Metzger's comment that there was an eyewitness to the crime who claimed that he, or she, saw Brad deliver the fatal blow with the kitchen knife. I was reluctant to raise either issue and waited for Kristen to mention them. I knew that Marcie's claim about the time that Brad came home that fateful night would not help his cause. As for there being an eyewitness, if *I* knew about it, Kristen would certainly have been made aware of that.

Without it — and I'm certainly not a lawyer — it seemed to me that she could have successfully demanded Brad's release based upon his being held with nothing but circumstantial evidence, at best.

Had Brad been told the unhappy news about an eyewitness? It was possible that he hadn't.

Brad vehemently denied having killed Leboeuf. He swore that he'd left the Fin & Claw about one o'clock and had gone directly home. While he acknowledged that his hateful feelings about Leboeuf ran deep, he would never be capable of killing him, or anyone else for that matter. At times I thought he might break into tears, but he held them — and his temper — in check.

I was relieved when Kristen brought up the crucial piece of evidence that had justified the authorities, led by Mort Metzger, to charge Brad with the murder.

"As your attorney, Brad, it's important that I know the truth," she said. "That doesn't mean that I would not defend you if you were guilty, but the scenario would demand different legal tactics to mitigate whatever punishment the court would impose on you. I want very much to believe that you are innocent of this serious crime and will do everything in my power to bring about that result. But there's something that you should know before we go any further."

Her serious tone captured his — and my — full attention.

"There is someone who claims to have seen you arguing with Gérard Leboeuf at a little before three in the morning, in his kitchen, the night he was killed. This person told the district attorney that he witnessed you picking up the knife that killed Mr. Leboeuf and stabbing him."

Brad started to say something, but the words didn't come out.

"Do you understand what I'm saying, Brad?"

"Yeah, I — it can't be. It's not true. Why would someone — ? Whoever said that is lying." With each utterance, I could see Brad's face getting redder.

"We know that this individual might not be telling the truth, but —"

"Of course it's not true. Who is it?" he asked forcefully.

"Someone who worked for you and for Gérard Leboeuf." She consulted her notes. "His name is Trotter, Jacob Trotter."

"Trotter?" Brad erupted. *"He* said that? The sheriff believes *him?"* Brad turned to me. "Tell her, Mrs. Fletcher. You know what a foul ball he is. You've seen him yelling and

303

screaming at me." He slumped back in his chair. "Jake Trotter," he muttered. "That SOB. He went to work for Leboeuf and now he says that I killed the louse." He came forward and shouted, "Let Trotter tell me to my face that he saw me kill Leboeuf. He's a dirty, rotten liar."

His loud voice alerted the deputy standing guard at the end of the hall. He came over to the cell and asked through the bars, "Everything all right here?"

"Yes, everything is fine," said Kristen.

"Keep it down, huh?" the deputy said, and walked away.

I'd been silent for the half hour that we'd been together. Now I spoke up. "Brad," I said, "you and Jake Trotter have had difficulty getting along, and that's no secret. I saw the confrontation the two of you had the first day I visited the Fin and Claw, before it even opened. He was furious with you, accused you of being an amateur when it comes to running a restaurant. And I was there when he quit and stormed out of your restaurant. But do you think that because of these personal ill feelings, he would deliberately lie to the authorities and place you in the precarious position you're in?"

"I don't know," was Brad's answer. "I don't know what he *thinks* he saw. What I

304

do know is that whatever he says, it's not the truth. It wasn't me. I did not kill Gérard Leboeuf!"

"Kristen, has Trotter made his accusation under oath?" I asked.

"Not to my knowledge," she replied, "but he'll have to at some point."

"Trotter went to work for Leboeuf after leaving Brad's restaurant," I said. "Isn't it possible that Trotter is accusing Brad of the murder in order to deflect suspicion from himself?"

Kristen nodded slowly. "We know what a volatile man he is. It's certainly something to consider."

"Yeah," Brad said, having mustered a sudden burst of energy, "that's got to be it. Trotter had run-ins with Leboeuf, too. Ask the other guys in the kitchen. Jake's got a mean streak, and everybody in town knows it. Sure, Trotter killed Leboeuf and he's trying to blame it on me so he can walk free."

Brad's hopeful analysis was within the realm of possibility, of course, although at that juncture it was just speculation on his part. He needed proof. I wondered whether Mort Metzger and the other investigators had probed deeply enough into Trotter's activities the night of the murder, and I intended to ask Mort about it at the first possible moment.

But this was a case where potential suspects were plentiful. It was frustrating to me that the authorities had zeroed in on Brad so early in the investigation. I wondered how much Brad's attorney knew of Leboeuf's alleged ties with organized crime and whether they might have played a part in his killing. And had Charles Compton, aka Warren Shulte, come to town earlier than he claimed to get even with his former employer?

What about Leboeuf's wife, Eva? *Cherchez la femme,* or *Look for the woman,* was the famous French phrase that Fritzi the waiter had quoted. Leboeuf had a reputation as a skirt chaser, as the saying goes, at least according to gossip at Sardi's in New York City, where Fritzi once worked. My casual observations of the interaction between Gérard and Eva had been that there was palpable tension between them. While not something to build a case on, there was a certain wisdom to it based upon many murders in history in which a wronged woman wielded the murder weapon or had enticed someone else to act for her.

Then there was Leboeuf's son. Mort had told me that the initial focus was on Wylie, but that line of inquiry had been abandoned once what they'd thought was Brad's fingerprint had been found and Trotter had made his claim. Had Mort or others on the case really spent a lot of time questioning Wylie about his father's death? Or did Trotter's claim bring the investigation to a jarring halt before all the interviews were concluded?

The deputy informed Kristen that her time with the prisoner was up.

"You've got to help me, Mrs. Fletcher," Brad said as he stood. "I didn't kill him."

"We'll do everything we can to prove that," his attorney said.

Kristen Syms and I left the courthouse together and continued our conversation on a bench outside.

"I want to believe Brad," I told her. "In addition, there are so many others who might have wanted Leboeuf dead. I feel like we're dealing with an incomplete investigation."

"That may be true, Jessica, but we — at least I — can't worry about other suspects at the moment," she said. "Later I'll want you to tell me about them, but right now I need to know everything you can pass along about Brad."

"All right, but I'd like a favor in return."

"What's that?"

"Do you have a copy of Jake Trotter's statement with you?"

Her hand slid down to the briefcase she'd set on the bench. "I can't give it to you."

"I'm not asking you to make me a copy for me. But would you let me read it? I'll just scan it and give it right back."

"I guess that won't hurt anything." She snapped open her case, pulled out two pages stapled together, and handed them to me. I gave them a quick once-over and gave them back to her.

"Did anything strike you?" she asked.

"I'll have to think about it a little, but you said something earlier that struck me."

"What's that?"

"You talked about Jake Trotter being a volatile man, and he is that. But what complicates this case is that we're dealing with three volatile men, not just one. Brad, Trotter, and Leboeuf. Brad goes off like a rocket at the first provocation. He and Jake were like oil and water. But Gerard Leboeuf was not a nice man either. He was known for crushing his competition in the business. You can find lots of material about him online. I was there when he insulted Brad's mother, Isabel, made fun of the Fin and Claw menu, and sneered at the food."

"Aren't you giving me more reasons why

Brad would want to kill Leboeuf?"

"It would seem so, but the point I'm making is that Leboeuf must have a trail of former rivals lined up wanting to see him dead, not to leave out how many others he may have abused with his elevated ego and sharp tongue."

"But how many of them were in town the night he died?"

I sighed. "I don't know. And there's something else I have to tell you, even though it pains me to do so." Reluctantly, I told the attorney what Marcie had said to me about Brad asking her to lie about the time he'd returned home the night of the murder. Kristen listened quietly. When I was finished, she grimaced, sat back, and directed a stream of air at an errant wisp of hair on her forehead. "That's not good," she said.

"Not good at all."

"It also wasn't in his favor that he tried to run from the police," she said.

I nodded my agreement.

"Have you told anyone else?" she asked.

"No, but I know that I'll have to at some point."

"And I'll have to share it with the prosecutor."

"I understand," I said. "I want to help,

309

not hurt Brad. If there's anything I can do, please let me know. I was so fond of Brad's mother, Isabel, and I want to see Brad and Marcie succeed with their restaurant. If Brad is innocent, I —"

"*If* he's innocent," Kristen said solemnly.

That word "if" stayed with me all the way home and far into the night.

CHAPTER TWENTY-TWO

The lead story on the front page of the next edition of the *Cabot Cove Gazette* was about Brad Fowler's arraignment. Evelyn Phillips's photographer had managed to grab a candid shot of Eva arriving at the courthouse with her entourage; a stock shot of Brad, taken when the Fin & Claw opened, also accompanied the article.

I read the piece with great interest. In it Evelyn retraced the path of events leading to Gérard Leboeuf's murder, ending it with a statement from Marcie Fowler: "My husband is innocent of this charge, and I'm confident it will be proved beyond a doubt." Evelyn didn't indicate where or how she had obtained Marcie's statement. I hadn't seen the *Gazette* editor in the packed courtroom, but the article made it sound as if she had been there in person.

When I moved on to the inside pages and caught up on happenings around town, a headline caught my eye: FOOD INSPECTOR CHARGED.

Harold Greene, a longtime employee of the Maine Center for Disease Control and Prevention, Division of Environmental Health, has been charged by the state attorney general with multiple counts of breach of duty. Among the charges are accusations that Greene, a state health inspector, solicited bribes from restaurants in exchange for withholding reports of violations of the State of Maine Food Code, and instead gave them a clean bill of health. Mr. Greene has denied all charges.

However, this reporter was also made aware of an incident in which a health inspector assigned to Cabot Cove allegedly falsely accused a merchant of sanitary violations posing an imminent health hazard. The merchant claims his reputation was so damaged by the false report, he was forced to close his business. The merchant, who prefers to remain anonymous at this time, would not name the health inspector but has told the *Gazette* that he is considering bringing his case to the attention of the attorney general's office. If so, Mr. Greene, who has been the only state inspector assigned to this town for many years, may have more charges leveled against him.

Mara apparently had been correct in her assessment of Harold Greene. And if Mr. Greene was guilty of accepting money for his silence regarding legitimate violations, it wasn't too far a stretch to think that the health inspector might have "seeded" a new restaurant like the Fin & Claw with rodent droppings as a way of establishing the power of his position, or as a warning to the restaurant owners to treat him generously. Was it also possible that a man willing to accept a bribe might also be willing to falsify a report at someone else's behest? Brad had claimed that someone — maybe Jake — had put evidence of rodent infestation where it didn't exist. But could Harold Greene have been paid off by someone else to find such a violation — someone like Gérard Leboeuf? Could it possibly be that Leboeuf would have gone so far as to pay Greene to trump up health violations against the Fowlers in order to gain a competitive advantage? I hated to believe that anyone would do such a thing to gain a financial advantage over another human being, but that kind of behavior obviously does exist.

And Leboeuf's reputation for having forced other competitors out of business argued that such action was not out of character for him.

As I read the article I couldn't help but think about Brad and Marcie Fowler's run-in with Harold Greene. I picked up the phone and called Evelyn at her newspaper.

"Good hearing from you, Jessica," she said. "Did you read today's story on Brad Fowler's arraignment?"

"Couldn't have missed it, Evelyn. It was thorough and well written."

"A welcome comment from someone with your writing skills. What can I do for you this morning?"

"Well, I was wondering whether you'd been provided with a list of restaurants that were alleged to have been shaken down by Mr. Greene."

"Why do I have the feeling that Jessica Fletcher has a hidden agenda in asking me that?"

"No hidden agenda, Evelyn. I'm curious because it was Harold Greene who inspected the Fowlers' Fin and Claw and claimed to have uncovered violations, including mouse droppings in the kitchen."

"Yes, I heard about that. You know how things like that get around. But I don't usually run a list of those who failed an inspection the first time around. They usually correct the violations and pass on their second try. I don't see tarnishing someone's reputation unless they're flagrant violators. *Then* it becomes a public service to expose it, and I write it up in the paper."

"That's very sensitive of you, Evelyn."

"I'm not always the bull in a china shop you seem to think I am," she said.

"Now, Evelyn —"

She laughed. "Just giving you a hard time," she said. "What would you like to know?"

"Can you tell me a little more about the man who closed his business after one of Greene's inspections? I'm not asking for his name, just a few more details than you wrote in your article."

"Interestingly enough, it was another situation where two restaurants were in competition. The man, who shall remain nameless, at least for now, opened his establishment down the street from an existing place and began having problems with the health inspector from his first day. He believes the other owner was paying off Greene to find violations in order to give his place a bad reputation, with the eventual goal of closing him down."

"And that's what happened?"

"Apparently so. The guy got weary of answering a series of what he says were unjustified and increasingly expensive citations — not to mention the tarring of his reputation for running an unsanitary and unhealthy restaurant."

"Why didn't he go over Greene's head?"

"He did. He appealed to the state, but the complaints he filed fell on deaf ears. He says he finally gave up and closed his doors. Nothing was ever proved against Greene, but that doesn't mean he wasn't involved. Mara down at the luncheonette told me the guy has a shady reputation."

So Evelyn had spoken with Mara as well.

"I talked with her, too. She said that she's never paid Greene a penny, but that he always seems to have his hand out." I laughed. "You know Mara. She'd sooner slug him than pay a bribe. She says that she always follows him around closely when he's doing an inspection."

Evelyn laughed, too. "I don't blame her," she said. "But to answer your earlier question, I don't have a list of the restaurants involved. Why your interest?"

"I was curious to know if Jake Trotter ever worked for any of the restaurants that received notices of violations."

"Oh, ho! Now we get to the crux of the reason for your call. I hear that Trotter was an eyewitness to the murder. Did you?"

"I had heard that, yes."

"But even if Trotter was in cahoots with Greene in setting up restaurant owners to get violations, how would that impact the case against Brad Fowler?"

"I don't know that it does." I said. "I'm just looking at the case from all angles. You know his mother, Isabel, was a friend of mine. I feel that, for Isabel's sake, I have to defend Brad."

"Even if he murdered Gerard Leboeuf?"

" 'If' is the operative word here, Evelyn."

"Hard to ignore an eyewitness, Jessica."

I could visualize her holding up her hand against what I was about to say.

"I know. I know," she said, adding words to her silent signal. "Jake's a flake, a less than savory character, plenty of problems with the law over the years. But he swears he saw Brad kill Leboeuf. From what I'm told, Trotter was stone-cold sober when he told Mort Metzger and the other investigators what he'd seen. Just because he's a troublesome hothead doesn't mean he's not telling the truth."

My silence prompted her to add, "You do agree with me — don't you, Jessica?"

"Yes, of course. But what if — ?"

"What if what?"

"Nothing. I was just coming up with scenarios."

"Like when you write your novels? This isn't fiction, Jessica. This is real life."

I didn't need to be reminded of that and told her that I appreciated what information she had and would be in touch again.

"Before you go," she said. "When I was in the courtroom, I saw you chatting with Fowler's attorney, Kristen Syms. What was that about?"

"We've been friends for a long time," I said.

Evelyn had responded to my questions about Greene and the restaurant owner who shut down his business. Should I thank her by revealing that I'd been invited to sit in on Kristen's interview with her client? Anything I said to Evelyn could end up in the pages of the *Gazette.* I wanted to be fair, but I decided I'd better not share that information, at least this time. I'd been in a privileged position and felt that it would be a violation of Kristen's trust in me, to say nothing of Brad's request that I be present.

After we hung up, I reviewed the notes I'd made when I returned from the arraignment. If the fingerprint Mort said the techs had found was indeed Brad's, there was nothing I could do to explain it away. But what about the eyewitness? I'd been given only a few minutes to skim his statement, but something *had* stood out in the report. Trotter claimed to have seen Brad arguing with Leboeuf, and in his fury, pick up a knife from the counter, raise it over his head, and bring it down on the famous chef.

I reached for the phone and dialed Seth Hazlitt, crossing my fingers I'd reach him at a good time.

CHAPTER TWENTY-THREE

Seth wasn't in his office when I called, but I managed to track him down at the hospital, where he was visiting patients and their families. He said that he'd have to call me back, and I waited in my office until he did.

"What can I do for you, Jessica?"

I'd prepared a list of questions to ask, and ran down the list.

"Anything else you'd like to know?" he said.

"No, that's it, Seth. Sorry to have bothered you while you made your rounds."

"It was a pleasant respite, Jessica. Mind telling me why you have these questions?"

"Just filling in some blanks, Seth. Nothing important."

Since I'd called him at the hospital, he probably didn't buy my "nothing important" protestation, but he didn't press and we ended the call.

While Seth had, indeed, helped fill in

some blanks for me, I didn't enjoy a sense of resolution. To the contrary, I spent much of the next few hours pacing the floor between bouts at my desk, where I pored over my notes. I decided to relieve my restlessness by taking out my bicycle and riding downtown. Even though most of the stores would close within the hour, I needed a little exercise to clear my mind of what had occupied it at home. I was brimming with nervous energy. When that occurs, I need to be moving, walking, focusing on anything and everything other than the cause of my angst and irritability.

I left my bicycle in a bike rack and ended up strolling through one of the parks in town that provides relaxing greenery. After a few minutes of sitting on a bench and watching squirrels scurry after one another, I walked to the pier, where I paused, looking back and forth from the Fin & Claw to Leboeuf's French Bistro, the respective parking lots of which testified to a busy night ahead for both. I suppose my aimless wandering was a way to put off an action that I'd been pondering all day. Convinced that I was making the right decision, I approached the rear entrance to the bistro. As I did, the door opened and two kitchen workers on a break came through it. One lit a cigarette; the other swigged water from a bottle.

"Excuse me," I said. "Is Jake Trotter in the kitchen?"

They looked at each other before the one with the cigarette said, "No, ma'am. Trotter doesn't work here anymore."

"Oh. When did that happen?"

The fellow with the water giggled. "Jake quit," he said. "He left right after the boss got killed!" His tone said loud and clear that he wasn't displeased at Trotter's absence.

"Do you know where he is?"

They looked at me strangely. *They must think I have a crush on Jake. Why else would a middle-aged woman follow him to his place of work — or former place of work, as I now knew?* I thanked them and walked to the seawall, feeling a mixture of frustration and relief. I'd gotten myself all worked up expecting to confront Jake Trotter and pin him down about important comments he'd made in his statement. And now he wasn't where I'd been expecting him to be.

I looked out over the water. A fishing boat was on its way in from a day at sea, accompanied by a flock of seagulls following the day's catch. I took in the first wave of tourists who'd come to town and were strolling the promenade, men, women, and children enjoying all that Cabot Cove has to offer. It seemed to me that there was probably plenty of business for both new restaurants to handle, and that all the bad feelings each owner had held for the other were unnecessary. Yet a murder had taken place, and people were thinking the motive had to do with who was going to emerge triumphant in this restaurant war. But there are no winners when one man is dead and another is accused of his murder.

I walked back through the park to where I'd left my bicycle and debated what to do next. Now that I knew Jake Trotter wasn't in the bistro's kitchen, I had another decision to make. It was going to get dark in an hour. Should I try to find him or let it go for another day? I consulted my cell phone, then climbed on my bike and headed home. Once in my driveway, I made up my mind. I called the taxi company and told them I needed a cab. One of their drivers pulled up to my house within fifteen minutes. The driver waved to me. "Just got the call, Mrs. Fletcher, that you need a taxi."

"Yes, I do," I said, sliding into the rear seat.

"Going downtown?" the driver asked as he slowly pulled away.

"As a matter of fact, no."

"To Dr. Hazlitt's house?"

"Not this time."

"Sheriff and Mrs. Metzger's place?"

"No." I gave him the address I'd found on my cell phone.

"That's out on the peninsula," he said.

"Yes, I know."

"There's not much out there, Mrs. Fletcher."

"I'm visiting someone who lives there," I said.

"Okay," he said. "Whatever you say."

The trip took almost a half hour. The route took us through the center of town and to a stretch of four-lane highway until it narrowed into a two-lane road. The final ten minutes found us on a poorly maintained gravel road that led down to a line of small houses — "shacks" might be a more apt term — behind a row of low industrial buildings. The six dwellings that constituted the small community were in various states of repair. A rusted vehicle sans tires rested on cement blocks in one yard. Clothes dried on a line in another, where someone had made an effort to dress up the house with small pots of geraniums on the steps.

Jake Trotter's address was 6; the black iron numeral hung from a single nail on the front of his home. I recognized the red pickup truck in Jake's driveway as one I'd seen parked near the restaurants, a distinguishing large dent on one fender and a coating of rust along the bottom of the door. A small porch ran the width of the cottage's front. Two green wicker rocking chairs flanked a table on it.

"You're sure this is the address?" my driver asked.

"If this is the address on the paper I gave you," I replied. "Yes, this is it."

"Want me to wait for you, Mrs. Fletcher?"

I was tempted to say yes. "That won't be necessary. I'm not sure how long I'll be here," I said, "but I have my cell phone with me. I'll call in plenty of time before I need a ride back."

I signed the chit with my name and account number on it, got out, and watched him drive away, seriously wondering whether I'd made a prudent decision. *Too late for second-guessing,* I told myself as I approached the front porch, climbed the three rickety steps, and knocked on the door. There was no response. I knocked again, louder and more prolonged this time. Still no reply.

"Mr. Trotter?" I said in a loud voice. "Are you home?"

There was silence, aside from the sound of water lapping onto the rocky shoreline and the long calls of gulls.

I called his name again, louder this time, and knocked with more force. To my surprise the door creaked open a little. I pushed it further and tried Trotter's name one more time. When he didn't answer, I stepped through the opening and took in the room. It was, to be kind, a mess. A rancid odor reached my nose, and a pervasive aroma of whiskey and stale cigarettes or cigars hung in the air.

I knew that I didn't have any business intruding into his home and considered leaving and calling back the taxi. But items on the counter of the Pullman kitchen caught my eye. Marcie had said that Brad accused Trotter of stealing things from the Fin & Claw's kitchen. What had she said was missing?

I circumvented a wooden box of tools on the floor and stepped over to the kitchen. The obvious newness of the pieces that Jake had left in a pile was in contrast to other scattered paraphernalia on the counter, which had seen longer wear. There were an obviously expensive frying pan, a set of stainless steel mixing bowls, and a long, narrow grater covered by a plastic shield. I

326

hesitated before picking up the grater, turning it to see what company made it. It was a Microplane, the same brand of grater Marcie had said was a gift to Brad from Isabel. As I examined it, a sound from behind caused me to stiffen. I didn't want to look behind me, but knew that I had to. I replaced the grater on the counter and turned to face Jake Trotter, who stood in the open doorway. He was dressed in a stained white T-shirt and dungarees. But what was more noticeable was the shotgun that he carried. It was pointed directly at me.

"Who the hell are you?" he growled, tipping up the gun's barrel for emphasis.

"I'm sorry to have barged in," I said brightly, "but you didn't answer when I called your name, and your door was open. I'm Jessica Fletcher, by the way. We've met before."

"We have?"

"Yes, Mr. Trotter, when you worked for the Fin and Claw. Remember?" I didn't elaborate that we'd never had a formal introduction. I'd simply been present two times when he'd been arguing with Brad Fowler.

"What are you doing in my house?"

I drew a deep breath, hoping it would

inflate me with confidence. "I came to talk to you," I said. "I knocked, more than once. The door swung open, and I came in, hoping you were here. And now you are."

"You're trespassing."

I forced a laugh. "Yes, I certainly am, although I don't mean you any harm. I simply wanted to talk."

"About what?"

"About Gérard Leboeuf's murder."

"I already told the cops all I know about it."

"Yes, I know that you gave a statement to the sheriff. Would you be kind enough to please put down that gun? It's making me uncomfortable."

He pondered what I'd asked, his long, angular face set in a question mark. I thought he might accommodate my request, but the shotgun remained aimed in my direction.

"People know that I'm here. I told them that I was coming to talk with you about the murder and the statement you gave the police."

It wasn't true, of course. Apart from the taxi driver who'd brought me to the house, no one had any idea of my whereabouts. But it seemed a sensible thing to say at the moment, and I wished that I *had* let others know of my plans.

"Do you mind if I sit?" I said, indicating one of two straight-back chairs at a slab of wood atop a barrel. A half-empty bottle of bourbon and a glass rested on it. "I'm feeling a little tired." I didn't wait for his permission, and settled myself in one of the chairs, figuring he was less likely to shoot a woman sitting down than one standing up. I didn't bother to wipe off the seat, which clearly had crumbs of some previous meal on it, not wanting to offend my host.

Host! That's a laugh, Jessica. Wouldn't it be ironic if your writing career ended right here in a shanty outside your beloved Cabot Cove? Seth would shake his head and say he'd always told me to mind my own business and leave the investigatin' to the police, but his stubborn friend would never listen.

I forced a smile. "You said that you witnessed Brad Fowler kill Gérard Leboeuf," I said, eager to get to my reason for being there.

"That's right."

"I'm sure you'd never lie to the police, Mr. Trotter, but somehow I have trouble accepting your story. And Brad — Brad Fowler, that is — denies having had anything to do with the murder."

He laughed, exposing a large set of yel-

329

lowing teeth. "What do you expect him to do?" he said. "He killed Leboeuf, plain and simple."

"And you saw him do it?"

"That's right. I gave my statement and I'm done with it. I'll be out of this cruddy town, and good riddance to it."

"You're leaving?"

"You bet I am. I've got me some money now. Been saving up. I'll be outta here before you can blink."

"But where will you go? And don't you have to come back to testify when Brad Fowler comes to trial?"

"I'll worry about that when the time comes."

If the police can find you by then. He said he'd saved some money, but for a man who didn't keep a job for very long, it was more likely that he'd come into money another way. I wondered if he'd pawned items that he'd stolen from his previous employers. Otherwise, where would a sudden influx of money come from?

I asked.

"None of your damn business," was his reply.

"Did you sell this house?" I asked, indicating with a sweep of my hand where we were talking.

"Not mine to sell," he said. "I rent this dump. I'll find me a lot better place once I get on the road. Plenty of places, nicer than this, for a man with my talents."

I decided to stay with the topic of money.

"I'm pleased for you, Mr. Trotter, that you now have enough money to leave and improve your living conditions."

"It's about time," he said, pulling the second chair away from the makeshift table and sitting heavily on it. He frowned, as though a thought had crossed his mind. He asked, "What's this to you anyway? What are you, a buddy of Fowler?"

"I was a very good friend of Brad Fowler's mother, Isabel. Remember her? She died, you know."

"I knew that. Had a stroke in Fowler's kitchen, at the restaurant. What a joke — him running a restaurant. Didn't know what he was doing."

"But you know your way around a commercial kitchen, don't you, Mr. Trotter?"

"I sure do. Only the clowns I've worked for never had the good sense to listen to me."

"Including Mr. Leboeuf?"

"He was okay; sorry when he died."

"And according to your statement, you

saw him die, saw him killed with a kitchen knife."

"That's right." He cocked his head and leaned closer to me. "You don't believe me, huh? Well, the cops believe me. That's what counts."

Now that he was sitting, the shotgun rested on his lap, no longer pointed in my direction. He poured himself a drink from the bottle, and as an afterthought asked whether I wanted a drink, too.

"No, thank you."

"You know," he said absently, as though speaking to a third person in the room, "I don't really blame Fowler for killing Leboeuf."

"Oh? Why do you say that?"

"Well, I mean, if my wife was playing around with another guy, I might do the same thing."

Was he implying that Marcie Fowler had been involved with Leboeuf in a romantic way?

"You know this for fact?"

"Yeah. I saw them together."

"When? Where?"

He laughed; it was more a cackle. "The night that Leboeuf got it. She was in the kitchen at his so-called bistro. 'Bistro.' Fancy name, huh?"

"Marcie Fowler was with Gérard Leboeuf the night he was murdered? What time was that?"

Trotter shrugged and drank. "Two, three, after the place was closed."

"Was that the only time you've seen them together?"

"It's enough, isn't it?"

"Did you see them — I mean did you see them in some sort of an embrace?"

Another shrug, another drink. He refilled his glass.

"Not exactly, but I wasn't born yesterday. I know hanky-panky when I see it. Never did understand why a looker like her would stick with a buffoon like Fowler. What's he got? Money? No. Looks? No. He's got a temper. That's what he's got. You know, I bet he beat her and that's why she turned to Leboeuf. For a little comfort." He chuckled. "I'd have given her a little comfort, too."

I hadn't expected this turn of events and had to grapple with my thoughts to put them in some semblance of order. "What exactly did you see take place between the two of them?"

"I saw him give her like a secret smile when she walked in the back door. 'I knew you would come,' he says, all tickled. And she goes, 'Were you serious about this?' holding up this love note he must have sent her. And then he pulls her toward him, and says 'I can be serious.' And I'm thinking, 'Oh, boy, wait till the wife sees this.' "

"Well, that's certainly news," I said.

"Hey, I'm a good guy. I like to help out."

"I appreciate you being candid with me, Mr. Trotter, so let me be candid with you. I don't know if you're telling me the truth about Marcie having an affair with Leboeuf."

"Believe what you want. It's no skin off my nose."

"What I do believe is that you were *not* telling the truth when you told the authorities that you saw Brad Fowler stab Gérard Leboeuf."

He squirmed in his chair, as though I'd poked him with a stick, and glared at me. "I tried to be helpful. If you don't appreciate it —"

"Let me tell you why," I quickly added. "I had the opportunity to read your statement to the police."

"You did?"

"Yes, and something you said stayed with me. It didn't fit with the facts."

"Everything I said was factual. I can't help it if you aren't up with what went down."

"You said that you saw Brad Fowler lift his hand and drive the knife down into Leboeuf."

"Yeah. He did."

"But Leboeuf was stabbed in the spleen, probably from the side. He was stabbed by someone who held the knife low and thrust it at him from that position."

He shrugged. "Yeah, well, what does it matter — up, down, sideways? So what?"

"It matters a great deal, Mr. Trotter. I'm sure that Sheriff Metzger and the other investigators will recognize that inconsistency, too, once they have a chance to go over your statement more carefully." I paused. "The punishment for perjury is pretty harsh."

My admonition had an effect on him. He fidgeted; at one point the shotgun almost slid off his lap. I sat quietly, waiting for him to speak. When he did, his voice packed the strength it had earlier in our confrontation. What he said surprised me.

"You're a big shot in town, aren't you?"

"I wouldn't say that."

"But you write all those books that sell millions of copies, right? I heard about you."

"What are you trying to say?"

"You want to get Fowler off the hook, I can tell. What I mean is that maybe I can change what I told the cops about seeing him kill Leboeuf. You would like that, right?"

"If what you told them originally wasn't true, then, yes, you should amend your statement to them."

"Yeah, I could do that, 'amen my statement' or whatever you said, but —"

"But what?"

"Look, I'll level with you. I've got to get what's coming to me. I've been kicked around by one boss after the other, guys who didn't know squat about running a restaurant compared to me. I got screwed when I was a cook in the army by sergeants who wouldn't know a dishwasher from a refrigerator. I should have had my own place, but there was never money to open a joint. I worked fifty, sixty hours a week for these clowns and got paid beans. You know what I mean?"

"I think so."

"So I'm entitled to something."

"I'm listening. But what does this have to do with me writing books?"

"Like I said, you must be rolling in dough. If you could — well, maybe top what I got for making that statement to the police, I could change it and —"

"You were *paid* to say that Brad Fowler

killed Leboeuf?" I tried to keep the shock out of my voice. "Who paid you?"

"Look, what's the difference? If you take care of me, I'll take care of you. You want your buddy Fowler off the hook, and I can get him off the hook — for a price. Make sense?"

I looked to where the restaurant items I'd examined earlier sat on the counter. "Did you take those from the Fin and Claw?" I asked, cocking my head toward them.

"Just stuff." He yawned and shook his head like a dog shaking off water. "So what? I figure I gave more than I got. He didn't even know how to divide a kitchen into stations, much less a dining room. He would've had everything mixed together. But he wouldn't listen to me. Jerk!"

I pulled my cell phone from my jacket pocket.

He blinked. "Who're you calling?" His words were slurred.

"I'm calling my cab company to take me home."

"But what about our deal?"

"Mr. Trotter, we don't have a deal. This was an enlightening conversation, but now it's time for me to leave."

I'd be lying if I didn't admit that I was frightened at that moment. Trotter had been steadily drinking since he sat down. He had a shotgun, presumably loaded, on his lap. He'd admitted to me that he'd been paid to make a false statement about having seen Brad Fowler kill Gérard Leboeuf, and he'd offered to make another false statement in return for money. It occurred to me as I reached the cab company and asked that I be picked up at his address that he had every reason to harm me, to raise the weapon and shoot me.

I stood, straightened my skirt, and walked to the door, expecting at any moment to hear — and feel — the blast of a sixteen-gauge shotgun. But there was nothing, just silence. I stepped out onto the front porch, drew in a series of deep breaths, and waited beneath the overhang of a small factory entrance for the taxi.

On the ride home I knew that I had to call Mort Metzger to tell him that Jake Trotter's statement about Brad Fowler was false. It had been paid for.

And then I had to talk to Marcie Fowler.

CHAPTER TWENTY-FOUR

Mort's wife, Maureen, answered my call at the sheriff's home.

"He's not here," Maureen said. "Working late on some case."

"Do you know how I can reach him?" I asked.

"He called a half hour ago from his office. He might still be there."

I caught Mort as he was preparing to leave.

"What's up, Mrs. F.?"

"I just left Jake Trotter's house," I said.

"What were you doing *there*?"

"Mort, have you had a chance to review Trotter's statement claiming that he saw Brad Fowler stab Leboeuf?"

"Haven't gotten around to it yet, Mrs. F. One of the detectives from the state took it down. Gave me the gist of it, that Trotter saw the murder."

"Trotter lied, Mort. I just returned after

confronting him."

"Now, Mrs. F. —"

"Wait, Mort. Please listen. Seth said Leboeuf was stabbed in the spleen. That's on his side, under his rib cage. Trotter said that he saw Brad raise the knife and bring it down from above."

"That doesn't mean he didn't see it happen, Mrs. F. He's not the brightest guy. Maybe he just put it wrong."

"No, Mort. He was paid to make his claim."

"*Paid?* Who paid him?"

"I don't know, but I intend to find out."

"No, Mrs. F. I'll do the finding out. That's my job, not yours."

"I don't want to interfere with your job, Mort. You know that. We had an agreement. If I run across something like what happened with Jake Trotter this evening, I'm supposed to call you first. That's what I'm doing."

"And I appreciate that, Mrs. F. I know I told you to pass along any information, but now you have. So leave the rest to me. Thanks for the report. I'll follow up on it."

He hung up before I had a chance to tell him about what Trotter had said about having seen Leboeuf and Marcie Fowler together the night of the murder. Could that have been true? Trotter was a liar. That was now an established fact. Worse, he was someone who would lie for money, even if it falsely accused another person of a heinous crime. Was there any truth to what he'd said about Leboeuf and Marcie? Could I believe *anything* he said?

I called the Fin & Claw and asked to speak with Marcie.

"She didn't come in tonight," Fritzi said. "Just as well. It's slowed down the past hour."

"Is she at home?"

"That'd be my guess."

His guess proved sound. She answered on the first ring.

"Marcie," I said, "I need to speak with you. It's urgent."

"Have you heard anything new about Brad?"

"Maybe," I said, "but that's why I want to sit down with you. May I come over?"

"Oh, I don't know, Mrs. Fletcher. It's getting late. Can't we talk on the phone?"

"No, we cannot. Would you prefer to come here?"

She hesitated before saying, "Yes, I guess I would prefer that. Can't you tell me what this is about?"

"Not on the phone, Marcie."

She sighed. "All right. I'll be there within the hour."

As I waited for her arrival, I did what I'd been doing ever since Gérard Leboeuf had been murdered. I added to my notes, which by now took up almost a full pad of yellow, lined, legal-size paper. I'd transcribed most of my observations to my computer as a backup, my version of a belt and suspenders, to make sure if one went missing the other was still available. As I wrote, I realized that Marcie had become an enigma. The thought that she might have been involved in some sort of liaison with Leboeuf was appalling. Was it true? If so, would she admit to it when confronted? I doubted it. When she'd confessed her doubts about Brad and said that maybe he *had* killed Leboeuf, I'd chalked it up to the strain she was under and dismissed it. But when she'd followed up later, telling me that Brad had asked her to lie about what time he'd returned home the night of the murder, I had to admit that her revelation wasn't what I would have expected from a wife fighting to establish her husband's innocence.

Originally I'd thought that Jake Trotter had provided the authorities with his alleged firsthand knowledge of the murder because he was attempting to deflect attention from himself as a possible suspect. That same thought now crossed my mind where Marcie was concerned. If she had been involved romantically with Leboeuf — and that was still a very big *if* — could that relationship have deteriorated to the extent that she would have plunged a knife into him during an argument? Although Trotter was an unreliable witness, I believed him when he'd said that he'd seen Marcie in the kitchen with Leboeuf the night of the murder. If that were true, why was she there?

Yet another question to ask when she arrived.

I put the kettle on for tea and waited anxiously for her to pull into the driveway. When she did, I opened the door before she rang the bell.

"Hello, Marcie. Thank you for coming."

"I wasn't going to," she said, "but my curiosity got the best of me. Since you wouldn't tell me what it was about over the phone, I figured it must be significant. I hope I haven't made the trip for nothing."

"I appreciate you coming. Would you like some tea, coffee, maybe wine?"

"No, nothing for me," she said.

I decided to forgo tea, and we settled in the living room.

343

"Well, I'm here," she said. "What's so important that it had to be discussed tonight?"

Her combative stance mirrored her attitude that night in the Fin & Claw, although she had called the next morning to apologize. Again, I was sensitive to what she'd been going through and was careful to not allow any pique I might be feeling to surface.

"Marcie," I said, "let me first begin with some good news."

She'd been pouting on the couch. My words caused her to sit up, and animation replaced her sullen expression.

"What is it?" she asked.

"Are you aware that Jake Trotter gave a statement to the police that he'd seen Brad kill Gérard Leboeuf?"

Her eyes narrowed and her mouth became a slash. "I learned about it this afternoon from Brad's attorney, Ms. Syms. I don't have words for what a contemptible liar he is, Mrs. Fletcher. How could any human being do such a thing, make up a story to put someone else in jeopardy? Brad is facing a lifetime in prison because of Trotter. Sure, they didn't get along, but that's no way to get even. It's despicable!"

I let her emotions settle down a bit before

saying, "I know that he lied, Marcie, and I've informed Sheriff Metzger about it."

"How do you know? Can you prove it?"

"Let's just say that Mr. Trotter admitted to me that he was paid to say that he saw Brad kill Leboeuf."

"*Paid?* Someone paid him to say that? Well, find that person and you've found your murderer. Who is it?"

"I don't have an answer for you yet, but Sheriff Metzger has assured me that he'll follow up. But while this is good news for you and Brad," I continued, "there's something troubling that I feel compelled to raise."

"What?"

"I find this awkward to ask, but did you and Gérard Leboeuf ever have an affair?"

I expected her to react emotionally, perhaps even angrily, but didn't expect the extent to which she responded. She leaped off the couch, went to the window, her hands clenched into fists, turned, and shouted, "How dare you even suggest such a thing? *How dare you?*"

"*I'm* not suggesting it, Marcie, but someone else has. I need to clear the air."

All the anger and resentment dissipated, as though someone had opened a valve. She returned to the couch and slumped onto it.

"I need to ask you another question," I said.

She raised her hand to stop me. "Whoever said that Leboeuf and I had some sort of relationship going must have been smoking dope. I detested the man. To think that —"

The sobs burst forth, and she wrapped her arms tightly about herself. I waited until she'd gained control of herself. I wasn't sure now if her emotional outbursts were genuine or a delaying tactic. Nevertheless, I forged ahead and asked the second question that was on my mind.

"Were you with Leboeuf in his kitchen the night he was killed? Be careful what you say."

"Why would you think that?" she asked.

"Because you were seen there after the restaurant closed."

She guffawed. "Who told you that — the same liar who said Leboeuf and I had had an affair?"

I began to think Jake Trotter had led me down a primrose path for his own amusement. Could he have been lying about both witnessing the murder and the visit to the bistro kitchen by Marcie Fowler? I hoped so, but something in Marcie's eyes convinced me to continue pursuing this line of questioning. "It doesn't matter who told

346

me, Marcie. What's important is that *you* tell the truth. No one is suggesting that you were involved in his death." I waited before adding, "But you were there, weren't you?"

I could almost see her mind working, as though it were being displayed on a computer screen. When she said nothing, I followed up with, "I'm sure you had a perfectly legitimate reason for being there, Marcie. Did he send you a note, asking you to stop by? Was that why you were there? Denying it will only cause the authorities to suspect you of having killed Leboeuf. You told them — and me — that you'd gone directly home from the restaurant after it closed, but that wasn't true, was it?"

After drawing a deep breath, she managed, "He sent one of his men over with a message for Brad. I intercepted it."

I immediately thought back to the phone call from Leboeuf in which he asked whether I thought that the Fowlers would be open to being bought out. Could that have been the message? I didn't want to put words in Marcie's mouth, so I waited for her to tell me more.

"He said he wanted to talk business, and I assumed he might make us an offer to buy us out."

"What made you think he would?" I

asked. "Had he approached you or Brad with that possibility?"

She shook her head. "No. But I hoped that was the case. I knew Brad would just tear his note into little pieces and throw it away. I couldn't take that chance."

"Why would you entertain being bought out? I thought that the Fin and Claw represented a lifelong dream."

"It was Brad's dream, not mine, although I told him it was mine, too. And it was for a while, but then it turned out to be a nightmare. Isabel put every cent she could raise into the restaurant, and we signed our lives away for the bank loan." She now took on a pleading tone. "Do you know what it's done to Brad, Jessica, to our marriage? He's become a tyrant, a monster. He's racked with guilt over his mother's death, feels that if he hadn't opened the restaurant she'd still be alive. Yet he can't let it go now. It was her dream, too."

"Isabel had health problems for many years, Marcie."

"I know that. Brad knows down deep that he wasn't responsible for her stroke — and neither was Leboeuf — but in his mind it's all bound up in the restaurant. It's not what he expected. The debt we've incurred, the undermining of our business, disloyal staff, broken promises, theft, a corrupt health inspector, all of it is cascading down on Brad and eating him up. It's been nothing but heartache since we decided to open the Fin and Claw."

Her tears came again but softer this time, tears of fatigue and abject frustration. I moved to the couch and put an arm around her. "It's okay," I said. "I understand."

She wiped her eyes with the back of her hand and said, "Brad didn't know I'd approached Leboeuf about buying us out. He would have been furious if he had. I didn't know what else to do. I couldn't talk to Brad. He snapped at everything I said and just kept cursing Leboeuf and saying that he'd make the Fin and Claw a big success and drive Leboeuf out of business." She managed a smile as she added, "He's so naive, Jessica, so naive. Drive Leboeuf out of business? Fat chance. I thought that if Leboeuf made a firm offer, I could take it to Brad and hope that he'd see it as a sensible way out. We had a good marriage and life before opening the restaurant. I had a good job, and Brad enjoyed working the lobster boats. The restaurant has torn us apart."

"Had you made a date to see Lebocuf at his restaurant after it closed that night?"

"No. I went home after we closed, but I couldn't sleep. I kept obsessing about selling the restaurant and getting us out from under. I finally decided that even though Brad would be angry if I approached Leboeuf, I had to do it. I couldn't live this way anymore."

"Brad said that when he returned home, you were sleeping."

"He was protecting me. I'd gone to Leboeuf's restaurant with the hope that he was still there and that we could have a discussion about selling to him."

"What time was that?"

"About two thirty, maybe a little later."

"Brad hadn't arrived home when you left?"

"No, and I was concerned about that."

"Did he usually come in very late after the restaurant closed?"

"He did then. We'd only been open a short time. I worried that Brad might have had a run-in with Leboeuf and that he'd be there when I arrived. Thankfully, he wasn't."

"What happened next?"

"The front door to the bistro was locked, so I went to the back door that leads into the kitchen. Leboeuf was standing there in the kitchen, drinking a glass of wine. Chang, his manager, was with him. I overheard

Chang say he had something to attend to but would be back. I waited until he left. I don't think he saw me. Then I stepped inside. I apologized for barging in, but waved the note and asked Leboeuf if we could have a talk. I think he was a little drunk. He laughed and said the note was meant for me, that he knew I would come. I asked if he was serious about talking business. He offered me a drink. I said no; it wasn't a social call, and got right to the point. I asked if the note meant he might be interested in buying the Fin and Claw."

"How did he respond?"

Her face twisted into anger. "I was leaning against one of the prep tables with my arms crossed. He wrapped his arms around me, so I couldn't move. He pressed himself against me and tried to kiss me. His hands were all over me. It was disgusting."

"What did you do?" I asked.

"I tried to push him off me, but he had my arms pinned. He was strong, too strong for me. I kept twisting my face away, telling him to let me go. He said something like, 'Maybe I'll buy your place if you come with it as a bonus.' "

Her tale was wrenching, and I grimaced as she replayed what had happened that night. I was hesitant to ask what happened next, but didn't have to.

"I was sure he was going to try to take it further, but thank goodness, that's when his wife walked in."

CHAPTER TWENTY-FIVE

Marcie's matter-of-fact statement that Eva Leboeuf had walked in on the scene she'd been describing brought me up short for a moment.

"She saw what her husband was doing to you?" I said.

"She did. She went ballistic, called me a slut and every other name she could think of. I told her she should yell at her husband, not me. By this time, he'd let go, but he didn't move away, and he didn't look sorry that she'd interrupted him. He told her to 'take it easy,' that nothing happened. So then she turned on him, using every four-letter word she could think of."

"It must have been traumatic for you," I said.

"It was awful, Mrs. Fletcher. I tried to explain why I'd come there, but I couldn't get a word in edgewise."

"How did it end up?" I asked.

"I was angry at what she called me, but instead of yelling back at her, I started to cry. I pushed Leboeuf away and ran out the door."

"Had Chang come back?" I asked.

"No, but he was the one who discovered Leboeuf's body later, wasn't he?"

"Yes. I wonder if he knew she was there. If so, he never mentioned it to the police. Marcie, if what you're telling me is accurate, Eva Leboeuf, in a furious state, was left alone with her husband at just about the time he was killed."

"That's right."

"What did you do once you'd run from the kitchen?"

"I went home."

"Was Brad there?"

"No. And that's the worst part."

"So had he gone to Leboeuf's kitchen looking for you?"

She cast her eyes down before answering in a quiet voice, "Yes."

"How do you know that?"

"I waited up for him. I wanted to know where he'd been. I was afraid that's what had happened."

"Did he think you were having an affair with Leboeuf?"

"Oh, no! He's knows me better than that.

But he did suspect I'd try to see if Leboeuf would buy us out."

"Did he and Leboeuf have another confrontation?"

She shook her head.

"They didn't argue?"

"Brad said that he went to the bistro's kitchen looking for me. When he got there, he saw Leboeuf's body on the floor with the knife in him."

"And?"

"He did what I did. He ran out, hoping he hadn't touched anything, and came home. We sat up the rest of the night talking about what it all meant for us. Brad was convinced that if people knew that he'd been there right after Leboeuf had been killed, they'd immediately point a finger at him, especially since he wasn't very subtle about his dislike of the man. He said that since I'd been there with Leboeuf, people might not believe that I rejected his advances; they might look to me as the logical suspect."

"What did you do with the note from Leboeuf?"

"We burned it. Was that bad?"

"Too late now."

"I'm sorry. We were scared it would tie us to the murder."

"So you decided between the two of you to hide the fact that you'd both been in that kitchen."

"It seemed the safest thing to do at the time."

"But if you'd told the authorities about Eva being there, it might have shined a light on her as a suspect."

"We didn't think anyone would believe that she'd killed her husband." After a long pause, she said, "Do you think she did?"

"From what you've said, she was very angry with him, but whether she was angry enough to kill him, I couldn't say. Even if it's a possibility, possibilities aren't solid evidence."

"If she did, then maybe she was the one who paid Jake Trotter to accuse Brad."

"I wouldn't doubt it, Marcie. But we need proof."

"Oh, she'll never admit it. And if she doesn't, that just leaves us as the scapegoats."

"Perhaps. But I have an idea."

"What is it?"

"Will you be willing to come with me tomorrow morning to see Sheriff Metzger and tell him what you've told me tonight?"

"Do you think he'll believe me?"

"I think if you come forward with the

truth, he'll listen. He's a smart man and a kind one."

"Will it help Brad?"

I sighed. "I can't promise anything, but I think it might. Without Jake Trotter's false testimony, the authorities don't have anything to justify holding Brad. It's one man's word against another."

"I'll do anything if this nightmare can be put behind us and Brad and I can have the sort of relationship we used to have."

"Be back here tomorrow morning at nine. I'll call ahead and arrange an appointment with the sheriff."

"Okay, Mrs. Fletcher. I hope you know what you're doing."

I hoped I knew what I was doing, too. I shared Marcie's desire to see the nightmare end. For me it would mean being able to shut down my racing mind, climb into bed at ten, and enjoy eight hours of uninterrupted sleep for the first time in days. For them it would be an opportunity to look at their future without the threat of jail and to decide whether they'd taken the right steps for their life together.

I was showered, dressed, and had had breakfast when Marcie arrived the following morning. I carried my shoulder bag with me, as usual, as well as the goody bag I'd received at Leboeuf's grand opening. Marcie gave me a strange look when she saw Leboeuf's name on the side of the little shopping bag, but she didn't ask and I didn't volunteer any information. We entered police headquarters, where the desk sergeant, who was expecting us, told us to go directly to Mort's office.

"Good morning, ladies." Mort directed us to two chairs that were usually covered with piles of paper but had been cleared for our visit. "So," he said once we'd been seated, "what's this all about? I hope it's important, because I've got a bear of a day ahead of me."

"You'll be the judge of how important it is, Sheriff." I hoped that my addressing him formally would capture his attention and keep it. "Did you have an opportunity to follow up with Jake Trotter and the lies he told in his statement about having seen Brad Fowler kill Leboeuf?"

"First thing this morning, Mrs. F. I spoke with the DA, who agrees with you that what Trotter said he saw could not have happened the way he described it. We picked Mr. Trotter up an hour ago. At the moment, he's in a holding cell, awaiting legal representation. He doesn't have very kind words to say about you, I might add. He said you had a deal, and he's furious you didn't keep to your part of the bargain."

"We never had a deal. I merely let him ramble on, thinking it was a possibility, so that he would reveal the truth."

"He admits he perjured himself, which means he's in for big trouble for having given a false statement to authorities."

Marcie leaned forward. "Does that mean you'll release Brad now?"

I put my hand on hers. "These things take time," I said. "There are procedures that have to be followed." I was afraid that if Mort let Brad go right away, Marcie might never tell the sheriff the truth about the night of the killing.

Mort looked from me to Marcie and leaned back in his seat. "Mrs. F. is correct. We have procedures to follow. Now, what is the reason for this little get-together this morning?"

"Did Mr. Trotter say who paid him to lie?" I asked.

"No, but I have a sneaky suspicion that you know the answer to that question."

"Well, I do have some ideas, but before we get to that, Marcie has something you should know."

"You have the floor, Mrs. Fowler," Mort

said, taking a pen from his breast pocket and pulling a legal pad toward him.

Ten minutes later Marcie finished recounting what she'd told me at my home the previous night. When she was done, Mort raised his eyebrows and said, "So according to you, Mr. Leboeuf was alive when you left him, and Mrs. Leboeuf was alone with her husband in the kitchen. Was anyone else there?"

"Not as far as I know," Marcie said.

"And your husband says that he saw the body and no one else when he went there looking for you, and then he took off."

"Yes, sir."

"Leboeuf's manager, Mr. Chang, was the one who reported finding the body."

"He'd left when I arrived, but said he was coming back," Marcie reiterated.

"Mort," I said, "I know that there was one readable print on the knife that killed Leboeuf."

"Right, origin unknown. Whoever left that print had never been fingerprinted before. We ran it through the FBI database in DC. No such print on record."

I held up the goody bag I'd received at the opening of Leboeuf's French Bistro. "This might help you," I said. I reached inside and, using a handkerchief, carefully extracted the fancy stemless wineglass with the fancy gold "Leboeuf" on its side.

"What's this?" Mort asked.

"The bag of favors the Leboeufs provided guests on their opening night. This glass was in it. You and Maureen must have received one, too."

Mort leaned forward to better see it. "Oh, yeah," he said. "Maureen has it on the fireplace mantel. So what?"

"When I received mine," I said, "I thanked Eva Leboeuf and held the glass in my hands. She took it, held it up to the light, and bragged about a glassblower in Venice who had made them exclusively for the bistro's opening night."

"I see where this is going," Mort said. "You think the print on the knife used to kill Leboeuf might match up with his wife's prints on this glass."

"That's what I'm hoping," I said, replacing the glass in the bag. "Of course my prints will be on it, too, but I assure you that I didn't kill Gérard Leboeuf."

Mort called in a deputy and instructed him to take the bag and run the glass to one of the state's regional crime labs a few hours away. "They have the print from the knife used in the Leboeuf murder. Tell 'em we need a fast answer."

That answer came back later that afternoon. The print on the glass was a perfect match to one on the murder weapon. Both prints belonged to Eva Leboeuf.

CHAPTER TWENTY-SIX

The aftermath of Gerard Leboeuf's murder played out in Cabot Cove, and in the media around the country and the world, over the ensuing six months. I used that time to continue documenting events as they occurred, filling notebook after notebook, transcribing my observations, and saving press reports and official documents as they became available.

In the meantime, all the players in the case found their way through the legal system. Naturally, Eva denied having stabbed her husband to death. The attorney she hired pointed out that it was not unusual for her fingerprints to be on the murder weapon; after all, she spent considerable time in the bistro's kitchen. That stance might have prevailed, except that her son, Wylie, himself under indictment for drug possession with the intent to sell, broke down during questioning and told Mort and the other investigators that he was awake when his mother returned to the house the night of the murder and that she'd had blood on her dress. When asked to produce the dress, Eva said that she had torn it and tossed it into the trash. No one believed her, and under continuing questioning, she eventually confessed to the murder but claimed it was self-defense. Leboeuf had grabbed her hand when she tried to slap him, she said, and had twisted her arm back. She told him that he was hurting her, but when he refused to let go, she swiped a knife off the counter and stabbed him in the side to make him release her. She wept sweetly when she took the stand, and the jury was sympathetic, convicting her of involuntary manslaughter and giving her a reduced sentence.

The shocking murder of noted restaurateur Gérard Leboeuf, and the conviction of his wife, former supermodel and businesswoman Eva Leboeuf, was certainly sensational enough to satisfy even the most inquisitive of onlookers. But the story expanded when the FBI, aided by the agent assigned to Cabot Cove following Leboeuf's death, Anthony Cale, filed federal charges against the chef's corporate organization for a variety of crimes, including money laundering, racketeering, tax eva-sion, and a half-dozen other violations of the law. In exchange for leniency, Charles Compton — aka Warren Shulte while he was hiding away on Cape Cod (Shulte happened to be the name the FBI had suggested for the Witness Protection Program he'd rejected) — gave devastating testimony as Leboeuf's accountant. Having nailed the case for federal prosecutors, Compton decided to take the government up on its offer this time, entered the Witness Protection Program, and has again disappeared. The two young men who constantly hovered over the Leboeuf family were charged with racketeering, having provided strong-arm manipulation for the Leboeuf empire, and they departed Cabot Cove in handcuffs.

As for Wylie Leboeuf, the judge gave him a suspended sentence, provided he enroll in an approved rehabilitation facility for thirty days, which he agreed to do. He'd been brought up in a tumultuous family atmosphere, and my good wishes and prayers went with him.

The only member of the Leboeuf family who emerged unscathed was Max, their German shepherd, who found a good and loving home with Mort Metzger's deputy, Chip.

Another player in this twisted, wrenching,

and sad saga was the state food inspector, Harold Greene. In return for pleading guilty to taking bribes from restaurant owners, he lost his job and pension and was prohibited from working for any government agency for three years. As part of his plea bargain, he admitted that Gérard Leboeuf had paid him to trump up sanitary violations at the Fin & Claw, which he'd also done with other restaurants during his shabby career.

As for the corrupt Jake Trotter, he was convicted of giving false testimony to the authorities and was sentenced to two years in a state penitentiary, where he served his time in the prison kitchen. I hoped he would find a different community in which to live when he was released.

The resolution of Leboeuf's murder and its accompanying sordid scenarios was announced at a press conference conducted by Mayor Shevlin and Sheriff Mort Metzger, who shared the stage with state investigators Anne Lucas and Clifford Mason. Mort had privately thanked me for my help in bringing Eva Leboeuf to justice but asked whether I would be offended if he didn't mention me in his public remarks.

"Of course I won't be offended, Mort," I told him. "All I did was put a few pieces together, which you would have done in due

366

time. You've done a wonderful job and deserve the gratitude of everyone in Cabot Cove."

Armed with that assurance, Mort took over the stage after being introduced by the mayor and heaped praise upon Lucas and Mason, who appeared to be uncomfortable with his words. In my opinion, they hadn't been instrumental in resolving the murder, but at least they hadn't gotten in the way. It pleased me to see Mort bask in the limelight, and the broad grin on his wife's face was all the thank-you I needed.

Once Cabot Cove had settled back into some semblance of normalcy, I got down to the task of telling the tale for my next book. I interviewed everyone involved who made themselves available — the Leboeuf family and their organized crime keepers the exceptions — and my excitement grew as the pages piled up and the story took shape to my satisfaction. Naturally, Brad and Marcie Fowler — their names changed — were front and center in my fictional recounting of the events and cooperated fully. They represented my "happy ending."

Brad's mother, Isabel, had taken out a life insurance policy for $200,000, with Brad as the beneficiary. Armed with that infusion of capital and free to devote their energies to the Fin & Claw, Brad and Marcie developed a new menu offering fewer dishes, but still with a page devoted to Isabel's recipes, including the divine lobster in butternut sauce that I'd loved. As a result, the restaurant grew more successful with each passing week.

Not long after, Marcie and Brad decided to start a family, with Marcie opting to be a stay-at-home mom during their child's early years. What especially warmed my heart was to see that the couple's relationship had solidified. "Brad is a different person," Marcie confided in me. "He puts things into perspective now and doesn't let trivial things get to him."

Brad made Fritzi Boering the Fin & Claw's general manager, a role for which Fritzi was well suited after his years keeping customers happy at Sardi's, Manhattan's famed show-business eatery. Fritzi regaled everyone who would listen with the tale that he alone had solved the murder of Gérard Leboeuf, way before Jessica Fletcher and the police had come up with the answers. *Cherchez la femme!*

I was a month away from finishing *Killer in the Kitchen* when my publisher, Vaughan Buckley, summoned me to New York to appear on a highly rated TV talk show. Following my appearance, we had dinner at our favorite French restaurant, L'Absinthe, where, as usual, we were enthusiastically greeted by Jean-Michel Bergougnoux, who showed us to Vaughan's usual booth.

"You were terrific on the show," Vaughan told me over appetizers — tartare de boeuf for him; I went along with something raw but made it salmon tartare. In honor of my being close to completing *Killer in the Kitchen,* he sprang for a bottle of 2005 Bordeaux Chateau Lynch Moussas Grand Cru, which, after tasting, he proclaimed was superb. I'm not a wine connoisseur, but I took his word for it. It was tasty.

When it came time to order our entrées, Vaughan asked if I was in the mood for boeuf bourguignon, steak in red wine sauce.

"Steak?" I said. "Beef? *Boeuf?* No, I think I've had enough *boeuf* to last me a long time. Anything but *boeuf.*"

I returned to Cabot Cove and eagerly dove into writing the final chapters. I declined lunch and dinner invitations from friends and, as usual, became a virtual recluse. When I thought that I'd written the final page, I came up for air and joined Seth, Evelyn Phillips, Mort and Maureen Metzger, and Jim and Susan Shevlin for dinner at the Fin & Claw, where we toasted Isabel Fowler and enjoyed dishes based on her recipes, which came from the kitchen cooked to perfection.

"So you finished the book," Evelyn said. "Congratulations!"

"Actually," I said, "I forgot to add one thing, so this celebration is a bit premature."

That didn't put a halt to the festivities, and I returned home sated with good food and scintillating conversation with some of my favorite people.

Before I got ready for bed, I turned off the lights throughout the house, with the exception of my office. I sat down at my computer, pulled up the manuscript of *Killer in the Kitchen,* smiled, and typed: "THE END." Now the story was complete.

ABOUT THE AUTHOR

Jessica Fletcher is a bestselling mystery writer who has a knack for stumbling upon real-life mysteries in her various travels. **Donald Bain**, her longtime collaborator, is the writer of more than one hundred other books, many of them bestsellers.